What the critics are saying...

About Prisoner of Desire

"...extremely erotic adventure that is fast-paced, intriguing and hard to stop reading once started. Pirates, more women than they could possibly handle and two Captains who give as good as they get, make PRISONER OF DESIRE an awesome, must read..." – *Tracey West, The Road To Romance*

"PRISONER OF DESIRE is Delilah Devlin's first novel. I can't wait to see what she can come up with next. This is a very erotic adventure that you won't want to put down...I highly recommend this novel for anyone who loves pirates and romance..." – *Patricia McGrew, Sensual Romance Reviews*

About Slave of Desire

"From the first steamy sex scene this book is red hot. It is amazing that Ms Devlin managed to get a plot written among all the sexual exploits of Calandra and Drago. But there is indeed a plot, and Ms Devlin's characters are well developed as to grab the reader's interest..." – *Penny, Fallen Angels Review*

"...Delilah Devlin is fast becoming one of the best erotic romance novel writers today. Her talent for creating characters and plots that intrigue and capture your attentions are legendary. Slave of Desire is a wonderful read full of action and adventure..." – *Angel Brewer, The Romance Studio*

Pirate's Desire
An Ellora's Cave Publication, July 2004

Ellora's Cave Publishing, Inc.
PO Box 787
Hudson, OH 44236-0787

ISBN #1843608960

Edited by BRIANA ST. JAMES
Cover art by DARRELL KING

Warning:

The following material contains graphic sexual content meant for mature readers. *Pirates' Desire* has been rated E–rotic by a minimum of three independent reviewers.

Ellora's Cave Publishing offers three levels of Romantica™ reading entertainment: S (S-ensuous), E (E-rotic), and X (X-treme).

S-*ensuous* love scenes are explicit and leave nothing to the imagination.

E-*rotic* love scenes are explicit, leave nothing to the imagination, and are high in volume per the overall word count. In addition, some E-rated titles might contain fantasy material that some readers find objectionable, such as bondage, submission, same sex encounters, forced seductions, etc. E-rated titles are the most graphic titles we carry; it is common, for instance, for an author to use words such as "fucking", "cock", "pussy", etc., within their work of literature.

X-*treme* titles differ from E-rated titles only in plot premise and storyline execution. Unlike E-rated titles, stories designated with the letter X tend to contain controversial subject matter not for the faint of heart.

PRISONER OF DESIRE

By Delilah Devlin

Thanks to my sister, Myla, for sharing this journey with me, and to Linda for her 'eagle eyes' and encouragement.

Chapter One

"Captain, I've picked up the ship's warning beacon."

Captain Adamarik Zingh straightened from the navigation console. At last. The final stage of his plan was about to unfold. The beacon was programmed to broadcast as soon as any ship approached within hailing distance of the penitentiary. "Let's hear it."

His communications mate pressed the intercom switch.

"Warning! You are entering Interplanetary Dominion controlled space." The computer-generated message transmitted in the Universal Language. "This ship is a Dominion Prison. Any vessel detected within a one hundred milli-league radius of the ship will be destroyed."

"Retract the visor," Adam ordered, ignoring the warning.

The whirring sound that accompanied the retracting curtain of metal grated, reminding Adam of the loss of his previous spacecraft. Its state-of-the-art bioluminescent screen would have recreated the view of space without leaving the ship's hull vulnerable.

But pirates couldn't be too choosy. The lumbering transport vessel he now captained had enabled his band of raiders to creep close to their target, beneath the blanket of the Dominion's detector beams. Its unremarkable appearance in this little-traveled part of the universe was a perfect ruse.

"I see her, Adam." The man at the helm, his first mate Cantor Marlow, dipped the prow of the ship leeward. The sudden change in tack caused the old barge to shudder violently. Then a low, ominous groan from the hull itself rattled the consoles, spilling cups and charts onto the floor.

Adam maintained his balance, barely, and turned to glower at his first mate. "Cookie'll dice your innards for that. He'll be cleaning grub from the ceiling for a week."

Cantor shrugged, a wicked twinkle in his eye. "I was just making sure the breaching crewmen were out of their bunks." His gaze shifted beyond Adam. "There she is."

Adam glanced through the open portal, searching the sky. The infinite, black night stretched before him. Full of endless possibilities. A siren's call that had beckoned him from his first voyage.

Then he saw it. The enormous hull of the prison ship loomed in the distance--anticipation leapt in his veins.

"Alert the breaching crew."

His first mate grinned. "Lucky sods!"

Three whistles shrilled, followed by the alert message.

"Cantor, you're in charge," Adam called over his shoulder as he headed toward the hold of the ship.

"Aye, sir. Good luck, and don't forget my list."

Adam slapped his palm against the hold door button, and it slid silently open. Within the hold, the breaching crew was assembling—or at least he thought it was his crew. Gone were their beards and rough pirate's clothing. In their place stood well-scrubbed, clean-chinned men.

His security officer, Darak, strode toward him wearing a deep, azure shirt, tucked into tan leather breeches.

"What in hell are you wearing?" Adam demanded.

"It's just a little something I picked up at our last port of call. Alarian silk." Darak shrugged, grinning sheepishly. "Quite sturdy material, actually."

"You look like a peacock," Adam complained. His gaze swept over the rest of his breaching party. "I'm capturing a ship with a bloody flock of peacocks!"

"The men await your orders, sir. They're eager for this mission. Every one of them volunteered."

Adam rolled his eyes. "They fought for the right to board. I'm lucky to have any crew left with blood enough for this capture. Is the breaching craft loaded?"

"Aye, aye sir. With eight days of supplies, should we need them."

"Very well. Let's get on with this."

Darak pivoted on his heels. "Attention," he shouted.

The crew leapt to obey, forming two ranks along the bulkhead.

Adam stomped down the line, his nose itching as he passed through a cloud of contesting colognes emanating from his bloodthirsty crew. "Are you planning on conquering them with smell?" he growled.

As he passed his medic, his eyes watered uncontrollably. He paused, sniffing.

Doc blinked rapidly, moisture welling in his eyes. "It's the scent of Alarian rose, sir—mixed with the pheromones of a Moldan yak. Very potent."

"Grrr," Adam glowered, then stomped back to the front of the formation. "We'll enter the prison through the docking station. Be quick. Let's have them contained before they realize we aren't the warden and her guards. We only have a narrow window of time to get aboard undetected by the Dominion's security system." As he delivered his last instruction, he narrowed his eyes. "Don't trip over your lace."

"Captain," Darak interjected.

"Yes, Darak?"

"Sir, the men want to know if we're certain this is the right prison ship."

"I paid 10,000 dinars in Earth gold for the information. If it's not the right ship, you'd best be ready to defend your virtue." Adam enjoyed a moment's satisfaction as his crew absorbed the message. "We've eight days to survive aboard ship before the Intrepid can rendezvous again without Dominion detection."

Another crewmember raised his hand. "Is it really a ship full of women convicts?"

"Aye, and ripe for rescue," Darak answered, producing laughter and cheers among his shipmates.

"How long have they been deployed?" another asked.

"Over three years," Adam answered. "They may all be dead. We might find only a ghost ship."

"Sir." Ivan, the science officer and youngest of his crew, raised his hand. "What if there aren't enough suitable women aboard for our purpose?"

"If they're fertile, they'll suit," he replied bluntly. "When does our window open?"

Ivan checked his wrist computer. "The asteroid, Cygnet, will block Dominion detector beams beginning in five minutes."

"Board up!" Adam shouted. He followed his crew into the breaching craft, scratching his beard and wondering if he should have changed his clothing.

* * * * *

Before the siren finished its first warning peal, Cell Block Captain Evena McClure rolled out of her bunk and onto her feet in one fluid movement.

"Damn HS block!" Two nights running she'd answered alarms in the high security cellblock. Although tired and cranky, she raced from her quarters to the cabinet that housed the behavior modification clubs, the only weapons permitted aboard the prison ship. Slapping her palm to the security reader, she waited impatiently until the door latch popped.

At the sound of the heavy thud of her CB Sergeant's footfalls behind her, she tossed her a weapon, and then shouldered her own club.

"Thought I'd get a decent night's sleep for once." Mary Grogan smiled, a flash of startling white against her dark chocolate face as she fell into step beside Evena. "You wanna bet on who's raising a ruckus this time?"

Evena shook her head. "No, I won't take that bet. I'd lose."

Together, the two women rushed down the corridor leading from the guard quarters directly to the security surveillance room. Entering, Evena noted the two women on night watch standing at the viewing panels.

"Calandra, what's the problem?"

The guard darted a glance over her shoulder. "That damn psychopath Celestine refused to don her uniform, again. I sent a couple of guards to persuade her, but she got the drop on them. Celestine's fashioned a wire whip." She moved to the side to allow Evena to see the viewing screen. "One guard is down. The other's doing her best to keep out of reach."

Evena frowned as she watched the battle in the cell. The guards' uniforms were shredded, and one was bleeding heavily. "Damn! I'm going in."

"Have a care. She's slicing ribbons off them." Calandra released the lock on the security gate to the high-risk cellblock then offered Evena a disgruntled grin. "Why don't you just kill her? No one'll miss that one."

"Sorry to disappoint, but she's not worth risking my pardon."

Evena slid back the door and jogged toward Celestine Monteval's cell, Mary once again at her heels. The occupants of the other cells didn't alert their fellow cellmate, evidence that even the most extreme of the violent offenders weren't rooting for that psychopath.

Grunts and curses sounded from the open cell door. Evena hefted her club, smacking it against her palm loudly as she stood in the doorframe.

Celestine spun toward her, then let the tail of her whip fall lax against the floor.

Evena spared a single glance at the bloodied guard, who slid down the wall, chest heaving, relief evident in her expression.

A throaty chuckle drew her attention back to the problem, and her eyes narrowed.

Celestine was naked except for the tattoo of a crimson snake, which undulated across her golden skin, emphasizing a figure that would inflame a monk—which was what Evena felt like these days. Celestine's perfect white teeth flashed in a triumphant smile. "Captain, did I wake you?" she asked mockingly.

Evena ignored the woman's taunt. Instead, she glanced over her shoulder at Mary. "While I keep her occupied, get the other two out of here."

"Yes, ma'am."

"And Mary, she doesn't come out of here alive."

Celestine's lips thinned into a malevolent grimace, emphasized by the ominous hiss of her homemade whip slapping against the floor.

Evena cocked her head left than right, popping the vertebrae in her neck, before she said in a bored tone, "Okay Celestine, I'm going to ask you once, nicely, to get back into your uniform."

"I hate to disappoint you, but I can't possibly. My skin doesn't breathe in that damn thing," she said, smoothing a hand down her naked flank.

Evena gritted her teeth. Celestine was going to refuse every reasonable offer. However, Evena's office demanded she offer a peaceable settlement. "Well, I'll make a deal with you," she said in a tone that implied she didn't think Celestine had the intellect to understand. "You put the uniform back on, and I won't withhold your water rations."

A frown darkened the stunning face of the psychopath. "You can't do that. Who made you God?"

13

"The majority of the women aboard the New Attica who elected me CB Captain."

"I don't recognize your right to order me around. You're no better than I am."

Oh yeah? Who's running this ship and who's stuck in an HS cage? Evena's pride kept the starch in her backbone and her retort behind her teeth. "The women have given me the right. I'm responsible for order aboard this ship. My first duty is to ensure that every prisoner abides by the recycling laws."

"Here's what I think of your rules." Celestine swung her arm wide, jerking it back at the top of the arc to produce a lightning crack of her whip.

Evena feinted right, narrowly escaping the razor-sharp metal.

Celestine advanced, her face red with rage. "It's not fair. Why do you get the run of the ship, while I'm locked in here?"

"Because you're nuts, Celestine." Evena forced herself to stand still, pretending unconcern for her opponent's approach. The bitch was unpredictable. While Evena was confident she could take her, and itched for an excuse to bring her down, she'd die before she let Celestine know she held a healthy respect for her brutality. "Our internal review board sentenced you to this block. I'm merely upholding their ruling."

Celestine's hands fisted at her sides. "I'm going fucking insane here. I'm from Arturia. I'm not made to be without a partner."

"You tried to take the face off your last lover, Celestine."

"The bitch threatened to leave me," Celestine screeched. "I was just helping her on her way."

Suddenly, the whip snaked out, wrapping around the end of Evena's club. Celestine jerked sharply.

The tug was meant to disarm Evena, but she'd anticipated the move and pulled back hard.

Celestine cried out and let go of the whip to avoid slicing her hands open. Before it hit the floor, she leapt at Evena.

Evena took the force of her charge and rolled with it, quickly pinning the woman to the ground. Grasping Celestine's hands, she stretched her arms above her head, and lowered her body to trap her opponent against the floor, careful to keep her face out of reach of the psychopath's sharp teeth.

Celestine shuddered beneath her, her expression morphing from enraged to sultry in a second. "Oooh, if I'd known you were that hard-up, I'd have issued another kind of invitation, Evena."

Evena wiped all emotion from her face. "Shut up."

"What's the matter? Want some?" she asked with a roll of her belly.

The smell of the woman's sweat was pungent yet strangely enticing. Evena glowered, disgusted she'd even noticed. "I'd sooner fuck my nightstick."

Celestine's sultry pout grew surly, and she resumed bucking beneath Evena, nearly unseating her.

Evena shifted, clamping her forearm over Celestine's and freeing a hand to grab Celestine's hair. She lifted the other woman's head off the floor, then slammed it down. "This is the way this is going down." Thump! "I'm going to get up slowly. You're not going to so much as twitch—" Thump! "—because if you do, Mary here is going to use her stick to lobotomize you." She twisted her fingers into the hair and tugged hard. "Do you understand me?"

"Yes." Celestine ground out.

Evena stared into the dangerous woman's eyes until she finally turned away. "I'm going to get up now. When I say so, you can start getting your uniform on."

"I'm not wearing it," Celestine's voice was petulant and small. "It smothers me."

Evena fisted a hand in her hair, forcing her to look at her. "Listen, you spoiled little bitch! You haven't the right to withhold your sweat or piss. If you don't comply, you won't get your ration of water. Do you understand me?"

Celestine snarled and pitched beneath her.

Evena's already bad mood soured. She wished like hell the woman would lay still. It had been too long since she'd touched another person's naked skin. That she was lying on top of a professional courtesan further frosted her ass.

Two shrill whistles sounded.

Evena's head snapped up. "Damn. The warden." She let Celestine's head thump back against the floor and sprang off her.

She swept her club from the floor and shot a glance to Mary. "I'll have to let you clean up here."

Mary grinned, slapping her club against her palm. "My pleasure."

With adrenaline still pumping through her veins, Evena passed the HS gate and loped toward the docking station. A visit from the warden could mean news of her pardon, if she wasn't just delivering new prisoners. At the very minimum, the prison galley would receive its quarterly shipment of protein packs and water to supplement their recycled stores.

As she approached the docking station, she heard screams from within. The door slid open and three of her guards ran out. "Captain, pirates are boarding!"

Cold dread settled in her stomach. "Get to the security room. Arm yourselves. Sound the general alert."

Evena raised her club and entered the room. It was overflowing with men—brightly dressed men. And more were climbing through the docking port. Four of her guards were struggling wildly to escape their captors' arms.

"Release the women," she shouted.

All eyes turned toward her. Evena wondered whether she should've waited for reinforcements as one man strode toward her. Unlike his comrades, he was dressed entirely in black. His dark, disheveled hair brushed the tops of his shoulders, and a many-days-old beard-stubbled his chin. Dark eyes swept over her in a single quick appraisal, burning her skin.

Evena's pulse pounded loudly in her ears, and a quiver of awareness fluttered deep in her belly. He was a large man, broad-shouldered and heavily muscled, and despite his wary scowl, a handsome one.

She raised her club higher and bent her knees, sinking into a fighting stance.

The bearded pirate raised a hand. "I come in peace."

Evena's glance dropped to the laser sword at his side, before mocking his claim with a cynical lift of her brow.

He spread his hands wide and took another step toward her. "We couldn't be sure who would be aboard."

She snorted. "What? You couldn't read the warning on the portal? This is the New Attica. A prison ship. The Dominion doesn't have a sense of humor about intruders. And weapons aren't permitted here."

His frown deepened, and he took another step forward. "That isn't exactly a toothpick you wield."

Evena resisted the urge to retreat. "I'll repeat. You and your men have trespassed on a Dominion prison. We've nothing of value to steal here."

"I take it you're in charge?"

"Yes, and I'm ordering you to depart immediately."

"I'm afraid we can't do that for at least another eight days, that is if we don't want to be caught in the security beams and obliterated."

"Not my problem."

The corners of his lips twitched. "You're a stubborn wench, and a bit bloodthirsty. I like that. Aren't you curious why we're here?"

"Nope," she said, shifting one foot to the other. Aware of movement around her, she was unable to look toward it, as the bearded man was within the reach of her club now. "Like I said, we've nothing here of value."

"That's where you're wrong. We're here to conduct a little business with you and your fellow inmates."

"Then you've wasted your time. What exactly do you think we have to bargain with?"

"Yourselves."

"Explain that before I beat in what's left of your brains."

"Very well. We seek wives."

Chapter Two

Adamarik admired the woman's fearless stance. Never mind she didn't stand a chance and probably knew it. Even now, Darak and Ivan crept along the wall, outside her peripheral vision, ready to pounce and disarm her when he gave the signal. First, he wanted to test her mettle. He needed a strong woman for his mate.

That she also possessed the body of an Amazon only sweetened the pot. The sleek, black reclamation suit she wore clung lovingly to her curves, revealing long, muscled flanks, a flat stomach and a full, luscious ass that inspired an immediate hard-on. The suit outlined the aureoles of her breasts and the buds springing from their centers expanded with each exhalation of her chest.

His gaze returned to her eyes, now narrowed green slits, as she rotated the club in a figure eight above her head. He realized she couldn't fight her body's instinctive response and was pissed about it. He grinned.

"Get whatever's going on behind those black eyes out of your head," she warned, swinging the club in a sudden arc at his shoulders.

He leapt to the side with a bark of laughter, raising a hand for his men to hold them back. "I could cut that club in two with a single slice of my saber."

"Only if you're fast enough." She stressed her point with a sudden feint to the left, and swept the club at his knees.

He jumped over it, but didn't get out of the way in time to miss the backstroke that clipped him in the ass. "Ooomph!" He needed to end the game before either of them was injured.

"I think you need to lose a few pounds before you can give me a real fight," she taunted.

Fat, was he? With an imperceptible nod to his men, he offered her a target she wouldn't be able to resist. He stepped forward within striking distance and grimaced as the club arced toward his head.

Darak lunged at her back and tapped her with the electro-stun. Adam caught the feisty beauty in his arms as she crumpled wide-eyed and slack-mouthed toward the floor. Having felt the effects of the electro-stun himself, Adam knew she was aware of everything happening around her, and likely distressed by her sudden paralysis. Smoothing his hand over her auburn hair, Adam crooned, "Shhh, now. Give it a few moments. Darak only stunned your body. You'll regain movement."

He took her to the ground, cupping the back of her head to lay it gently against the floor. A wisp of fire-colored hair caught at the corner of her mouth. He pushed it away with a finger, tracing a path along the cream-colored skin of her cheek. Hot color bloomed in her cheeks—anger he was sure.

"Tsk, tsk. Spitfire, I bet you'll be ready to carve my heart out with a spoon when you come back to full strength." To give her something to really be angry about, he chuckled and traced her lips—pink, pouting lips.

"Now that I have your full attention, you will listen to me," he said, placing his face close to hers. "I was telling you the truth. My crew and I are looking for mates—willing mates."

He admired the fierce concentration that produced the frown drawing her dark brows together.

"We're pirates, yes," he continued, enjoying the advantage he held, "...but still we're honorable men."

Her green eyes glared back at him.

"I really don't make it a habit of using electro-stuns to get women to fall into my arms," he said with a wicked smile. "They are usually quite willing."

A faint gurgling sound emanated from the back of her throat.

Adam stretched out beside her on the floor, resting his head on his palm. With a finger, he tilted her chin toward him so that her gaze met his.

He marveled at her expressive cat-green eyes as she stared mutinously back at him. Her show of spirit pleased him, and he felt his loins stir.

Casually, he raked a thumbnail across the nipple nearest him. "Yes, I can tell you and I are going to be spending a lot of time together."

The gurgle was now a low growl that increased in volume when he palmed her breast and gently massaged the round mass. The bud at the center rose against his hand, and he rewarded its response with a tweak.

"Getting into the spirit of things so soon, Captain?" Darak interrupted his play, a lopsided grin on his face. "The men are aboard, and the breaching craft has returned to the Intrepid."

"Well, love," he said with another quick tug of her nipple. "Looks like you are stuck with us for the next eight days."

The woman surprised him with a blow to the side of his face. It lacked power for she had yet to regain control of her body, and her arm fell back limply to her side.

He rose over her, straddling her middle, applying only light pressure to her arms to restrain her. Averse to causing real damage or distress to a woman, nevertheless he had a job to do. Her continued resistance would only alarm her shipmates. The sooner they understood he and his band meant no harm, the sooner he could move forward with his plan.

Sighing regretfully, he said over his shoulder, "Darak bring me rope. This one's not going to listen to reason."

She squirmed weakly beneath his spread thighs, and his cock reared uncomfortably high within the confines of his breeches. Damn, but wasn't she a feisty wench? Taming this one would be pure pleasure. She'd sheathe her claws and purr, and he'd soothe the ache she was building in his groin. But first things first, he had to subdue her—for her own safety.

She squirmed again.

He cursed and stretched his legs beside hers, before nudging them apart to nestle his groin between. His cock rode the crest of her mons and surged. "Move again, and I'll consider it an invitation," he growled, at the same time he ground his cock against the apex of her thighs.

Her eyes widened and her lips moved slowly to form words. "Bu...Bu..."

"Bastard?"

She snorted.

"Need a hand?" Darak dropped rope on the floor beside him.

Regretfully, Adam lifted himself off the woman, then rolled her to her stomach. "Darak, be prepared. Their security force will attempt a rescue. No one must be harmed."

He tied her hands together. Then with an arm encircling her middle, he hefted the woman to her feet. Immediately, she sagged against his side.

Suddenly, the door to the docking station slid open. A large black woman stormed inside, followed by a contingent of guards. They looked mad as hell.

The black woman's gaze flickered over the woman at his side whose head lolled on her shoulders. Her eyes narrowed dangerously. "Bastard!" she spat at him. "You wanna fight? You're gonna be sorry you ever messed with us."

Hoisting his hostage until she stood on wobbly legs in front of him, he slid a knife from the top of his boot and held it against her throat. He hoped they wouldn't guess his bluff. The last thing he was looking to do was spill her blood.

The black guard stilled instantly, as did her companions.

"Drop your clubs," he commanded.

The guards looked to the black woman. Her mouth tightened, but she nodded. Clubs thudded against the floor and rolled away from the group.

Instantly, Adam realized the woman in his arms was the key to a peaceful capture.

His hostage protested incoherently,

"Hmmm. Looks as though your friends hold you in some esteem. I'll be keeping you near."

"Bu...Bu..."

"Yes, my dear. I expect I am, but be a good girl and shut up. You're exciting your guards."

* * * * *

Evena seethed, silently condemning her captor to die a torturously slow death. At her own hands, of course. Her face would be the last thing he saw. When he cried out for mercy at the end, she'd laugh. Then she'd stomp on the fingers clinging desperately to the door of the garbage hatch—just before she jettisoned him, and the rest of the refuse, into space.

She clung to that wistful dream when the needling pain began to usher sensation back into the muscles of her body.

How she wished the electro-stun had been as effective at numbing the rest of her. How dare he use her own body against her? Well before her muscles began to flare back to life, every erogenous zone she possessed had awakened, screaming with awareness.

And he'd known—the bastard! The fingers that had gently twisted the tips of her breasts knew exactly how much pleasure-pain to apply. She'd been unable to hide the telltale signs of her arousal. Heat had flushed in a red-hot wave across her skin, raising goose bumps and constricting her nipples to form nerve-rich points.

When he'd lowered his body over hers to restrain her movement, his weight drew an anguish from her soul she didn't recognize. She felt small and feminine. Helpless. Aroused. Unlike the person she'd made herself into. Her hard-fought independence and confidence in her ability to resist all temptation--gone in an instant of male domination. His immense size was a blanket of hard, pulsing heat. While overwhelming to her starved senses, it was also strangely comforting. Why in the galaxy did that appeal?

The scent of him nearly drove her mad. Faint traces of soap mixed with male musk had filled her nostrils with every intake of breath.

The long ridge of his cock had made her feel powerful and weak. Moisture pooled between her thighs. Then he'd ground his cock against her crotch, and the muscles deep inside her belly had contracted, instinctually seeking to draw him deep inside her.

She hadn't had a man between her thighs in five years. The first would have to be a ravaging pirate.

When her guard had entered the room to find her subdued, humiliation painted her cheeks a deeper red. She'd struggled too hard for their respect.

"You can let her go, now." Mary Grogan wasn't suggesting. Her tone demanded.

"I don't think I will. I like this one," Evena's pirate replied silkily. "I may keep her for a while."

An inarticulate gurgle rattled in the back of Evena's throat. Sheer willpower would not return the function of her limbs. She dangled in the pirate's arms like a boneless rag doll. And she was beginning to feel just as witless.

"What have you done to her?" Mary demanded.

His arm shifted, circling her like a steel band, her breasts resting on his forearm. "This woman's in no danger. She's merely stunned. Are you next in command?"

Evena knew by the silence that Mary wore her bulldog expression. The pirate wouldn't get his answer from her.

"God's ballocks!" he swore. Abruptly, he turned her in his arms, his fingers snaking through her hair to bring her face close to his. "Are you all this stubborn?"

Evena could only groan as another wave of pain rolled over her.

"Darak!" the pirate barked, his eyes never leaving hers.

Footfalls sounded behind her. "Aye, sir!"

"You're in charge. I've got to get this one to a bed," he said, a speculative gleam in his eyes.

"Ummmm!" Evena groaned, the only evidence of her silent scream of protest.

"Organize the men. The women who aren't quartered must be brought into a common area. I'll find you there."

Evena heard a click of heels, then footsteps retreating. In a movement that left her head swimming, she suddenly found herself dangling over his shoulder, the ground before her eyes.

"Ladies," the pirate addressed her guard, "you are to do precisely what my crew orders. No one will be harmed. I've business to conduct."

As the pirate exited the docking station and strode down the corridor toward the living quarters, Evena's view was limited to his impressive ass. Almost giddy from the rush of blood to her head, she'd never pondered a man's ass before, but she supposed his ranked among the galaxy's most prodigious. Hard and deeply muscled, it flexed enticingly with each step. What would it look like flexing to drive his cock inside her overheated flesh?

Where was he taking her? Would he "take" her? Could she resist? Regardless of her diminished strength, she wasn't sure whether she'd want him to stop. He'd primed a fire inside her that threatened to consume any remnant of common sense. This prime specimen of a man could scratch her five-year-old itch.

They entered a cell, and he dumped her on a mattress, then sat down on the bed beside her. His black eyes swept over her, lingering on her breasts. "I've never seen a reclamation suit before. I've heard about them, but only deep spacers use them. Look damned uncomfortable."

The muscles of Evena's face spasmed and she gasped.

He leaned forward and pressed his fingers to her temples, slowly rubbing circles that swirled lower to her cheeks. Her lids fluttered shut, and his touch swept softly over her closed eyes.

She sighed as the muscles in her cheeks relaxed, and the pain ebbed from her face.

"You must stink."

Her eyes opened to glare at him, then the next spasms racked her torso and legs.

His hands cupped her shoulders, pulling, lifting—easing the cramps. "I'd guess that if it breathed, it wouldn't do its work. But you have to reek."

She realized he was deliberately baiting her. Was he trying to keep her mind off the agony? She found she could open her mouth, "Lining of suit...absorbs water...pulls it away from skin...Don't stink!"

"Well, I'm going to find out," he said, reaching for the fastening at the neck of her suit.

"Like...hell...you are." She tried to rise up, but her belly clenched in a paroxysm of agony.

Despite her protest, he opened her suit and peeled it from her body. Then his hands settled on her tummy and kneaded gently, until the convulsions resided.

He moved down to massage her thighs, then her calves. When he reached her feet, she didn't care he was a pirate, or that he had been the cause of her pain in the first place. Drifting toward sleep, she was just grateful the pain was finally gone.

She heard him inhale deeply. "Amazing," he said.

She opened her eyes to find him staring at her, his nostrils flaring, ruddy color staining his cheeks. Control over her limbs was fully restored, but every place he'd touched her remembered his teasing rubs and tweaks. When his gaze traveled down her naked body, she felt the caress to her toes.

"Just a little musky." His voice sounded strained.

"Bastard!" Her voice lacked conviction.

"You need a bath."

Her heart stuttered, then began a pounding rhythm that grew so loud in her ears she was sure he would hear.

He swung a leg across her middle, straddling her, his cock heavy on her belly. Her breath grew ragged. He'd do it now. And the size of him and the determined set of his jaw told her he knew exactly how to wield his "weapon." Her cunt softened and grew damp.

Please do it now. He leaned forward, nuzzling against her ear, then she felt the moist, hot lap of his tongue along her jaw. An explosion of pleasure erupted inside her. Yes! I want this. I need this. The years of self-imposed abstinence while she'd tamped down any hint of desire was swept aside. Her head rolled to the side, giving him access to her neck and signaling her surrender.

When he licked her collarbone, then moved lower to cleanse her breasts, Evena didn't care she didn't know his name. Didn't care he was a ruthless pirate. He was a man. A man with a prodigious ass.

A man who licked his way around her breast, but missed the point. Raising her arms, she clamped her hands to the back of his head and guided his mouth to her nipple. "Christ...do I have...to draw you a map?"

His shoulders shook with a single bark of laughter.

She gasped when his teeth latched on, nibbling and swirling his tongue around the tip, until she pushed him to the other breast. This time he fluttered his tongue against the nipple, frustrating her, denying her a deeper pleasure.

Evena lowered her hands to his waist and tugged desperately at the fabric of his shirt, freeing it from the waist of his breeches. His skin was hot as hers and firm. Hard muscle tensed. Plunging her hands beneath the cloth, she raked his back, reveling in his sharp intake of breath that told her he enjoyed her touch. I'll make you burn too. Then she pulled him down on top of her.

When his hips slammed against her groin, she arched beneath him, tilting her hips to rub the distended nub at the center of her pleasure against the fabric covering his cock.

Despite the layer of his clothing, the shock of contact and the flowing-ebbing pressure from his rolling hips, almost unleashed the storm threatening to break over her.

Braced on his forearms, Adam rocked against the woman, watching the expressions on her face change from desire to pain when she neared the precipice. But he had no intention of balling her to paradise.

Although his cock would gladly explode inside his pants, Adam needed this woman's cooperation to peacefully acquire the women he and his men needed for mates. Abruptly, he rolled off her, determined to woo her slowly.

The woman had other ideas and followed, spreading her legs wide over his hips. Leaning forward to nip his collarbone, she scraped her pubis against the long column in his trousers.

She tempted him. Her breasts were a rare dessert—round apples covered in milk-white flesh tipped with puckered raspberries. They hovered above his mouth—ripe for picking. Rather than sucking them deeply into his mouth, he covered them with his hands and pushed her back.

"What?" she asked breathlessly, her chest heaving. Her own hands rose to press his tightly to her breasts, encouraging him to massage, but he slipped his hands from beneath hers. "Why did you stop?" she demanded stridently. "This is what you came for, isn't it?"

Chapter Three

She was exactly where he wanted her--so ready for release, she'd promise anything. Now was the time to press his advantage.

The scent of her arousal wafted around him. Trailing a hand from her breast to her hip, he paused, watching her eyelids drift close. With one hand he spread the lips of her cunt, and with the thumb of the other he scraped the pad across the hard, red pearl — once.

Her breath caught, and her eyes opened to glare at him. She'd beg for him to take her. He'd give her sweet release — *after* she granted him his request. If he could resist her lure long enough to remember what the hell he was about.

"Get on your back," he ordered, not recognizing the gruffness of his voice.

She scowled, but slid to his side.

He rose on his knees and opened the buckle of his belt. He took a deep breath and willed his cock to obey his mind.

Eagerly, she settled a leg on either side of him, raised her knees, and let her thighs splay wide. Rose-red petals parted. Wet with dew they made a sucking sound as they opened, exposing the entrance to her channel.

His hands shook as he slid the breeches past his rump, and his cock sprang free. He gritted his teeth against the urge to plunge inside her damp, waiting channel.

She groaned and tilted her pussy toward him. An invitation his cock was eager to accept. The opening to her vagina pulsed and released a thin trickle of cream. Her greedy hands reached for him, but he held them away, pushing them to the pillow beside her head. If she touched him now, he'd lose.

Lowering his hand to her cunt, he rimmed her with his thumb, then pressed it inside. Her hips rose, seeking deeper penetration. He pulled his thumb out and offered a second flicker across her clitoris, and she bucked.

"Finish this!" she demanded.

He placed his dick at the opening of her cunt, and pushed forward, just far enough to sink an inch or so inside her heat. Christ! She was tight. Hot. Heaven. His balls tightened, readying for release.

Placing his hands over hers on the bed, he held back despite the quivering flesh that pulsed and milked the head of his cock. Her cheeks were red, her expression ferocious. His warrior woman looked ready to battle for his surrender. How she tempted him! "I want something from you, first."

She rolled her hips, inviting him to deepen his penetration. "It's right here, dammit."

He fought his desire, sweat breaking on his brow, rolling to plop on her flushed breast. "Not what I meant," he said between clenched teeth.

She groaned and arched, circling her hips on his cock. "Talk later. Fuck me."

Yes! He ground his teeth and pulled back, until only the muscles of her vagina clenched around the ridge circling the head of his dick kept him from falling out. "Not until you agree—"

"I won't. Can't think. Later. Fuck meeeee," she keened.

He'd pushed her too far. Miscalculated her rising desire. He'd have to take her first. Thank God! Cursing his weakened will, he pressed into her. Hot, steamy. Smaller than he'd expected. His balls were so taut he thought he might explode before he was fully seated within her.

"Ahh," she gasped, "wait."

His head dropped to her shoulder and he held himself still. Every fiber of his being screamed for release. Instead, he drew in a deep breath and lifted his head, ready to withdraw rather than cause her pain.

The woman's expression stunned him. Fierce and determined, she stared into his face while she eased her legs around his back clasping his body, and pulled him inexorably into her.

A gush of warm liquid bathed his cock. Adam shuddered and withdrew before pushing back inside her, cramming his dick into her tight passage. Again and again he eased out and drove forward, each time inching further inside until she sheathed him to the hilt. Faster and faster he pumped, his balls banging against her ass.

Feet planted firmly in the mattress, the woman raised her hips to greet each stroke. He continued to pound into her, pistoning in and out so hard, so fast, her breath came in guttural grunts. Awash in her juices, each thrust was accompanied by slapping, slurping, sucking sounds.

Suddenly she screamed.

Then release was upon him. He roared as the tingling wave washed over his balls, tightening them hard as stones, moments before the explosive spurt of come drained him. He collapsed onto the bed next to her, dragging air into his starved lungs.

After he found his breath, he glanced to the side to find her staring at him, her expression mirroring the stunned feeling inside him. He'd never had a ride like that.

* * * * *

Evena struggled to catch her breath. She couldn't believe what had just happened. She'd been swept into a vortex of sensation that had swirled and constricted until her only point of light had been his gaze. Then her body had convulsed around his cock. Pulsing, squeezing— every red blood cell in her body delivered to the muscles of her vagina to hold him inside. She'd never had a ride like that.

Not that she'd had any recent experience to compare. No. She'd never had any experience like that to compare. And if memory served, no one had ever made her scream.

She took another deep breath and glanced at her pirate. He stared back at her. Neither spoke. Perhaps he too was trying to remember how to breathe. Or maybe, she'd inadvertently let him see how powerful the moment had been for her.

She swallowed, surprised by the burning lump at the back of her throat and closed her eyes, denying tears she refused to shed.

It had been so damn long.

That must be the reason her orgasm had been so powerful. It had wrung a primal scream from deep inside her soul. There had been times in last three years she'd despaired of ever feeling a man move inside her again.

The one lying next to her could have been conjured from her fantasies. Hard, ridged muscles, whorls of black chest hair tapering to a line before flaring to frame his sex. Her gaze swept lower and her eyes widened. Although shrunken and spent, she wondered how she'd accommodated his cock. It was enormous. Easily the width of her wrist, it was a purplish-red and still glistened with their combined come. While she watched, it twitched against his leg and lengthened.

She swallowed hard and slowly raised her gaze.

His expression was thoughtful, assessing.

No way, would she let him think her vulnerable just because he'd made her scream. She lifted her chin. "Were you telling the truth before? You're seeking wives?"

His gaze became shuttered. "Yes. We're offering transport from this prison to a planet on the edge of the galaxy. Far from the Dominion."

"For some of the women," she replied thoughtfully, "this could be their only chance for freedom. If what you say is true, it'd be cruel for me to oppose you."

"And you, little warrior? Will you not seek your freedom with us?"

Did he mean he wanted her for himself? Her heart thrilled, but she shook her head. "No. I'll remain behind."

His gaze shuttered. "Because you don't believe in me?"

"Because I'm going back to Earth," she stated firmly.

He drew a deep breath. "Then what of the other women? Do you trust that I will deal fairly with them?"

"I'm not sure yet. We've only just met. And our first 'meeting' wasn't exactly conducive to rational thought."

He exhaled and rose on one elbow to look down at her. "How can I convince you?"

Gazing up at him, she couldn't help the desire that tightened her belly and brought heat to her face. Dark and hard and bearded, he was the embodiment of her most secret fantasies. *Am I letting my fantasies rule my heart and mind?* She wanted to believe him.

She crooked her arm around his neck and pulled his face close to hers. "I don't know," she said truthfully. *Only time will tell me the truth. Don't let me down.* "Perhaps you'll have to show me some milk of human kindness," she quipped.

His lips twisted in a smirk, then his shoulders began to shake. "And perhaps, I'll wring sweet cream from you."

Her mouth stretched into a grin and she reached up to kiss him. She'd barely touched her lips to his, when she heard the slide of the door opening.

"They're in here," a man's voice shouted. "See? He didn't kill her." He sounded exasperated.

"Evena? What are you doin' without your suit? Do I have to go an' kill myself a pirate?" Mary Grogan's outraged voice preceded her into the room. It was followed by a low whistle. "Damn, girl! I see why you're takin' your time."

Evena looked over her pirate's shoulder to see Mary staring at his dick. She didn't blame her one bit. "Um, Mary. I'm fine. This is…" Color flooded her cheeks when she realized she didn't know her lover's name.

"Adamarik. Call me Adam, Mary." The pirate smiled, and extended his hand.

Mary shook her head. "Uh-uh. I know where that hand's been. Later." She nodded to Evena. "The women are gathered in the atrium. This one, Darak," she said with a grimace at a man wearing a peacock blue shirt, "says his captain, the man who's playing with your tit by the way, is going to tell us what they're doin' here."

Evena noticed the younger man standing behind Mary for the first time. He was handsome—dark hair, blue eyes, with dimples that creased his cheeks on either side of his smile .

Her pirate, Adam, growled and nuzzled her neck. "I'll be there shortly, Darak."

"Looks like you've already been, Captain."

Adam growled, tickling her neck.

Evena understood Adam's frustration. She wasn't ready to face anyone, either. "Mary, we'll get dressed."

"I'll wait outside, and so will you!" she said, shoving a grinning Darak out the door.

Once the door slid shut, Evena pushed at Adam's broad chest until he lay flat on his back, then crawled on top of him, aligning her body with his. Folding her hands on his chest, she rested her chin atop them to look into his face. "I think we missed a step or two, somewhere."

"Big on following the directions, are you?"

31

"Yes. Sometimes." Her face grew serious. "Don't give me a reason to regret not killing you."

He snorted. "You never stood a chance. Our arms are far superior."

She smiled sweetly. "And where is your weapon, now?"

He glanced at the floor toward the clothing heaped beside the bed to find his sword. He smiled, but his eyes held suspicion. "Do you really think you could take me?"

"Let's not find out."

"So what step did I miss?" he asked, tucking a hand beneath his head. "I began my journey in the north and worked my way south. Don't think I missed anything in between. X marked the spot—I dug for treasure."

"You're a pirate." Dropping her gaze, she combed his chest hairs with her fingers. "How do you know you arrived at the correct destination, if you didn't start in the right place?" she asked, darting a glance at him.

His eyes narrowed.

"Never mind," she said, exasperated. Funny, she'd forgotten how tree-trunk dense men could be. She pushed up, intending to get dressed.

His hands anchored her at the waist. "If you want a kiss, why not just ask?"

"I don't anymore. You can let me up."

"What if I ask for one?"

"Not in the mood."

"You're a stubborn wench." His hand cupped the back of her head and forced her downward.

She thinned her lips and scowled at him.

"Then again, I could start in the south and work my way northward..."

"For Pete's sake!" She kissed him, intending to give him a quick, non-passionate smack—just something to get the lummox to let go of her. But his lips moved. And she was lost again.

"Dammit! I told you we shouldn't leave those two alone, again."

* * * * *

As they neared the atrium, the roar of several hundred voices raised in animated conversation could be heard. Evena paused in the corridor and turned to face Adam. "The women will be offered the choice to go with you, right?" Misgivings about the pirate's offer soured her stomach.

Adam's gaze didn't waiver. "We'll take no unwilling women."

"The ones you leave behind may riot. How do you intend to prevent this?"

"I won't announce the names until the last day. And I'll make it clear from the beginning that I'm taking only a hundred women. We'll set up an orderly interview process."

Mary stepped close to Evena. "It could get really ugly when you leave. Your boys better be gentlemen."

"Too late for that," Darak said, peering around the corner.

Mary joined him. "Damn, horn dogs!"

Adam grabbed Evena's hand. "Trust me. I'm offering a hundred of them a second chance."

Evena hoped she wasn't letting her hormones lead her astray. She steeled her back and walked toward the entry. "Mary, let's get some order here."

"Yes, ma'am!" Mary followed. Placing two fingers in her mouth, she blew and issued an ear-splitting whistle. "I may as well have pissed in the wind," she grumbled when the noise didn't abate.

The large atrium was usually a place for serene contemplation. The high-ceilinged room with its moist, humid air and terraced planting beds was the living center of the prison ship. It teemed with trees, grass, flowers, and plants that provided life-giving oxygen, food, and beauty to soothe the prisoners' feminine souls. By unspoken agreement, the prisoners spoke in whispers, moved slowly about their gardening chores — but not so tonight. Tonight, men were in the ship. Handsome, colorfully dressed, sweet-smelling men.

The pirates never stood a chance. Most had lost their shirts and shoes, stripped from them by laughing women. Not that they looked concerned. Most were laughing right back, at least those whose mouths weren't otherwise engaged.

"Attention!"

The loud male roar sounding from behind her made Evena jump, but it was effective. The room grew still in an instant.

Her dark pirate strode down the flagstone path to the central patio, hands on his hips, looking unbelievably sexy and stern in his black clothing and even blacker expression.

Evena noted the interested stares of the women, devouring him with their eyes, stripping him mentally and measuring his masculinity. She wanted to step in front of him to cut off their avid gazes. He's mine.

Mine? Jealousy smacked her in the face. She tried to shake it off — she didn't have a right to that emotion. Sure, she'd fucked him, but he belonged to the woman who would be his wife. And that woman certainly wouldn't be her. She had a pardon in the works.

But Evena hated the woman already. She would have him for life. This unknown woman would hold his body, bear his children — own his smiles and hot loving.

"Ladies, if I may have your attention, please." Adam's voice was a rumbling baritone. "Men, take your seats," he said more firmly.

His voice vibrated down her spine. By the shivers she witnessed from the women in the audience, Evena could tell his voice had the same impact on them. They seated themselves on the ground before him.

"You may be wondering what interest pirates have with a prison ship..." he said, with a smile curling one side of his mouth, "...not the obvious one that comes to mind, now." He waggled an admonishing finger at them.

The women tittered in laughter as he had intended Evena was sure.

"My men and I are weary of our lawless ways. We've captured many a Dominion ship, pillaged their cargoes...," he raised a single black brow, "...pleasured their women, and thumbed our noses at the Dominion all the way back to our ship."

The women cheered his jab at their common nemesis.

"But pirating is a lonely business."

Mary dug her elbow in Evena's side. When Evena darted a glance at her, Mary rolled her eyes.

She grinned. The pirate was laying it on a little thick. "Mary, what do you think?"

"Are you asking if I trust them? Hell no!"

"Am I fool to cooperate?"

"Don't see as we have much choice. They're a rough bunch, but so far no one's been harmed."

"If they do free some of the women," Evena said thoughtfully, "their lives couldn't get any worse, could they?"

Mary shrugged. "I don't know. But I do know it's gonna to be hell keepin' order. Especially once they've made their choices."

"What about you, Mary? Would you do this?"

"I'm a lifer. And I don't have a family willing to pay for a pardon. This may be my only chance for freedom."

"What if you aren't chosen?"

"What are you talkin' about? I'm gonna do the choosing!" Mary's broad white smile flashed. Then she gave Evena a sideways glance. "Looks like you did some choosing of your own already."

"Not me. That was just sex. I'm going home."

Mary shook her head, her expression disbelieving. "Uh-huh? Does Captain Blackbeard know that?"

Evena didn't answer, and turned her gaze back to the pirate captain.

"Along the way," he continued, "we've searched for a home. A place where we could set down roots, self-govern without Dominion interference, and raise families. We've found her."

Evena's breath caught at the intensity of Adam's expression. This wasn't for the benefit of wooing the women to his point of view. He'd revealed his heart.

"There's a small planet on the edge of the galaxy—beyond the Dominion influence. She possesses everything we'll need to build a new colony. Her atmosphere can sustain human life. The air smells sweet with breezes that carry the scent of a rose-like flower that grows there. There's plenty of fresh water in streams and lakes to support the crops we'll raise. She's green with trees and plants we've determined are edible, and her seasons are temperate."

A woman in the group gathered at his feet raised her hand timidly.

"Yes?" Adam smiled encouraging her to speak.

"Does this planet have a name?"

Adam paused before answering. "I'd thought to let our wives select the name."

"But your men said they weren't married. None of your crew is," another woman from the crowd said.

"'Tis exactly why we're here."

Dawning understanding produced faces wreathed with grins.

"How many?" another shouted from the rear of the group.

"About a hundred."

"How will you choose?" "Will we get to meet the other men?" "Can I bring—" The questions flew, until Adam raised his hand for silence.

"My men and I will be here for eight days. We'll conduct interviews with all the women who wish to leave, determine those eligible, then have them draw lots."

"What do you mean by eligible?" the now not-so-timid woman in the front asked.

"Only fertile women in their child-bearing years. We want to raise families. The women must be able to produce children."

"Then who will help us with the work?" "What about those with mid-wifery skills?" "I can't leave my Clara behind, she's been a mother to me!" The women's questions and complaints rose to a crescendo.

"Silence!" Adam bellowed, then added, "please." His exasperated gaze sought Evena's, and she walked over to join him in front of the group that was rapidly growing contentious.

"He's offering an opportunity for freedom for a hundred of our sisters," she shouted. Sullen expressions grew thoughtful, and the women settled back down. "Let's not impede him. I'm sure he'll deal fairly with you. In the meantime, we've guests. Let's enjoy them while they're here."

Adam spread his hands wide. "I've brought foods and wine I suspect you haven't enjoyed in some time. I'll have the men deliver it to your galley. I propose we have a party to get to know each other."

Cheers greeted his announcement.

Alarmed, Evena tugged on his sleeve. "Wine? A party? Just how do you suppose we'll keep order?"

"That my dear, is your job."

Chapter Four

Adam congratulated himself. The party was well underway, and although debauchery ruled, violence was absent as a party guest.

He sat amid cushions that festooned the lawn of the atrium, drinking a glass of the precious French wine he'd "acquired" from a freighter a month past. Women pressed food upon him, dangling Arturian berries above his lips for him to nibble, and offering slices of Samureen cheese, which they fed him with their fingers.

Looking around the garden, he could imagine how the sight must appear to the dour CB Captain McClure. He'd caught glimpses of her and her guard walking through the crowd. They were instantly recognizable, being the only prisoners present who wore their reclamation suits.

The rest of the women had searched their meager stashes for feminine attire and wore odd combinations of clothing, no doubt most of it intended to be worn as underwear. His men thought they looked delightful.

Laughter drew his attention back to his companions. Darak and Ivan reclined nearby. Two women, one a young blond, the other an older redhead, were struggling to strip the shirt from his young science officer. Ivan groaned as the blond leaned over him to flutter her tongue against his flat brown nipple, while the other traced a path lower, licking her way through the sparse hair on his chest toward his navel.

Abruptly, the women halted and pulled off their clothing. At Ivan's urging, the blond straddled his face, the other tore at his pants, pulling them low enough to free his cock. Leaning over him, she opened her mouth wide to clasp him to the root, her cheeks hollowing as she sucked.

The woman with her legs splayed wide above Ivan's mouth moaned, her head thrown back, her fingers pinching and tugging at her rosy nipples. The woman working over his cock, rose up to impale herself on him and leaned forward to take the other woman's breast into her mouth. Together, the women rocked, moaning loudly. Ivan's body bucked, his hands reached behind his head to grasp the ass of the woman whose pussy he plundered with his tongue.

Adam's cock rose in his pants. Where the hell was Evena when he wanted her? The woman next to him slid a hand over him, caressing his dick through his clothing. Adam closed his fingers over hers to stop her exploration.

A glimpse of black in the crowd drew his attention. Evena stood, her arms crossed in front of her, a look of disgust on her face. She'd seen the woman's action and made her own mind up about whether he'd invited it. Anger, swift and righteous, billowed his chest. What right has Evena to judge me? She refused me. He raised one brow and settled back against a woman whose breasts now served as his pillow. What will you do now?

Evena's expression grew impossibly darker.

Good! He patted the ground beside him, an invitation to join them.

With a scathing look, she turned her back on him and walked out of sight. She wasn't immune to his barbs. A fact he'd add to his arsenal of seduction.

"Damn, I didn't know the boy had it in him," Darak exclaimed hoarsely, watching Ivan and his small harem. The three women surrounding Darak, who'd been petting his body through his clothing, shrugged out of theirs, giggling.

Amused, Adam watched Darak feverishly push his pants down, then flip the young brunette nearest him onto her stomach. She quickly came to her knees, her caramel-colored, heart-shaped buttocks in the air, wagging her ass playfully. Darak's large hands reached for a buttock each, squeezing and separating, giving Adam an excellent view of the woman's open cunt and rosebud anus. Another of the women, 40-ish, big-breasted and blond, slid beneath the black woman, and latched onto her breast with her mouth.

The last woman, an attractive blond with a thin scar that curved along her cheekbone, rose behind Darak and licked and kissed his back and ass, finally kneeling behind him to separate his buttocks and tongue his asshole. With a roar of pleasure, Darak plunged into the black woman, who squealed her delight.

All around Adam, women surged over the men, and over each other in an orgiastic frenzy. He felt the opening to his own pants give, and his cock bounded out, pointing toward the ceiling. "A moment, ladies," he tried to protest, but was shoved onto his back. A dozen hands divested him of his clothing. Mouths and fingers converged over his cock, licking, squeezing.

"Never saw one so big."

"That's not going up me," another said flatly, but she still tongued the vein that pulsed along the underside of his dick.

"He'll tickle my tonsils."

Adam chuckled uneasily. Never having had his cock be the recipient of so much consternation, he was a little taken aback over the avid attention it was receiving.

"Captain Zingh, may I have a word with you?" Mary's upside down face appeared above his.

"Yes?" he asked absently, then realized she'd provided him the perfect excuse. "Yes! Ladies, duty calls," he said pompously, rising to his feet. "Uh...my clothing?"

The ladies giggled, and shrugged, pretending ignorance.

He gave them a narrow-eyed glare, and then turned to Mary.

"Point that thing the other way, please!" she shuddered. "That should be registered as a lethal weapon."

Amused she'd noticed, and that she wasn't unimpressed, Adam crossed his arms over his chest. "All right, what was it you wanted to tell me?"

Mary glanced away from him, then her eyes widened. "Damn, horn dog!" she exclaimed. She was staring at Darak who was pounding away at the black woman. The younger blond stood in front of him now, her legs on either side of the black woman. She'd pulled her cunt lips up to expose her clit, and Darak's face was buried in her pussy.

Mary didn't appear angry. Her gaze was assessing.

"Mary."

She dragged her gaze back to him.

"What was it you wanted to say to me?"

"Oh. Nothing. Just thought you'd like to know that Evena left in huff a few minutes ago, heading toward the galley."

"And you thought I'd want to know?"

"Guess I also thought you were looking a little scared back there. Surrounded by all those women."

"Do you think I was afraid for my virtue?

"Nah! I know the pirate's motto. So little time, so many cunts to plunder.'"

"It's ships, Mary. Ships. I don't plunder women, I woo them."

"And you gotta spread it around, huh?" She said, nodding toward the crowd of waiting women.

"Truthfully, I was afraid they would make a meal of me. Wear it to a nub."

She laughed, a loud deep rumble. "They'd have a long way to go. And I mean long."

"Mary, which way did she go?"

She didn't even pretend not to know which she he meant. "Out that door, second corridor on the right. Galley's at the end."

"Thanks. Make sure my men don't make asses of themselves."

She snorted, her attention already riveted to Darak's pumping buttocks. "Mmmm-mmm-mm. That boy's full of surprises."

* * * * *

Adam snagged a pair of breeches hanging from a tree limb. After hopping one foot to the other as he shrugged them on, he headed barefoot for the galley.

The noise and boisterous atmosphere of the party had lost its luster the moment Evena had stomped out of the room. He wasn't sure why he'd flaunted the other women—he truly hadn't been interested in their attentions, but he'd felt a need to assert his primacy. After all, she'd refused him. Irritation swelled his chest.

He was a pirate, dammit! Scourge of seven solar systems. Master of his own destiny. He took what he wanted, no apologies given. Orgies and debauchery were his calling card.

His shoulders slumped. Actually, although he'd often shared women with his crew, and engaged in gratuitous sex with multiple partners, lately he'd longed for sex involving fewer gymnastics, and for a partner who'd help him shoulder some of the burden of his new world.

Why he pursued the one woman who appeared uninterested in what he could offer puzzled him. Except for sex, that is. He knew she wanted that. The way her eyes had burned as she'd watched the women climb over his body betrayed her.

But he needed to know, one way or another, whether she was willing to be his mate. If not, then he'd join the rest of his men in seeking a compatible partner. Although he couldn't fathom how life aboard a Dominion penitentiary could possibly compare with conquering a new world.

The galley door slid open silently and he stepped inside. The long, white dining tables and benches gleamed brightly, but the room was empty. A sound from within the kitchen itself alerted him of Evena's location.

She was rooting in one of the large refrigeration units, her back to the door. Adam stood in the entry, his gaze devouring the rounded buttocks defined by the form-fitting reclamation suit as she knelt to reach inside.

His cock pressed against the placket of his too-small breeches. He hadn't seen her naked in that position yet, but vowed he'd have her doggie-style before the night was over.

She grunted, reached a little farther to the back of the fridge, then wiggled backward with her prize in her hands.

Adam released the top two fasteners of his borrowed breeches to relieve some of the pressure strangling his cock. Rearranging himself again, he willed his erection to lose some starch. Conversation with Evena was challenging enough without the distraction of a hard-on diverting blood from his brain cells.

She stood, turned with the package in her hands and gasped when she saw him. Her gaze narrowed immediately, and she looked away, placing the package on a counter. "Did you make a wrong turn? The head's at the other end of the corridor."

"I don't need that kind of relief."

"Oh, then I'm surprised you aren't back at the party enjoying the other kind."

"Of relief?"

"No, head," she replied curtly, opening the box and removing a mud-colored nugget from inside.

Frustrated by her anger, he sighed deeply. "Look, what happened before was nothing. I was waiting for you."

"Sorry, I don't perform with an audience. Strictly solo." She plopped the nugget in her mouth and grimaced.

He tried to keep reign on his own temper, but the woman gave the word stubborn a bad name. "I don't either...um, not anymore that is."

"Not since ten minutes ago, huh?" She swallowed another brown lump.

He wished she'd at least look at him, when she skewered him. "Look, I didn't want that. I was just trying to be polite, a good host—"

She rolled her eyes.

"—then things got carried away. There were so many of them."

"Oh yeah, I forgot. Darak mentioned your motto—'So many women, so many cunts to plunder,'" she said, from around a mouthful of partly consumed mess.

"It's ships, for fuck's sake. Ships! And what the hell are you eating?"

"'Protein Poo.' One of our cook's own recipes. Mmmm-mmm," she said with a superior smile and held one out to him. "Cookies. Do you want one?"

"Hell no. That—that's disgusting." He looked into the box and could see why they'd earned their hideous moniker. "If you didn't want anything to do with me, why the hell didn't you at least eat the food I brought aboard?"

She shrugged and popped the one she held into her own mouth. "When you're gone, I'll still be eating these tasty little nuggets. I won't miss what I didn't have."

"Will you miss me?"

Her lips tightened, the only evidence he'd scored a direct hit. She busied herself selecting another cookie. Finally, she straightened and looked him in the eye. "Look, I'm not judging you. There are nearly four hundred women aboard this ship. Only a hundred will be lucky enough to leave with you. The least you and your men can do is give those left behind a pleasant memory."

"I'm not here to service four hundred women. I'm seeking a wife." He took a deep breath. "I'd gladly take you to wife," he said starkly.

Her expression grew bleak. "No."

Something akin to pain burned in his chest. "Why not?"

"Because I'm going home—to Earth. My family's arranging a pardon for me from the Dominion President himself. I'll get to go back to my own home and my own life."

Adam hated the man instantly. "Is there someone waiting for you? Another man?"

Her eyes looked past him, her expression far away. "No. There was, but the bastard's the one responsible for my being here. I'm going back to find him."

"To exact revenge?"

"Something like that." She looked at the nugget in her hand, and tossed it back into the box. "It's my mission in life to make his a misery. He's stolen five years from me."

Adam drew back. Revenge was something he understood. "Will making him pay give you happiness?"

"Huh!" she snorted. Her eyes flashed with hatred. "Happiness? I'll settle for satisfaction. Five stinking years I rotted in jail, first in an Earth penitentiary, now in this rust bucket." Her voice caught at the last word, and she spun to return the box to the refrigeration unit.

Adam stepped toward her resting a hand on her shoulder to calm her and felt the ragged breaths she drew.

She shrugged his hand away, but didn't turn. The box fell to the floor.

With his mouth close to her ear, he said, "I know about betrayal and anger so strong it twists your gut." He placed his hands on the cool metal of the fridge on either side of her and leaned into her back. He wouldn't give her space to pull her defenses around her like a cloak. "Are you afraid to let go of it?"

She pushed back against him, but he resisted, holding her in place. She stood rigidly in the circle of his arms. "This conversation's over." Her tone was steady, but he felt a shudder roll down her back.

"Very well, but my offer remains."

"Don't waist your precious eight days on me, Captain, or you'll be leaving empty-handed."

Since a direct approach hadn't achieved his goal, Adam decided to try another tack. He pressed his lips to the side of her throat. "You know the women aboard this ship. I want more time with you." His hand crept around her stomach, then lower, to cover the hot core of her sex. Pressing the fabric, he insinuated his fingers between her nether lips and rubbed.

Her breath caught, and her head fell back against his shoulder. "What do you want from me?" she asked, her voice breathless now.

"Help me find a wife." He pressed his rigid cock to her buttocks and began to rock against her.

"You want me to choose your wife?" she asked, her tone incredulous as she reached a hand backwards to clutch his hair.

"Yes." He rolled his hips, centering his cock on the crevice separating her buttocks. "You know what I like. I want someone like you."

She gasped, and rolled her head to face him. "We'll have to consult—"

He bent his knees slightly and lunged his hips upward, lifting her off her feet.

"—often." Her butt rested in the cradle of his hips, her legs spread wide, dangling on either side of his hips.

Friction burned his cock and he rubbed his fingers harder against her clit. "Yes. We'll consult." His hand reached for the neck of her suit and slid it open, baring her from her breasts to the nest of wiry curls.

He straightened his legs and released her. Turning her, he stripped the suit down her long legs, kneeling to help her step out of it. When she was naked, he placed one leg over his shoulder and nuzzled his face into the dark-red curls, spearing her cunt with his tongue.

Her hands curved around his head, clutching at his hair, pressing his face to her. No encouragement was needed as he lapped at the salty-sweet flesh that began to pulse and squeeze. He pushed a single finger inside and sucked hard against her clit. A wash of creamy female come coated his finger and he inserted two more fingers, pushing upward while he continued his assault on the rosy-pink nub.

"Adam!" Her hands twisted hard in his hair as she tightened around him, taught as a bow, only moments from climax.

He pulled away, rising to strip his breeches off while she watched, her hands cupping and squeezing her breasts. Christ! *She needs this as badly as I do.* Triumph, along with the urgent need to be inside her, swelled his cock painfully.

"Get on your knees," he said, his voice hard as his ripening balls.

Her eyes widened, but she complied, facing away from him as she leaned forward to rest her head on folded arms.

Dropping to his knees behind her, he palmed the cheeks of her ass, then reached down to press against her inner thighs.

She widened her legs and her waist dipped lower, giving him an excellent view of her moist, swollen vagina and rosy-pink anus.

With a hand guiding his cock, he traced a path from the top of the line separating her buttocks, pausing at the pink lips to press a teasing dick-kiss, rubbing a drop of pre-cum in tantalizing circles around the puckered mouth.

She moaned and pressed back against him, but he was determined to provide her an orgasm she'd never forget. He moved his cock lower to her weeping cunt and held himself at her opening. Dripping spit over her asshole, he plunged his thumb inside her at the same time his cock drove into her vagina.

Instantly, Adam's cock was engulfed in her femininity — moist, pulsating heat that threatened to sweep through him like a forest fire. Her anus constricted around his thumb, a tight ring that filled his mind with endless possibilities for exploration.

Evena released a muffled scream and surged backwards to meet his next thrust. She'd not deny he could bring her the sweetest completion.

Circling his hips, he screwed her, pressing hard inside, tilting her hips to expose her clit to the rough hairs on his balls. Soon her buttocks rubbed his belly, as she pressed back harder, higher, seeking the hot friction.

His balls tightened, ready to explode with the grinding motion of her hips. He pulled out slowly, then pressed forward concentrating on the feel of the walls of her vagina, rippling and squeezing, pulling him inward.

"Faster!" Evena demanded and pushed back to take him deeper inside her, but he forced himself to stop and slapped her buttocks.

"Adam?" The word was a question and a moan, and her cunt tightened impossibly around him.

Gratified this was another new experience he could give her, he growled, "You liked that?"

"Please?" she responded, her voice was high and thin.

"Baby, whatever it takes." He slapped her again, and her ass wiggled as she tried to deepen his penetration, but still he restrained her hips. Several more slaps against her tender flesh and she was gasping, pleading with him to end it.

Adam's control was slipping. The woman wiggling on his cock was coming undone. The reddened cheeks of her ass trembled and her breath came in pants. Adam steadied her hips then rammed home. In, out, faster and faster. The only sounds were the rhythmic slap of his belly against her ass, and her deep grunts as he plowed deeper and deeper still—until he felt the hot wave of his climax roll over him in a red wave.

He thought he must have shouted, but heard only her long scream before she collapsed, suspended only by his hands still wrapped around her hips.

With his heart hammering inside his chest, he drew Evena into his arms. Still connected, their hearts gradually slowed. Adam found it impossible to stop the motion of his hands as they glided over the smooth skin of her belly to her high, round breasts and back again.

To his knowledge, he'd never petted a woman. Never reveled in the aftermath. But he wished this joining would never end.

"I suppose it would be more practical for me to do the initial screening," Evena murmured.

Adam had to think hard to pick up the trail of their conversation. When he realized she was talking about his ludicrous plan to have her choose his wife, he became annoyed. He'd intended to get a rise out of her. Perhaps make her jealous with the thought he might take another as wife. Evena was a stubborn wench. But if she wanted to play this game...

"Yes. Remember, I'll need a strong partner. Someone of your build. We'll have to do some...research to test the fit, so to speak." Adam felt a perverse satisfaction, as she grew rigid in his arms. He wanted her outrage. Wanted her to refuse.

"You are a rather large man. We definitely don't want a woman who can stand up to your...appetites," she said, her words clipped.

Adam smiled and nuzzled the back of her neck. He was going to enjoy seeing how far Evena would go with this plan.

Chapter Five

Evena simmered. So the lout wanted her to find him a mate? As she felt his cock lengthen inside her, her outrage grew. The thought of all the interviewing he would have to do before he found the perfect fit must be arousing the bastard.

It galled her knowing his desire was ripening at the thought of "dipping his wick" into another woman's well, and she was getting turned on.

"Perhaps we should retire to your room to discuss this further," he murmured.

As his cock hardened more, she squirmed and sank further down onto his rod. Tomorrow, she told herself, she'd get down to the business of finding him the perfect mate. Someone with black teeth and an ass the size of a Samureen cow.

In the meantime, she shivered and circled her hips around his cock.

"Enough! I'll have a bed beneath me," he growled and lifted her off him.

When she bent to retrieve her suit, he grabbed it from her. "You won't be needing that."

As he stalked out of the galley, she could only admire the broad shoulders tapering to a lean waist, and the buttocks that flexed above massive thighs.

She sighed and followed. Everyone would be in the atrium. What did it matter if she chased down the hallway after a naked man?

* * * * *

"Captain McClure!" Calandra's voice halted her. The guard stood at the door of the security surveillance room, her eyes wide as she looked from Adam to Evena. When Adam tossed Evena's reclamation suit over his shoulder and nonchalantly stood with his arms crossed over his chest, Evena could have killed him. His cock thrust straight out from the nest of dark hair, still glistening with their come.

For his part, Adam didn't seem to notice there was anything unseemly about his nakedness or blatant arousal.

Evena cleared her throat and attempted a similarly nonchalant pose, hoping the guard would miss the blush that burned on her cheeks and chest.

She needn't have worried. Calandra's gaze was fixed on the pirate's waving mast.

"Calandra," Evena tried a second time to draw the woman's attention.

Calandra blinked, then turned to Evena. "Captain..."

"Yes?" Evena prompted.

The woman's gaze slid from Evena to Adam. "Perhaps, this should wait," she murmured.

Impatient with the woman's fascination for Adam, Evena replied, "It's all right, Calandra. What was it you needed to tell me?"

Calandra's gaze returned to Evena.

Evena regretted the attention immediately, when she realized she was shielding her crotch with her hand. Evena straightened and tried to pretend that standing naked in a corridor, next to a man whose arousal was large enough to give a mare pause, was an everyday occurrence.

"Captain McClure, shift change is going according to schedule. As we speak, the guards in the atrium are switching out, and Tina's here to relieve me. She's already reviewing my logs."

Growing more mortified by the moment, Evena crossed her arms over her chest, but uncrossed them quickly when she realized she'd only pressed her boobs higher. "Good. Just remember the two-ale limit, in case there's trouble later." Evena felt a rough palm slide over her buttocks, a not so subtle hint they should hurry along.

Calandra's lips pressed together to suppress her mirth. "I don't suppose there are more like him at the party, ma'am?"

Ignoring Adam's blatant attempt at distraction, Evena replied grumpily, "There are nineteen more of the horny bastards. Don't worry about being late. I'm sure they've exhausted their current partners." That comment earned her a pinch on her already inflamed buttocks.

Evena's legs turned to jelly. A hand slid around her waist to steady her. Strangely, Calandra's avid stare only heightened Evena's growing arousal.

"Sure you wouldn't like some company?" Calandra asked, her eyes fixed to the hardened pebbles of Evena's breasts.

"Perhaps this would be an opportunity to begin our search?" Adam's raspy whisper curled her toes. "I'll let you do the interviewing—I'll just watch."

At first, she didn't understand his meaning—but her body recognized the challenge immediately. Evena's blood thrummed through her, engorging her nipples and clit, and releasing a gush of creamy response that began to trickle down her thighs. Her mind reeled with shock. *I want him to watch me make it with a woman.*

Adam took charge. Evena's arousal was so potent his head swam. He'd bet his last dinar, Evena had never made love with a woman, so strong was her body's response to the suggestion. Shock and desire warred in her expression.

With a nod of invitation to the buxom blonde, Adam herded Evena down the corridor with one hand on her ass.

"Name's Calandra, by the way," the blonde said dryly.

"Call me Adam." He glanced back at Calandra. "She's never..."

Calandra grinned, "Not from a lack of offers, believe me."

When they reached Evena's room, Calandra entered first and began to strip immediately.

At his raised brow, she shrugged. "Don't want to give you two the chance to rethink this."

As the suit puddled around her feet, Calandra's melon-sized breasts made Adam's mouth go dry and his cock jerk higher. What would Evena be tempted to do? What were the secret fantasies she'd denied herself for so long? He pushed Evena into the room, then pulled a chair next to the bed. He straddled it backward, and looked expectantly toward the women. He'd gotten them both here, the rest was up to Evena. He wondered if she'd have the courage to follow the desire he read in her flushed cheeks and avid stare.

Evena's heart hammered in her chest. Although no prude, she'd never before considered a sexual liaison with a woman. Strangely, Calandra's "attributes" made her mouth water with the thought of taking her breasts into her mouth. She'd tease her nipples into hard points. The blonde hair covering Calandra's mons beckoned her lower. How would woman-flesh taste on her tongue?

Let Adam squirm. He'd issued the challenge. She'd answer with one of her own. And there was something deliciously wicked about going with the flow while Adam watched. *How quickly will he succumb to my seduction?*

Somehow, the thought of sharing him with Calandra like this didn't generate any jealously. Perhaps it had something to do with his relinquishing control to her. He probably didn't understand how much control he'd given her.

Still unsure how to proceed, Evena knelt on the bed, then lifted a hand to invite Calandra to join her.

The blonde knelt in front of her and flipped her long hair behind her shoulders, exposing her breasts to Evena's fascinated stare.

Evena reached a tentative hand toward a large breast. The velvety texture of the peach-colored nipple invited further exploration. Evena leaned down and lapped at the nipple. The bud rose easily against her tongue, and Evena couldn't resist giving it a flicker. Calandra's gasp encouraged her to deepen the caress, so she swirled her tongue around the nipple, at the same time sucking it into her mouth.

Calandra's hands dug into Evena's hair, pressing her face closer. "More. Suck it harder," she whispered.

Emboldened by her success, Evena widened her mouth to take more of the breast inside the cavern of her mouth and increased the suction until the woman's nipples lengthened. At Calandra's urging, Evena chewed gently on the distended tips. Calandra's breath hitched and her breasts tightened. Feeling powerful and infinitely sensual, Evena buried her face in lush breast. *So this is how it feels. No wonder, men love to play with tits!*

Calandra fell backward onto the bed, her arms open, inviting Evena to join her.

Evena followed her, straddling the woman's hips, continuing her assault on her nipples, alternately abrading them with her teeth, then licking to soothe.

Calandra's hips undulated upwards, her bush scraping Evena's open cunt.

Both women moaned.

Flexing her hips, Evena met the next stroke. The flesh between her legs quivered with excitement. *How does a man feel when he blankets a woman?* Licking a path up Calandra's neck, she aligned their bodies, so they faced each other.

Calandra's smile was sultry, her face flushed with excitement. Remembering they had an audience, Evena gave a sideways glance at Adam to gauge his reaction. His cheeks were ruddy, his chest rising and falling rapidly. A single eyebrow raised—a challenge to see whether she would go on.

Evena looked down at Calandra. "He hasn't suffered enough yet."

Calandra grinned and gripped Evena's ass, pressing them closer, until they lay mons-to-mons.

Evena savored the moment. Soft on top of softer. Warm skin, spiced musk—they traded soft murmurs of appreciation.

Evena lapped at Calandra tongue. "I didn't know," she whispered. "It's so powerful."

"I know. Empowering. I've been waiting to show you," Calandra said, then licked over Evena's mouth.

Evena forgot Adam's watchful gaze. Instead, she couldn't help the thought-consuming passion that kept her awareness glued to every inch of skin where their bodies pressed intimately together. *Bush, tummy, and dear God, breasts.* Evena's mounds flattened against Calandra's, her nipples stabbing the other woman's breasts.

She circled her tits on the other's breasts, all the while staring at her lips. She'd never kissed a woman, but wondered how different her mouth would feel from a man's when it was pressed to hers.

Calandra's lips moved. "Shall we?" She stuck out her tongue again and drew a line along the seam of Evena's mouth.

Eyes drifting shut, Evena gasped and closed her mouth over soft lips, deepening the kiss, her hands framing the other woman's face. Her face, her lips. *So soft, so hot.* Calandra's tongue dove inside her mouth, sweeping over her tongue and teeth. The kiss deepened and liquid response trickled from Evena's cunt.

Evena slipped a leg between Calandra's, rubbing her thigh against the woman's moist cunt. Calandra reciprocated, and Evena ground down, riding her leg.

Hands separated her buttocks, and fingers traced the path between. Small slender fingertips, rubbed a small circle around Evena's anus, pressing inward until the finger slipped inside.

Unraveling, Evena flung her head back and rocked, but it wasn't enough. She pushed away, sliding lower, and Calandra's hands pushed her shoulders, encouraging her to explore.

Evena sat up and cupped her own breasts in her hands, pressing them together, then tugging on the nipples to harden them further. Then with a hand guiding one breast, Evena bent, ass rising in the air, to trace the contours of Calandra's body with her distended nipple — over mountainous breasts, pouting nipples, then lower across her downy belly, dipping into the concave well of her belly button.

When she reached the nest of dark blonde hair, Evena paused to part Calandra's legs, and then knelt between them. She spread Calandra's nether lips and rubbed her nipple over the hard kernel of the woman's clit.

"Christ, you learn fast!" Calandra's hands twisted in Evena's hair as she writhed, her hips pumping. "Ohmygod! Eat me!" she pleaded.

Evena's already drenched pussy, spasmed producing a sucking sound. She smiled when she heard Adam's groan, but was too far gone to pay attention to him, now. Calandra's excitement was a drum beating a pulse, throbbing between her legs.

She sank her face down between the vee of Calandra's thighs, and rolled her chin and mouth around her sopping pussy. She tasted. *Salty, musky — like mine on Adam's lips — but different.*

"Yes, yes. Oh Christ, eat me," Calandra keened, pumping her hips so vigorously, Evena gripped her ass to hold her pussy to her mouth.

Evena's own cunt wept, pulsing as she licked along the seam of Calandra's. Then Evena darted her tongue inside as far as she could reach. With her fingers, she pulled back the hood that protected the swollen clit and rubbed her fingers in vigorous circles over it.

Calandra thrashed on the bed, then cried, "Please, please, please. I need his dick inside me."

Wanting to see that too, Evena lifted her gaze to look at Adam. His head was lowered, his gaze as dark and intent as a raging bull. She lapped at Calandra's pussy while she held his stare. *Will he break before I ask him to do it?*

His jaw clenched, nostrils flaring. His hands clenched the back of the chair.

Calandra bucked. "I need his dick. Now!"

Satisfied Adam was leaving her in charge, Evena withdrew from the end of the bed. Looking down at Adam, she pointed toward the woman's open thighs. "Check the fit," she commanded.

Adam's eyes never left hers as he stood, his cock impossibly huge, a drop of pre-ejaculate glistening at the tip. Evena reached a finger to wipe the drop from his dick, then brought it to her mouth. "Mine," she said, licking her finger clean, a warning in her eyes.

Adam's cheeks grew redder, his chest and shoulders rippling as he clenched his fists. "Tell me what you want," he demanded, his voice hoarse.

Evena mocked him with a raised eyebrow. "Fuck her doggie-style." *Did I just say that?* When Adam approached, her gaze fell to his cock. *It really is mine to command.* Excitement threatened to overcome her need to control.

Adam knelt on the edge of the bed and grasped Calandra's legs, flipping her to her stomach. She rose eagerly on her knees and presented her ass.

Pausing to check how she felt about the couple's eagerness to comply, Evena decided her curiosity was too aroused to want to stop them now.

Adam pulsed forward, his cock touching the woman's asshole, then glanced at Evena.

His submission thrilled Evena. She shook her head, no.

He pulsed forward again, this time touching the woman's gaping pussy.

Evena nodded and held her breath. He slammed forward, sheathing himself inside the woman's cunt.

Calandra yelped and tilted her hips higher to meet his thrusts.

Evena noted with satisfaction that a good three inches of his cock remained unsheathed each time he pumped inside. Walking around behind them, she watched as his buttocks flexed, in and out, and imagined herself in Calandra's place receiving his powerful thrusts. She laid a hand on his ass, and followed his movement, the muscle beneath her palm, shuddered slightly at the end of each thrust. She hadn't noticed that before.

Calandra looked over her shoulder. "Evena, join us." She gasped, as he lunged forward, spearing her again.

Curiosity seemed to rule Evena's actions. At Calandra's urging, Evena walked to the head of the bed and seated herself, with her back against the wall, her knees drawn up and splayed wide. She held her breath.

Calandra sank her face into Evena's pussy, and began licking and sucking as Adam pumped into her from behind, her head bobbing in time to his thrusts.

Adam stared at Evena's spread thighs, and his hips pistoned faster, the sound of his belly slapping Calandra's ass creating an indescribable excitement inside Evena. She raised her hands to her breasts and squeezed them, almost painfully, as Calandra sucked hard on her clit.

Suddenly, Calandra stiffened, and she threw her head back with a loud bellow, orgasm shuddering through her. When her release ended, she fell to the side of the mattress, pulling away from Adam's cock.

Adam stared at Evena, her thighs still spread wide for his perusal.

Her gaze dropped to his cock — red, veined and glistening.

"Yours, you commanded," he said, bending to catch her ankles, pulling her down the bed to him.

Evena fell back onto the mattress, and her gaze locked with his. "Fuck me."

Hooking his forearms beneath her knees, he raised her butt from the bed and plunged into her with a yell.

Hot, roiling tension began to build in her, radiating from her belly to her cunt as he pumped his hips, slamming deeper and deeper into her.

Calandra crawled to her, taking the breast nearest her into her mouth, clamping onto the nipple, suctioning it, and strafing it with her teeth. A hand crept lower, until her fingers found Evena's clit, and she plucked and rolled it between her fingers.

Surrendering completely to their loving, Evena's back arched off the bed as a wave of sensation unfurled in her belly, and her vagina tightened around Adams' cock, milking it.

With a roar, his seed spilled into her, washing her in a warm tide.

As Evena fought back to consciousness, she heard Calandra giggle. "Captain McClure, I didn't know you had it in you. God, I'm exhausted." She slumped beside her on the bed, an arm flung across Evena's belly.

Adam stretched out beside Evena, a hand beneath his head, his chest still dragging in ragged lungfuls of air. His outstretched arm landed on the mattress above her head, and she raised her neck for him to slip it beneath her.

Sandwiched between two warm bodies, Evena drifted into sleep.

* * * * *

Adam awoke in the dark to the sweet sensation of two tongues licking his balls.

A small hand wrapped around his ripening cock, and one of the women giggled, Calandra, he remembered. "He's awake," she whispered.

"Never mind, let's suck him off," Evena ordered.

Adam's dick hardened to stone in a second. The woman's aura of command, especially in bedroom matters, was the ultimate aphrodisiac. Accustomed to leading, giving control to Evena to do what she pleased was pure torment. To find her also directing the other woman's actions, left him a little nervous.

Tongues resumed their sweet torture, sliding along the length of him, pausing to mate noisily along the way while he waited impatient for them to remember he was the object of their quest. Then they parted, one heading back to his balls, the other licking a wet, hot path upwards to curve around the ridged head of his cock. *Heaven.*

Adam's head slammed against the pillow and his hips lifted from the bed. Lips below mouthed his testicles, then sucked them inside a steaming hot mouth to bathe them with a vigorous tonguing. Lips above sank around his cock, suctioning as they pulled up, strafing him lightly with teeth. Unable to hold still, he returned shallow thrusts.

Needing to do some touching of his own, he reached for the women, his hands finding their heads, but they pushed his hands aside.

The women shifted on the bed, and Adam held his breath, dying to know what they would do next.

The bed dipped beside his head, and at the same time, warm thighs straddled his hips. The heat of a fragrant pussy settled down over his face as another slid down the pole of his sex. With a groan, Adam lifted his face to rub it in the moist flesh poised above his mouth, circling his bearded chin over the woman's clit. Her taste was unfamiliar....Calandra.

Evena was playing on his cock. Her hips circled, grinding down on his dick, then pumped in short, hard strokes that rubbed her clit in the wiry hair that framed the apex of his sex.

"Give me your breasts," Calandra said, and Adam felt the women lean toward each other, then heard Evena's gasp and the wet, sucking sounds Calandra made as she latched onto a nipple. He could only imagine Evena's expression. Picture her first flight of abandonment as a woman sucked on her tits, and she used his cock like a dildo to pleasure herself. *I'm in Hell. How to wrest back control?*

Remove one from the equation.

Evena's hips pumped faster on him, and Adam renewed his assault on Calandra's cunt, tonguing her clit as he slipped two fingers inside her. She reared back, urging him deeper. Cupping his hand, he slowly inserted his fist, and Calandra ceased moving, her thighs trembling against his cheeks. He started to withdraw.

"No, don't stop," she pleaded, and pushed backward, taking his fist deeper into her, her vaginal walls rippling around his fingers.

A-hah! I almost have you.

Then a hand closed around his balls, rolling them inside their sack, squeezing gently. Feet planted in the mattress, Adam bucked beneath Evena, then started a pounding rhythm of his own.

Evena countered his strokes, her breath coming in short, throaty grunts.

Calandra moaned and pumped her hips, while Adam gave up precision for fluttering flicks of his tongue in the vicinity of her clit. When her orgasm hit, the walls tightened around his hand, pulsing in time to the chorus of her moans. "Oh, oh, oh...."

When the spasms ended, Adam gave her pussy one last kiss, then lifted her off his face. Evena had stopped moving on his dick, and her harsh breathing indicated she needed him to take over the strenuous work.

He smiled at Evena, ready to wreak revenge. "Oh Calandra, love," Adam prompted.

"Hmmm, pirate?"

"Are you up to helping Evena find her bliss?"

"Sure," she replied, her voice hoarse. "Just tell me what you want me to do."

Chapter Six

Evena panted, trying to calm her racing heart, but Adam's voice, low and intimate in the dark, along with his huge erection, was causing her belly and thighs to tremble with excitement.

She waited while he instructed Calandra. The timber of their voices, one dark and rumbling, the other light and flirtatious, made her lose the train of their conversation.

"Climb off me, Evena," Adam said. His hands at her waist assisted her as she awkwardly complied with his commands. "Turn around, love. Back up to me. Now, bend over."

Vulnerable and exposed, her cunt wept. Ripening heat in her belly grew to a raging blaze when his hands caressed her ass.

"Spread your legs, love."

She widened her stance.

His hands brushed down the inside of her thighs. "More."

She widened them further, feeling her labial lips open wide. Cool air licked her tender inner flesh.

Thank God, it's dark! Or I would never have the courage to surrender to them both. Waiting for their next moves was an agony of suspense.

Supporting herself on her trembling arms, she gasped when Calandra slid beneath Evena's tummy on her back, her soft hair brushing Evena's belly. "Ready when you are, pirate," she said.

"Now," he replied.

Please, please, please let it be now! Evena felt him slide partway inside her at the same time Calandra blew air against Evena's exposed clit. Her thighs quivered.

Adam slid out, then back in, slowly, twisting his hips to circle inside Evena. Calandra's warm breath continued to blow over her, and her hand sought Evena's breast, palming it. They were going to drive her mad, slowly torture her. *I won't beg. I won't…*

Evena leaned into Calandra's hand, urging her silently to deepen the caress. Calandra flicked her thumb over Evena's nipple and Evena moaned. But that was as far as the caress went.

Suddenly, wet, warm liquid trickled into the crease of her ass, followed by Adam's large thumb rubbing it over her asshole.

Evena shook, so great was her anticipation. Adam gave her another shallow thrust of his cock, and Evena waited with bated breath for him to unleash a storm.

"Ready, little girl?" he asked.

"Please, Adam," she begged, her inner walls already convulsing around his cock.

He lunged forward, burying himself to the hilt inside her cunt, while sliding two fingers inside her ass.

Unbearably full, she sobbed. It was too much!

Then Calandra sucked hard against her clit.

Heat, fingers, tongue, and cock rocked Evena, spiraling her down until her only conscious thought was the desperate need to climb the precipice.

With her breath coming in ragged gasps, her voice grunting in time to the rapid staccato of Adam's pistoning hips, she exploded, soaring over.

She collapsed onto Calandra, who wriggled from beneath her, laughing. "You nearly smothered me to death," she complained cheerily.

Evena grunted, too overcome to speak, still full with Adam's raging erection.

Calandra pressed a kiss to her shoulder. "I'll leave you two alone. Thanks for sharing, Evena."

Evena murmured drowsily, aware of the rustle of clothing in the dark, then the slide of the door as the other woman left.

Warm lips glided along the side of her neck. "I'm not finished with you."

Evena groaned. "I beg to differ. You've finished me off."

He laughed, a rumble that jerked his cock inside her.

Evena's toes curled. "You're inhuman," she complained.

He withdrew his erection in a long slow slide.

Evena murmured an unintelligible protest to the loss of his warmth and the connection.

He rolled her to her back, and then lowered his body until she was blanketed by him. Sliding a leg between hers, he pushed hers open, settling inside them, his cock resting, wet and heavy on her belly.

His hands tenderly smoothed her hair from her face. "Don't you know you're made for me?"

Evena conceded that was probably true, but it wouldn't do either of them any good. She was going home.

Biting her lip, she was glad for the darkness as a tear trickled down the side of her face. Try as she might, she couldn't deny the longing growing inside her to give herself to this man, body and soul.

Instead of speaking, she raised her lips, finding his unerringly, kissing him with all the want in her heart.

Adam gently entered her, rocking in an even rhythm, comforting, yet igniting the banked fire of her passion.

She raised her legs to circle his waist, holding him tight to her, and together they found sweet release.

* * * * *

The overhead lights flickered dimly, mimicking the early morning light of Earth. Evena squinted against it. For once she'd slept the night through without a single emergency to respond to.

Strong arms tightened around her waist, and Evena realized she was laying spoon-fashion with Adam warming her back. She snuggled closer.

"You do realize, she will never suit," Adam murmured near her ear.

"She?" Evan asked, her mind still full of cobwebs.

"Calandra. She doesn't fit."

Evena knew in an instant, they were back on the subject of mate-finding for the irascible pirate. She stiffened in his arms. "And why not? She's beautiful," she grumbled.

"There were still three inches of me left over after I was seated inside her."

Coarsely put, but true. Evena became alarmed. While their little ménage a trois had been a nice experiment, she did not want to share cozy threesomes with every woman aboard the ship until Adam found one who was his perfect "fit."

"Just how do you propose we find a woman who does—fit, that is? We only have seven days."

"We begin our interviews today. The first part of the process is the physical."

"Physical? As in examination?"

"Yes. Doc will ascertain every woman's fertility. I could ask him to do an internal exam to measure the length of their channels."

Outraged, Evena sputtered. "Measure their channels? How revolting!"

"I wouldn't make every woman do it. Only those who wish to be considered for my mate."

Evena attempted to rise from the bed, but his arms held her like a steel manacles. "Not no—hell no! I won't condone it."

"I'm only thinking of their welfare, my dear," he continued, his voice annoyingly reasonable. "If I should forget myself in a moment of passion, I might do my woman harm. Of course, the men might like to know their circumference, as well."

"What?" she asked, her voice rising as his meaning became clear.

She felt his chest shaking against her back.

"You were joking, right?"

Loud guffaws rumbled from behind her. "Heaven help me, but you're priceless."

"Bastard!"

"Yes, I expect I am."

Adam's cock nudged her buttocks.

Without a word, Evena opened her legs.

When he slid between, he grazed her cunt. Evena gasped.

"Are you sore?" he murmured.

"A little," she replied, feeling a little unnerved and very feminine.

His fingers dipped between her legs, pressing into her cunt. "You're awfully warm. Still swollen. I'm afraid we'll have to wait a while for you to recover, my dear."

"Sorry," she said, disappointed, but happy he intended to make love with her again.

"Don't be. I'm guessing you haven't indulged in wild orgies with pirates for some time."

"You're right about that," she replied wryly.

"Well, I suppose the thing to do now, is rouse my crew from their beds and get started."

"What about you?"

"What about me?"

She turned in his arms. "Are you sore?"

He eyed her warily. "No."

She smiled a woman's smile and reached for his cock. It pulsed within her hand. "Eager for attention, is he?"

"Ask him."

Evena grinned. "I think I will." She scooted down the bed until her face was even with his erection.

Adam held his breath, excited and wary of what she would do next.

"I've never been up close and personal, so to speak, with anyone's cock."

Adam wondered what kind of morons she'd been with before her incarceration. Her expression of wonder as she stared at him was unnerving—innocent and intent.

She traced a vein with her finger causing his cock to jerk with anticipation. "Does he have a name?"

"Well, he's never been christened." Adam pulled a pillow beneath his head to gain a better view.

It jerked again. "He appears to have a mind of his own. He needs a name."

Amused, he asked, "What would you suggest?"

"An impressive little man like this should have an equally impressive name, don't you think?" She looked up at him, devilment in her eyes. "How about Herbert?"

"Herbert!" he responded, trying to sound offended.

"No? Is Edgar any better?"

He grimaced.

"This is harder than I thought," she murmured, her hand gliding along his length. "He's a very important little man, and he should have a name that means something."

Grinning now, Adam watched as Evena's eyes narrowed. Moments ticked by, as she thought.

"I have it. I'll call him Rufus."

"Why Rufus?" he asked, curious.

"Well, in ancient times in merry old England there was a ruthless king who was very large, named Rufus the Red."

Adam liked the idea that she thought his dick was ruthless and very large. "Rufus, hmm?"

His dick jerked again.

"He likes it."

"Then Rufus it is," Adam agreed.

"Now that we've settled on a name, we should christen him, don't you think?"

Adam agreed wholeheartedly.

Her hand closed over the head, squeezing gently. "He's so soft."

Adam snorted.

"His skin, silly. It's like velvet. Almost as soft as my nipples." Her hand slipped from his cock to a nipple, testing the texture, then returning to caress him again.

The sight was unbelievably erotic. Adam had to check to make sure his tongue was still behind his teeth.

Her thumb circled the tiny eye at the tip, and Adam groaned.

Her head jerked up, and she circled again. "Rufus likes that?"

"Uh huh."

Her face lowered and her tongue stuck out, narrowed to a point, and dipped into the eye.

"Look at that!" Evena exclaimed, pointing his dick toward his face. A drop of pre-cum, white and round as a pearl, glistened on the eye.

Evena swirled her tongue over it, then licked her lips in a circle, before pressing a gooey kiss to Rufus's crown. "What a good little man you are."

Sweat broke on Adam's forehead. Evena appeared satisfied taking her time, but the minutes ticking by were becoming pure torture for him—his cock was hard as a rock. "Evena?"

"Yes, Adam?"

"He's Rufus the Ready," he growled.

"Did I mention, it was rumored that Rufus was gay?"

"He's not gay," Adam replied flatly.

"He's never—"

"Not once."

"Hmmm." She looked disappointed.

"Evena."

"Yes, Adam."

"Quit stalling."

"Spoilsport." Then, "He has a funny shape."

Adam gritted his teeth. "What's funny about it?"

"Well, it's straight, until just here," she touched the underside of Rufus, just below the ridge of his crown, "then he crooks inward a tad."

"He's straight as an arrow," he disagreed.

"'Fraid not. Rufus isn't perfect."

"Argh!"

Evena's hands circled Rufus, warm and tight. Adam closed his eyes and pushed upwards between her hands, relief moments away.

"Would you look at that?"

He cracked one eyelid open.

"My hands aren't small, but my fingers can't reach around—"

She was killing him by inches. "Evena!"

"All right!" she replied grumpily. "How long would you say he is—"

"God's Ballocks!"

"No need to curse. I can sure tell Rufus runs the show." Her hands slid down and up, then her lips closed over Rufus's smooth head.

With a hard-on so painful his teeth hurt, Adam willed his body to relax.

"You're squirming," she complained.

"I don't squirm," he denied and pushed between her clasped hands again, telling her with his body he was ready for her to get on with it.

"Anyone ever tell you you're grumpy in the morning?"

"Woman, right now there's only one way to get me in a better mood."

Wearing a frown of concentration, Evena slowly masturbated him with her hands—tugging, sliding, and twisting—her face so close her breath washed over the super-sensitized flesh. She'd learned fast how to drive him insane. Now that she'd settled into the task, he closed his eyes, his attention focused on the feel of her two strong hands rubbing the skin of his dick up and down his rigid pole.

As her hands moved faster, his heart thudded louder in his chest, his breath quickened, and blood thrummed through his veins, constricting his balls. He groaned and his hands fisted in her hair, drawing her face down to his cock.

Enough!

"Baby, suck me off," he pleaded hoarsely.

Evena swirled her tongue on his crown before sinking down on him. Up and down, her mouth followed the motion of her hands, gauging his arousal by his gasps and how tightly he gripped her hair. No way was he letting her up to make any further observations.

And Evena could have gone on and on about the taste of his warm, salty flesh and the musky scent of his arousal. And how about the feel of his huge cock ramming past her tongue to the back of her throat?

She sucked harder, and moisture lubricated her hands. She began to twist them slightly as she pumped on him.

"Like that...Christ, just like that, baby."

Evena increased the speed of her motions, and squeezed hard on his dick, adding the gentle scrape of her teeth.

Adam surged upward into her mouth, and spurts of salty-sweet liquid coated her throat. The rhythm of his gasps matched the pumping of his hips and the pulsing release of his come.

For several long moments after he'd ejaculated, he pumped into her mouth. Evena didn't mind. She bathed him with her tongue, soothing the poor little man she'd tortured so thoroughly.

Adam's hand smoothed over the back of her head, then urged her up his body. With his come still on her tongue, Evena kissed him, sweeping inside his mouth to share the fruit of her labor.

Strong arms pulled her on top of him and Evena snuggled her face on his chest, listening to the powerful, thudding heart within. A quiet thrill washed over her. This was what it felt like to have man cherish her. If only with his body. As his hand slowly stroked her back, Evena savored the moment. It was one she'd treasure in the lonely years to come. A moment that could wipe away the lonely years already lost.

"What brought you here, Evena?"

Startled his thoughts had followed a similar path, Evena tensed.

"I'm not judging you. I'd be the last to do that. I'm just curious."

She tried to evade. "There's not much to it."

The moments stretched while he waited for her to continue, and she finally sighed. "I worked for a universal financial institution. In the AI department. Cellular technologies were my forte."

"Brainy as well as beautiful," he teased.

She snorted. "Not so smart. I was having an affair with my supervisor. The bastard was embezzling money. Used my retinal ID. I still don't know how. Anyway, when it was discovered, my imprint was all over the transactions."

"What happened, then?"

"He dumped me." Feeling embarrassed for her stupidity, she continued unable to hide the bitterness. "At my trial he cried on the stand. Said he'd loved me, and didn't realize I'd been using him all the time to steal from our customers."

"What about your family? Did they stand up for you?"

Closing her eyes, she replied, "My family is well-connected. They were mortified when the family name was smeared all over the tabloids. They didn't really care whether I was guilty of the crime or not. They were angry I'd sullied their reputation."

"Then why return, Evena?"

The same question she'd begun to ask herself. Raising her head, she let him see her tears. "For five years this has burned a hole in my gut. I almost gave up. I was ready to take my twenty years and then disappear. My family has already distanced themselves from me and the scandal I caused.

"But then I got mad. I was robbed of my profession. Robbed of my virginity by a predator who used my naiveté to frame me for his crime. I want to see him pay."

He smoothed her hair from her forehead, his touch soothing and gentle. "You mentioned a pardon. Why is your family helping you with this if they'd rather you disappeared?"

Her mouth stretched into a smile, a cynical twist of her lips. "I know where the family skeletons are buried."

Humor glinted in his eyes. "Ah. The kitten grew claws."

"Something like that."

Adam curved his hand around hers and brought her fingers to his lips. "Just remember, my offer stands."

Her lips trembled. "I will."

He kissed her, his lips gently pressing hers. "Well pussy-kitty, the hour grows late. What do you say we find out what the rest of my crew's been up to?"

Chapter Seven

Evena followed Adam to the atrium, tugging at the snug fit of her reclamation suit. Funny, she'd never noticed before how closely it hugged her crotch. She hoped like hell it wasn't obvious to anyone who looked that her labia were swollen to twice their normal size.

Adam's predicament was far more amusing. Even a bedcover wrapped around his middle didn't lessen the masculine impact of his hard-edged features. He still looked like one dangerous dude—regardless of the pink sheet.

They entered the atrium, the place of solace and nurturing. Evena sniffed at the air inside and wrinkled her nose. Where the scent of greenery and blooming flowers should have lingered, the ripe aroma of sex permeated the air.

A hundred nude bodies littered the ground, some snoring lightly, others beginning to stir and interweave their limbs, moaning in lazy, unfrenzied coupling.

Adam looked over his shoulder at her. His expression was guarded. She wondered if he thought she'd be repulsed. With a wry shrug, she made her way over to him.

"Help me find my clothing," he whispered.

They made their way to the spot he'd laid the previous night. Reaching beneath the buttocks of a sleeping woman, he pulled out his breeches. Evena found his black shirt, wadded beneath the head of another, who grinned sleepily at Evena and amiably lifted her head to relinquish her pillow.

As Adam dressed, Evena looked for members of her security force. Calandra she found with Adam's young science officer, her head pillowed on his belly, his flaccid sex beside her mouth.

Evena nudged her with her toe, and Calandra blinked owlishly for a moment, before rolling onto her back and stretching.

The sight of the woman's swollen breasts made Evena's fluids stir. The delicious memory of those tits stabbing at her tongue made her mouth water. Odd, but the naughty things they'd done together in the dark didn't embarrass Evena a bit. Calandra grinned and parted her legs, an invitation Evena regretfully ignored.

Shaking her head, she said, "We need to get the guards up to make their rounds. This place is going to be hopping in a little while."

"Darn." Calandra sat up, rubbing her crotch. With an indrawn whistle, she replied sheepishly. "Don't think I'm up to it anyway."

Knowing how she felt, Evena gave her a hand up. Calandra surprised her by leaning into her, and Evena's hand lifted automatically to caress her bare breast, massaging the heavy globe. When Calandra pressed her lips to hers, Evena couldn't resist the welcome swirl of her tongue. They shared a long kiss, before drawing away to catch their breath. Calandra gave her a slow, wicked smile, a promise of more to come, and then Evena went in search of more of her officers.

One by one, she found her enterprising guards and woke them or drew their attention from their fucking to let them know they needed to get to work.

The last person she found was Mary. Evena stood over her for a long moment, staring. Mary rested on her back, Darak draped over her body, his cock still embedded in the short curls of Mary's sex, his lips sucking a breast like a baby as he slept. Mary's muscled arms enfolded him as gently as any mother.

She'd never seen her CB sergeant nude. Evena's tongue stuck to the top of her mouth, instantly dry.

The black woman's body was anything but masculine. With her newfound appreciation for the female form, Evena's heated gaze raked the dark, purple-brown nipples crowning her large breasts. The tips extended like the long, slender stamens of a rare orchid she'd seen once in the garden of a family friend. They invited a mouth to suckle.

Her gaze swept lower. Mary's belly was taut, the musculature evident beneath the satiny skin. Her dark labia were furled like a flower around Darak's pale cock. Evena's newly awakened sexuality made her wonder whether the curls that framed that amazing cunt would have the same texture as the close-cropped curls on the woman's head.

Mary stirred and her eyes opened. Seeing Evena, her mouth stretched into an impish grin, exposing her white teeth with the gap in the center. "Hey there."

Evena shifted on her feet, embarrassed to be caught ogling her friend.

"Don't be ashamed," Mary said softly. "I've been watching you for a long while, too." Glancing at Evena's crotch, she smirked. "Looks like you had a little too much action yourself last night, girl."

Darak moaned against Mary's breast and she gave a throaty laugh, "Come to mama!"

"Not again, Mary. My dick's numb." Without opening his eyes, he smacked his lips, found the nipple and tugged. "Mmmm." Darak centered himself between Mary's thighs and pumped halfheartedly at her cunt.

A large hand encircled Evena's waist, and Adam's warm breath stirred the hair beside her ear. "I almost feel sorry for him," he whispered.

"He's a lucky guy," she protested.

"She's more than he deserves."

"And don't I know it," Mary interjected, wrapping her substantial thighs around Darak's lean waist.

"Bring him to the galley as soon as he's up," Adam said.

"Poor word choice," Evena murmured, earning a rebuke in the form of squeeze to her buttocks.

"Sure thing, Captain," Mary replied.

Adam led Evena away, his hand at the small of her back. "The interviews will begin after the crew breaks their fast. Do you suppose you could place an announcement over your ship's intercom to let the ladies know we'll be expecting them?"

"Not a problem. I have to remind the women to get back into their suits, as well. Yesterday was nice, but we still have to recycle."

Adam smoothed a hand over her hip. "Do your women not know how revealing those suits are?"

"Are you saying you like the way we look in them?"

They reached the place where the corridor branched. Adam turned her to face him and drew her into his arms.

"Truthfully," he said, his voice dipping low, "I'd like better to see you in nothing at all, but the material of the suits fit close to your curves. It leaves little to the imagination."

"So when you first saw me—"

He traced a finger along her breast. "I could discern the shape of your breasts and the outline of your areoles and nipples. I knew the sight of me aroused you. Even now I can tell how swollen you are from our love play."

Evena blushed. His blunt talk aroused her, even as the knowledge that her body's visible response to him embarrassed her. Hell, her body was an open book for anyone to read!

Adam bent to kiss her lips, before heading to the galley. Evena mused that she was becoming accustomed to his attentions, even craved them.

And she'd only known him for a day.

* * * * *

With Calandra following on her heels, Evena set out on an inspection of the HS block cells. Frequent searches were required to ensure the prisoners weren't up to any mischief. So far this morning, no homemade weapons or evidence of security lock tampering had been uncovered.

As they neared Celestine's cell, Evena's back stiffened. She really, really didn't like the woman.

"Celestine's been kinda quiet," Calandra said.

So had Calandra. Evena appreciated the fact the other woman pretended nothing out of the ordinary had occurred between them. As the hours passed, she grew unsure how she felt about their lovemaking. "Is she aware we have pirates aboard?"

"Probably. You know how the prison grapevine works."

"Brace yourself. She's likely to be especially obnoxious."

"My club is ready. I really wish she'd slit her own throat with that whip, yesterday."

Evena silently agreed.

At Celestine's cell door, Evena raised her hand in front of the scanner until her palm print was verified, and the laser bars flickered off.

Celestine lay on the bed on her side, her head resting on one hand. Her reclamation suit gaped open, slit to her waist with the sides pushed apart to frame her breasts.

"We're back to full suits today, Celestine. You need to zip it up," Evena said.

Celestine swept a hand over one breast, plumping it, then rolled the nipple between her fingers. "I bet you saw hundreds of breasts yesterday." Her tongue snaked out and she licked her fingertips, then resumed twisting her nipple.

Her sharp-eyed gaze lifted to glare at Evena. "Heard you even had a couple of these in your own mouth."

Evena shot a quick glance at Calandra who shook her head, confirming that Celestine's sources were her own. That worried Evena. The psychopath was supposed to be isolated from the rest of the prison population.

Celestine's gaze remained on Evena. "Bet you didn't see any as beautiful as mine," she said while continuing to caress her breast until the tip blushed a deep red.

Keeping her face expressionless, Evena said, "Get up. You know the routine."

Celestine smiled and shimmied off the bed, her breasts jiggling becomingly. Brushing past Evena, she deliberately grazed Evena's arm with her nipple.

When she stood against the wall opposite the bed, Evena began her search. She was disappointed when she found nothing. She'd wanted an excuse to bust the psychopath's chops. With a jerk of her head, she indicated that Celestine could return to her bed.

As she sauntered past Evena, she leaned close to Evena and sniffed loudly.

Evena pushed her away, and Calandra raised her club.

Celestine laughed and moved away. "I smell man all over you, Evena. Can't get enough, can you? Who will you turn to when they leave, hmmm?" She lay back down on her bed. Ignoring the two women, she pushed her hand inside her suit and began to masturbate herself.

Evena's lip curled in disgust and she turned on her heel to leave the cell.

Once outside, she turned to Calandra. "I want to know who's talking to her. Log every visitor. Double up the guards. Someone's playing a dangerous game."

Celestine's mocking laughter followed them down the corridor.

* * * * *

Adam surveyed the dining room, satisfied all was progressing nicely. A line of women waited their turn to see Doc, who extracted a small blood sample from their earlobes to run through his portable diagnostic chamber. Multiple samples, with the women's blood smeared on blotter tissues, were set in the tray inside the chamber. The women didn't have time take their seats again before the monitor on the chamber gave readouts for each sample, the test of primary importance being the fertility reading.

Several women had already been turned away for fertility problems, but the rest waited in the next line to speak individually with one of the twelve pirates who were conducting interviews.

No internal examinations were being conducted this day. Once the field was narrowed, Doc intended to examine every woman to ensure she would be able to bear a child without complications.

Adam grinned when he remembered how enraged Evena had become when he suggested the women's circumference should be measured. It was a lucky thing his men hadn't hit on that very idea.

Adam stood behind one of his men, Milton Everhardt, as he interviewed the blond woman with the scar across her cheek that Adam had seen among Darak's harem the previous evening.

The scar did little to detract from her loveliness. Her long, sandy-blonde hair and cream-colored skin would please any number of his crew.

He leaned closer to gauge how the interview was going.

"So Miss Aurelia, have you ever worked on a farm?"

"No, but I've worked in a brothel."

"Well, that's a fine profession. Some of our men have very particular sexual requirements. Let me see." Milton removed his wrist computer, laid it on the table and pushed a button to raise a holographic display of a list.

"Here's Akron's list. His first requirement is 'Must love anal sex.'"

"What's this Akron look like?"

"I have a picture here." He pressed another button.

Adam nearly burst his gut trying not to laugh when a picture of Akron Kelly's nude body flashed above the table.

"Oh, my. Is this picture to scale?" Aurelia asked, while staring at the man's engorged cock.

"Pretty much so," replied Milton. "I took the picture myself."

"Tell Akron, I adore anal sex, bondage with chains, spanking...anything he desires," she replied eagerly.

"Yes, well. I guess I don't need to ask you anything else. Akron didn't care whether his woman could cook or clean or help him with his farm."

Aurelia grinned and leaned forward to plant a kiss on Milton's lips. "Look me up later, if you need to verify my qualifications."

Milton's cheeks grew red, but he nodded. As she walked away, hips rolling, Adam heard the younger man release a loud sigh.

"I take it everything is going well?" Adam asked.

The younger man jerked to his feet. "Aye, sir. It's been an interesting morning."

From the corner of his eye, Adam saw Evena enter the room. With a brief nod to Milton, he hurried to head her off. There was no telling what she might take offense to, given his men's lack of social etiquette.

Evena stood behind Ivan's chair as he interviewed a buxom brunette. Her scowl grew as Ivan read the qualities one of his crew desired.

"'Must have meat on her bones.'" He eyed the woman's fleshy thighs and check marked the first item on the list.

"'Must be willing to perform fallatio, and often.'" He looked up expectantly.

"Oh, of course," the woman replied, then grimaced, "Um, what exactly is that?"

A blush colored Ivan's cheeks spreading to the tips of his ears. "That's, you know, sucking his dick."

"Oh. I love that. I can do that."

Ivan added another checkmark. "Must like spankings. And giving them."

The woman's eyes rounded. "Now, I don't think I'd like that. Maybe I could give them, but I wouldn't want some man paddling my behind."

Adam crept behind Evena and caressed her bottom. Without looking around she leaned into his body, her buttocks rubbing against his growing erection.

"I hope, Madam," he said whispering next to her ear, "that you know very well whose cock you toy with."

"Adam? Is that you?" The minx turned, her expression pure innocence.

Adam's eyes narrowed, promising retribution. "Does our operation meet your approval?"

"So far. I haven't heard any mention of the measurements of a woman's circumference."

"That'll be tomorrow," he teased. "After we narrow the field."

"Now, Adam..."

He glanced up and spied Darak and Mary walking their way. "Your friend Mary's here."

Mary's face glowed. "I passed the fertility test."

"I could have told Doc she'd have no problems there," Darak grumbled, but then he too smiled broadly.

"Congratulations," Evena murmured.

"The only thing you've to do now is submit to an interview," Adam said.

"I've already taken care of that," Darak interjected. "She's met all my requirements. Top of the list."

"Better be the only one on your list," Mary said, her eyes narrowed in warning.

"You're right, dear. Just teasing."

Adam's brow lifted.

Evena hid a laugh with a cough.

"We're going to be interviewing for the better part of the day, here," Adam said. "If you ladies have other matters to attend to..."

Mary gave him a questioning look, then nodded. "Come on, Evena. Let's make sure our garden's been set to rights."

Evena nodded, knowing Adam had his own interviews to conduct, and that she'd just as soon not see whom his interest settled on. She gave him one last lingering gaze, then followed Mary into the corridor.

Chapter Eight

Shaking off her melancholy, Evena squared her shoulders and headed for the security room with Mary. Not slowing the pace, their long strides matched, heels clicking in time as they strode down the long hallway.

"Lord, I don't know about you, but that boy wore me out. You'd think he was the one who hadn't fucked in three years. Then to take on four women—boy's got possibilities."

Evena cleared her throat. "Mary, what you said this morning, about...looking at me for a long time. What did you mean by that?"

Mary's steps slowed. The look she shot Evena said she thought she wasn't particularly bright. "Evena, honey, you and I have watched each other's backs a long time. Usually, you learn a thing or two about your partner when faced with challenges."

Her brows drew together and her lips tightened. "But you've built one hell of a wall around your heart. Believe me, if I'd seen so much as a crack, I'd have been in like Flynn."

Evena's shock must have mirrored on her face.

"Don't look at me like that, girl. There's all kinds of love—and we're friends. I'd have scratched your itch, if I'd ever seen you wanted it."

"Mary, I'm s—"

Mary halted, facing Evena with her hands on her hips. "Jesus Christ, don't you tell me you're goddammed sorry. It doesn't matter. Not really. It's not like I did without, just because you weren't interested." Her lips twisted in a wry grin. "'Sides, I got some world-class ass last night. And more's coming."

Evena returned her grin, relieved her friend's heart was recovering.

"Guess I was just pissed that the first time you decide to try girl-pie, it's with Calandra, not me."

Evena blushed. "It...it just happened. She was there..."

"Shit! That makes me feel so much better," Mary replied, rolling her eyes. She started to walk again. "Come on, let's make sure those floozies cleaned up their mess after the party."

Quietly digesting Mary's comments, Evena realized she was right. She'd been so wrapped up in her old bitterness, she hadn't recognized the other woman's offer of love and solace. "So you're definitely going after Darak?"

"Yeah. He's comin' round to the idea. It won't take long for him to realize, I'm the one. But I'm willin' to share, if that's what he wants, too."

"You'd share him with another wife?" Evena asked.

"Sure. Some men feel suffocated, just one-on-one. Darak's a young pirate—still full of his oats. I don't want him to get bored and screw around behind my back. The man has a powerful sex drive. I want him honest. And I really won't mind him fuckin' another woman—so long as he lets me participate," she added with a wicked waggle of her eyebrows.

"Aren't you afraid of jealousy from the other wives?"

"Don't get me wrong. There will be only one 'number one' wife. We'll get along 'cause I won't let there be any game playing," she said, flexing her arm to produce an impressive muscle.

Evena shook her head. She had a hard time thinking of Adam with any wife—any woman, not herself.

"Evena, we're women. We hold the real power. We'll bear the children. We'll help each other and hold the community together. So long as we try not to make the same mistakes our old society made."

"But how do you fight human nature?"

"By remembering where we come from. Not this hell hole—Mother Earth. Now, I wanna hear about you."

"What about me?" Evena said, her back stiffening.

"I see the way you look at Adam—you're face all full of longing. When are you gonna to give up the past? Bitterness and revenge will destroy your woman-soul."

"I don't know if I can." Even as she spoke the words, she understood how hollow they sounded. Somewhere, between her emotional awakening and Adam's not-so-gentle sexual persuasion, she'd already started to change.

Mary snorted. "You better figure it out sooner than later, girlfriend. As we speak, that man's makin' plans for the future. And I'd sure as hell hate to conquer a new world without you watchin' my back."

Mary slipped her arm around Evena's waist, and Evena awkwardly returned the gesture. Funny, how only yesterday she'd felt a million miles removed from every other human in the known galaxy, and today she'd discovered she'd had a sister all along.

* * * * *

Adam watched Evena as she moved from table to table in the dining room, speaking with the women huddled in groups. At the start of the meal, a committee of women whose expressions indicated they had a bone to chew had drawn her from his side.

By the number of times the women gestured toward the men, he knew with a sinking feeling his well-laid plans were about to be dealt a blow.

"Doesn't look good," Darak said around the rim of his mug of ale.

"What started all this? Did anyone mention any problems with any of the girls?"

"Not really," Darak mumbled.

Adam gave him a sharp glance. "What? There was an issue and no one brought it to my attention?"

"Well, it wasn't an issue, really."

Annoyed, Adam drummed his fingers on the tabletop.

A frown darkened Darak's expression. "It's just that some of the women were asking whether they could bring people with them."

"As in, more of the women?"

"Yes."

"They were told in the beginning, we needed only a hundred."

"Right, but I don't think they realized how much work was ahead of them — until we spoke with them during the interviews today."

"I specifically said we would be starting a colony. What part of my briefing did they not understand?"

"The part about their taking care of their husbands' homes, helping with the crops in the fields, and raising the babies. They said the division of labor sounded a little uneven."

"Uneven? That's how it's done!"

Darak shrugged. "I'm just telling you what I heard."

"Well, they will just have to get over it. Besides, I'm sure the men will help out with the women's chores, if they become too onerous."

Darak cast him a doubtful glance.

Adam caught Evena's gaze and indicated with a crook of his finger that he needed her.

Evena's brows rose, but she kept right on talking.

"See how well they obey? And you thought they'd be so grateful they'd be an easy sell," Darak chortled.

Adam placed a hand in the center of Darak's chest and shoved him off the bench. While Darak sputtered in a pool of spilt beer, Adam noted with a great deal of satisfaction his shirt made of Alarian silk was drenched.

The men nearest him laughed, drawing the women's attention. Evena rose to her feet and strode toward him. Disgruntled that it had taken an altercation to bring her to his side, Adam folded his arms over his chest and waited.

Evena climbed over the bench opposite him and took a seat. She opened her mouth to speak, but he forestalled her, gesturing for more food to be brought to the table.

"What would you like to eat tonight, love? We've yak and Samureen beef, fresh vegetables we acquired from a freighter just a week from Earth, and fruit. Strawberries and apples."

Evena glowered at him, but picked up a fork and stabbed a slab of beef, moving it to her plate.

Adam hid a smile. Tonight, she wasn't so quick to refuse his offering. A quick glance around the room and he noted the women had begun to disperse, finding seats among the men. Perhaps he'd worried for nothing.

"Adam, the women have asked me to negotiate the terms of your bargain."

"I'm a reasonable man, Evena. I'll hear you out, but if this has anything to do with adding numbers to the passenger list, well that's just not going to happen."

"And where does the reasonable part enter into this?" she said sarcastically.

"Evena, I've supplies stockpiled to support my men and a hundred women for one year. If I take more people, we may starve before we can harvest our first crops."

"And you think the women will last the year with the work you and your men expect from them? Haven't you considered that perhaps more hands will increase productivity? You're asking an awful lot of women who aren't used to hard physical labor. And beyond the first harvest, who will be there to support the men's wives when they start to bear children?"

Adam reigned in his temper. The women's concerns were valid. There had to be room for compromise. "What do you propose?"

"The women who are selected want the right to select one woman to bring along as their partner."

"Two hundred women?" He knew he must have shouted his question, when the room grew silent. He took a deep breath.

"Your face is growing red. There's no need to get angry about this. It just makes sense. The men get their choice of wives. The women get their choice of helpmates. This can work out to everyone's advantage."

He took another deep breath. "As I said, I'm a reasonable man. What advantages?" he asked, his voice clipped.

"Some of the women would like to bring partners with them. They would be willing for their husbands to take a second wife."

Adam knew that suggestion would earn favor among his men. They'd have two wives to serve their every need, never mind they'd have two women to nag them, too.

"Some of the women would like to bring older prisoners to serve as grandmothers, midwives, and teachers for the children."

Adam's anger deflated. She was right. It took women to civilize a world. The wives would have their hands full, as it was. His colony would need unmarried women to fill those roles. "All right, but just two hundred."

Evena flashed a triumphant smile. "I told them you wouldn't be hard to persuade, once you saw the logic."

"That's my last compromise."

"Of course," she said, a little too quickly.

His eyes narrowed in suspicion.

Evena grinned and stuck a bite of asparagus into her mouth. "Oh, this is incredible. We tried to raise asparagus, but the conditions in the atrium didn't favor it."

Adam acknowledged her tactic to neatly change the topic of the conversation, and didn't miss the thumbs up signal she gave the women in the room.

A loud cheer arose, and one of the women stood, Aurelia, the ex-prostitute he remembered. Raising a glass, she shouted, "To the best band of cutthroats in the galaxy!"

Adam wasn't sure he was flattered, but he raised his glass anyway. Evena was looking entirely too pleased with herself.

"I think I'll ask doc to take her measure, tomorrow. What do you think, Evena? She's plenty of experience."

Evena slammed her glass to the table, uncaring that the contents, a fine French Burgundy, sloshed over the side. "If you don't mind a woman who's probably seen more d—"

"'Twas just a thought," he replied reasonably. "I'm getting a bit anxious. I've only six days left to find my wife."

"Captain McClure!"

Adam looked up to see a woman step near Evena. She appeared agitated.

"Yes, Mika?"

"We've received a transmission from the warden."

Evena's alarmed gaze found his.

"Tina hasn't responded. She wants to know what you think we should do."

Evena rose. "I'll take the call." To Adam she said, "This can't be good. The warden doesn't communicate with us unless she detects a problem."

Adam stood to follow here. "I'll go with you."

"All right, but listen from outside the security room. The transmission is two-way. I don't want her to see you."

This was the Evena he'd first met—all business and tough as nails. Adam followed her swiftly moving figure out the dining room, down the long corridor to the security room.

"Do you suppose they've somehow discovered our presence?" Adam asked, as he drew alongside her.

"Christ, that's all we need."

"How much might the outside know?" Adam asked.

Her long indrawn sigh didn't comfort him. "I really don't know what sort of sensing devices they have in the New Attica. Any computer hardware systems on board are completely inaccessible to the prisoners. Believe me, when we were first set in orbit, I inspected the ship from top to bottom." She shot him a wry glance. "I was bored."

"So you checked behind wall panels, in light fixtures—everywhere surveillance equipment is usually planted."

"Yeah. I didn't find any viewing or listening devices. Guess they knew we'd just paint over the lenses or yank the mikes out."

"So, why waste the money?"

"Exactly. But if they have heat-sensing capability, they'll know exactly how many people we have aboard this ship. Basically, your worst case scenario."

As a pirate, Adam always went with the worst-case scenario. "If they know we're here, what do you think they'll do? Would they destroy the ship?"

"Hardly, this prison is a costly experiment. One the Dominion has a vested interest in succeeding. The Central Council thought this one up themselves. Solves all their problems."

Adam heard the bitterness in her voice. He could well imagine how she'd felt being sent so far from everything she'd ever known.

Evena continued, her voice growing harder. "It's a great investment for them. And a real win for those who believe inmates need punishment and hard work to rehabilitate them. They don't have to pay for staff to maintain order—if we don't keep it ourselves, we'll die. We have to cooperate to grow food and produce our own water and air. They don't have to worry about constituents writing to complain of prison outbreaks, or the price of their real estate plummeting with a jail in their back yards. They just send us into a distant orbit and forget us. Out of sight, out of mind."

"If they're not likely to blast us out of space, what might they do?"

"I don't know. Let's see what the warden wants, before we get too worried."

Reaching the door, Adam pulled Evena back. "If she knows we're on board, you have to put the blame on me."

"I'll play it by ear."

"You're a clever woman. Do what's best for the women who elected you to keep them safe." He gave her swift kiss, then watched her step inside.

* * * * *

Evena pressed the hailing switch and Warden Driscoll's stony face came into view. "Red Hibiscus," she said.

Stunned, Evena motioned Tina out of the room. The code word meant the transmission was for Evena's ears only. Somehow, the woman knew about their visitors.

She quickly answered the challenge with the password that meant she was alone, "Blue Moon."

"Prisoner McClure, tell me about the situation aboard the New Attica."

Not knowing exactly how much the woman knew, but guessing it was probably more than she'd like, Evena chose to stick close to the truth. Never having learned how to lie well, Evena answered nervously, "Ma'am, the ship's been overtaken by a pirates."

"Why didn't you report this incident to us as soon as it occurred?"

Careful not to break with the warden's hard stare, Evena replied, "Ma'am, the pirates got the drop on us. They're armed, and they've taken hostages. I've been trying to diffuse the situation myself."

"What do pirates want with a prison ship?" she asked, suspicion in her steely stare. "And to what end? Have they mentioned a ransom? The Dominion won't pay it! We don't negotiate with criminals."

"No ma'am, they've mentioned no ransom demands. They have said they intend to take some of the women with them."

"Is this an organized breakout?"

"I don't believe so. None of the women appear to have any prior acquaintance with the pirates."

"McClure, an outbreak will cast a shadow over every woman on board that ship. If one prisoner leaves, all of your sentences may be affected."

Evena froze. "Ma'am, are you saying that even the women who don't participate in an outbreak will be punished?"

"Yes. And McClure, I have your pardon on my desk awaiting my signature. If the women leave, your family won't be able to buy your way out of this one."

"I understand." Evena's heart sank. Everything she'd wanted and worked for the past five years was slipping from her grasp. She'd been left few options.

"Do you? Persuade the men to leave alone, or better yet, detain them until I arrive with the fleet to retake the ship. It's your choice. I'll look kindly upon your pardon, should you help us to capture the brigands."

Evena nodded, numbed by what she'd heard. The force retaking the ship wouldn't discriminate between pirate and prisoner. "Ma'am, how long do I have to hold out?"

Warden Driscoll gave her an assessing stare, then replied, "Seventy-six hours."

An icy calm fell over her. "I'll do my best, ma'am."

"Don't let me down, Evena McClure. Your family would be very embarrassed if you were found complicit with a prison outbreak."

The screen went black, and Evena walked like an automaton out the door of the surveillance room. She gave a vague nod to Tina, and the woman returned to her station. Then she turned to Adam.

"I heard. Do you think we really have seventy-six hours?"

"Of course not. It's probably more like forty-eight. She'd hardly trust a prisoner with the true timetable."

He nodded. "She probably already has her team assembled." He reached for her hands and held them cupped within his own. "Evena, you must see now that you can't remain on this ship."

Evena shook her head. "My family won't stand…"

"Your family won't be able to help you."

The warmth she borrowed from their clasped hands began to thaw the chill that had fallen over her. He was right. They were on their own. She couldn't rely on any clout her family held on the other side of the galaxy.

Her mind began to sift through the possibilities, searching for a plan to prevent the devastation that would surely befall them.

"Do you want me to leave without the women to spare your pardon?" Adam asked softly. "I'd do that for you."

She looked at him incredulously. "Do you really think I'm that selfish?"

"No, just scared."

Anger brushed away the fog. "I wouldn't steal an opportunity for freedom for two hundred of these women to save my own skin."

Adam's lips curved in a little smile, but his expression was patient.

She shot a narrow-eyed glare his way. "How do you do that? How do you know precisely which button to press?"

He shrugged. "Anger dispels shock for me, too. See how much we have in common?"

"So what are you going to do? Your timetable's been moved up. And you can't hail your ship from ours. We've a set frequency—to the warden's office, only."

"Well, it's a good thing I had contingency plans for this operation. I have my own transmitter. I'll contact the Intrepid and have them prepare to return to the prison, immediately."

"How will your ship get past the detector beams? I thought you said you had to wait eight days for a window?"

"I lied. There were several windows of opportunity. We simply wanted sufficient time to look your ladies over—in order to make an informed decision. I don't pirate by the seat of my pants."

Relieved, that Adam would be able to organize an early escape, she teased him. "So you're saying you're just a little bit anal for a pirate?"

"I'm prepared, Evena. How do you think I've survived all this time?"

"Since I've never heard any of your exploits, I might have assumed you'd started your lawless life with this well-orchestrated event," she said dryly.

"There isn't time now for me to regale you with my adventures. If you were to come away with me, I'd gladly entertain you. What do you say?"

Torn between her longing for this man and her need to prove her innocence, Evena replied, "I don't know. I have to think about it."

"Well, that's better than an outright 'no.' I'm making progress. Maybe, I'll just have to bring to bear my considerable powers of persuasion. Why, I'll have you know I've been told—"

"I don't care to know by whom," Evena interrupted quickly. She was finding she had very little sense of humor when it involved Adam and the opposite sex.

"Perhaps I'll just have to demonstrate…"

Chapter Nine

"I've a proposition for you."

The raspy sound of Adam's voice in the dim light of simulated dusk startled Evena. They hadn't spoken a word since they'd entered her cell moments before. The only sounds had been the rustle of their clothing as they'd stripped, and the gasps they'd traded as they desperately sought to fit their bodies together as quickly and tightly as they could.

Then there followed a long silence while they'd savored the connection and their intimate caresses. For now, it seemed enough that they lay pressed together, as close as two people could be without inhabiting each other's skin.

Combing the hair on his chest with her fingers, Evena asked, "Have you thought of a solution to our mutual problem?"

"Now, that's a rather open-ended question," he said, his hands curving over her ass.

"I'm talking about the women—" she frowned, when his smile broadened, "—the additional prisoners the women wish to bring." She tugged his chest hair hard.

"All right! I offer to take with me every woman you deem mentally fit."

She patted his chest in approval of his good behavior. "You would take those who might not be able to contribute much due to disability or age?"

"Any woman who wants to come with us, and isn't a danger to the community, may join us."

"What about your well-laid plans? You said yourself you have provisions for only a hundred women."

"I can't in good conscience leave any woman behind to suffer a punishment for my actions."

"How will you provide for them?"

"I do have a trade, my dear," he said, his voice sardonic.

She raised her head to look into his face. "You'll continue committing piracy?"

Determination etched his features. "I will provide for the women, however I must. They won't starve. No woman will do without."

"You'll have many more women than men in your new colony. Don't you think that might cause problems?"

"I've decided to allow a more natural selection to occur. Give everyone time to know one another before selecting mates. If the women are willing to accept more than one wife in a marriage, everyone who wishes to form a family may do so."

"So back to the pirating thing. You'd do that for the women? Risk your life?"

"It's true I'd hoped to retire to the new planet and watch over its development, but one last go would be…"

"Fun?"

He shrugged. "Yes."

"Why did you become a pirate in the first place?"

"For the same reason responsible businessmen became revolutionaries in the old U.S.A."

Evena raised her eyebrows. "Hmm?"

"History wasn't your strong suit in school, was it love?"

Feeling like a dolt, she admitted, "If it didn't have a number—"

He pushed her hand toward his cock. "Long as you remember this is Number One."

She wrapped her fingers around him and caressed him. "Seriously. Why pirating?"

"Taxes on privately-owned ships were raised so high, I couldn't afford it. I refused to pay. I was labeled a pirate henceforth. " His gaze narrowed. "You look disappointed in my answer."

"I was expecting something more—"

"—blood and guts?"

She wrinkled her nose. "Well, more exciting."

"I promise you, I've had plenty of excitement ever since. I'll tell you about it once we're out of here."

Evena laid her head on his shoulder, not wanting him to see her vulnerability. "You haven't asked me what I've decided to do."

With a powerful surge, he rolled them, until he lay above her. "I promised a subtle persuasion." He kissed her lips. "Tell me afterwards, if it was effective."

Evena lifted her head to deepen the kiss, understanding that he didn't want to hear her response if she were going to deny him. She raised her knees on either side of him, taking him deeper. Her hands reached for his ass, and she sank her nails into his backside to encourage his strong thrusts.

With her eyes squeezed tightly, she concentrated on the sensations his cock produced as he pumped into her. She was so incredibly full — he reached so deep. His cock pounded against the mouth of her womb. Evena lifted up her buttocks to wrap her legs tightly around his waist. She needed him closer, deeper.

"You can breathe, you know," Adam's amused voice broke her concentration.

Realizing she'd been straining, she gasped, then opened her eyes to find Adam staring down at her.

His expression was fierce and dark. His jaw clenched tightly. Slowly, he withdrew, pulling away from the tight clasp of her thighs.

Evena moaned a protest and reached to pull him back down.

Adam caught her hands and placed them beside her head on the pillow. "They stay here." Then he knelt between her thighs and put a hand beneath each knee, encouraging her to lift them and spread them wide.

Cool air drifted over the opening of her wet cunt. Evena's breath quivered, as did the flesh guarding her portal.

Adam's rough hands caressed her inner thighs, pushing them even wider until she felt the lips of her pussy part, making a faint, moist sucking sound. He circled her opening with a finger, then pressed it inside.

Her hips rose to carry him further inside. "More. I need more."

Instead, he leaned over her and tongued a tightly beaded nipple.

Desire stabbed at her belly, curling her hips upward.

He sucked the nipple into his mouth, gently closing his teeth around the tip while continuing his fluttery licks. A second and third finger was insinuated into her vagina, stretching her.

Evena groaned. "This isn't persuasion — it's torture. Come into me," she pleaded. *Like you have my heart!*

Instead, he released her breast and moved to the other, opening his mouth wide to capture its fullness, suctioning and releasing it, while his fingers rooted deeper inside her cunt.

Evena gripped the pillow beneath her head. *Not enough! More!* Her legs trembled as she thrust against his fingers. Forgetting pride for the ache he'd created built between her legs, she begged him, "Adam, I'm going to come. Please, oh please, don't stop. Deeper!"

Adam deposited one last kiss on her breast, then licked a path down her quivering belly, tunneled his tongue into her belly button, then moved lower still, nuzzling the crisp hair at her mound. Finding the nerve-rich bud hidden in the nest, he swathed it with his tongue, then enclosed it with his lips and sucked. Hard.

Evena's startled shriek echoed in the tiny room. Her hips vibrated on the curled fist he'd fitted inside her vagina. A spurt of feminine come, warm and fragrant, bathed his hand, easing his way deeper into her tight passage.

"Tell me, you'll come with me," Adam said.

"Baby, I'm coming now!"

"No, Evena. You'll be my mate. Tell me!" he demanded, twisting his fist slightly, eliciting a shudder that racked her belly.

"Ohmygod! If you stop now, I'll die."

"Tell me, Evena. Tell me, and I'll end it."

"I love you, Adam. I love you."

"Not the answer I was looking for," his amused voice responded. "But good enough for now."

He withdrew his fist and straightened. Locking his elbows beneath her thighs he hoisted her up, placing his cock at the entrance of her dripping pussy. "Look at me, Evena."

Her eyes opened, widening as she watched her dark pirate poised at the mouth of her femininity.

"Know who takes your love, Evena. It's mine now. I won't ever let you go." He rammed into her, pressing endlessly forward, until he was sheathed to the hilt.

"OH MY GOD!" Evena screamed, coming undone as Adam began pounding against her, her orgasm spiraling tightly inside her.

When she came back to herself, Evena realized Adam had shifted her in his arms and they now lay on their sides, his body spooned to her back. He was pressing inside her once again, and she groaned. "Too much."

"Shhh, love. Relax," he whispered into her ear. Lifting her leg to ride along the top of his thigh, he moved inside her with short, rolling strokes.

As she gave herself over to his tender lovemaking, a calm settled over her. She stretched like a cat, rubbing her buttocks against his groin.

His breath hitched, and his strokes lengthened. The chest behind her grew warmer. Sweat broke on his skin, easing the slide as they moved in opposition of each other's slow thrusts.

A hand rose to caress her breast, pressing the flesh, molding and gently squeezing it, before taking the ripening nipple between his fingers. His clever fingers rolled and tugged at it, until the tip stood erect and exquisitely sensitive to his touch.

Evena became a mindless thing. Sensation ruled her movements. When his hand slid down to find her clit, a spring wound tightly, deep inside her belly. Incoherent moans rose from her throat. "Ah...ah..."

"Almost there, baby," he murmured. "Almost."

Abruptly, he pushed her onto her stomach, following to maintain the connection. Knowing what he wanted, she spread her thighs beneath him, and he lifted her to her knees with an arm around her belly, until her ass was in the air.

"Tell me how you want this?" he asked, his voice hoarse, almost strangled.

Remembering another time when she'd been on her knees before him, she buried her face in her arms and asked for the thing she craved most. "Spank me, please. Make me burn."

His response was swift. Large hands palmed her buttocks, then a sharp slap was administered to each cheek, followed by two quick, deep thrusts of his cock.

Evena moaned and lifted her ass higher, yearning toward the tender violence of his hands.

Slaps fell in rapid succession, warming her ass, while his hips pumped against her, driving his cock deeper and deeper. Finally, with her skin tingling and hot, he leaned over her, grasped her breasts in his hands and slammed into her, fiercely pounding against her backside.

The mingled scents of their arousal perfumed the air. Their voices grunted and gasped in time to slapping of his belly to her ass. Friction burned her, hotter and hotter, as her ass and cunt took his punishing thrusts.

Then her orgasm was upon her, constricting her nipples into deliciously pain-filled points, while her pussy rippled with contractions, squeezing and pulsing around Adam's cock, drawing it deeper into her.

A sudden wash of liquid heat burst inside her. She heard his bellow of ecstasy, then went flying after him.

Afterwards, Adam's arms cradled her as her breaths came in short sobs. A hand tangled in her hair and stroked her head, while the other rubbed her stinging ass. As she listened with her ear pressed to his chest, his heart slowed.

Wrapped in each other's arms they slept.

* * * * *

The peal of the siren, sounding from far away, pierced through the fog of sleep. Adam awoke to find Evena already stirring.

"Something's wrong," she said, as she stepped into the reclamation suit, sliding it over her hips.

"I'll come with you."

Together, they finished dressing, then entered the hallway to encounter chaos. Guards rushed through the corridor, armed with clubs. Evena took off at a lope, heading toward the security room, Adam at her heels.

Calandra was at the console, her face ashen when she turned to face them.

"What's happened?" Evena demanded.

"Aurelia's been murdered."

Adam recalled the pretty prostitute, who'd been eager to become a pirate's wife, and felt a deep sadness.

"Do we know who did it?" Evena asked.

Calandra nodded, her face stricken. "Celestine."

Evena's expression grew angry. "What was Aurelia doing anywhere near her cell? Celestine nearly killed her the last time they were together."

"It's my fault," Calandra replied, her eyes downcast.

"Explain how it happened. How did she get past this room?"

"I...I had company," Calandra whispered.

Evena stood as still as a statue.

Adam knew when she realized what had really happened, red flags of color rose on her cheeks.

"You weren't even in this room, were you Calandra?"

Tears leaked down the sides of her face. Calandra raised her head, her eyes pleading for understanding. "I stepped out for a few minutes. One of the men came to see me."

Adam's heart plummeted.

"Get on the speaker," Evena said, her voice hard. "Tell all prisoners to return to their cells. Have the guards report to HS block." Evena walked to the monitor still trained on what was presumably the interior of Celestine's cell.

Adam followed her. In the cell, a woman sat on the floor, her knees drawn up to her chest. She was slowly rocking, back and forth. Aurelia's body lay beside her atop a growing pool of blood.

Evena, her face closed and haunted, walked toward the doorway. "Open the gate to the cellblock," she said to Calandra, without looking back.

She walked purposefully down the long line of cells with their red laser-light bars. Pausing before one, she raised her palm to a scanner on the wall, and the lights flickered off.

Adam followed her inside, standing guard over her, as she turned her back to the rocking woman and knelt to feel for a pulse at Aurelia's neck.

Up close, Celestine was stunning, regardless of the vacant expression on her face. As he looked at her, she grew still, her features suddenly alert. Her head tilted toward him, and she smiled.

Adam stared back at her, schooling his face into a stony mask.

Her eyes narrowed. "You must be Evena's pirate. I almost feel sorry for you. There can't be much fire in her pussy." Her expression changed suddenly, growing soft and seductive.

A chill ran down his spine and he straightened, his hand reaching unconsciously to his laser-sword. He forced himself to remain unmoved by her words.

Finally, Evena rose from Aurelia's side. Her profile revealed her anguish, but while he watched Evena pulled on some inner well of strength and straightened her shoulders. She shot a glance over her shoulder at Celestine. "Just so you know Celestine, everyone except you and your friends in HS block is leaving this place. You'll be on your own. Let's hope the warden doesn't take too long getting here. You could get very hungry."

Celestine snarled, her teeth bared like a wild creature. "Then it will just be you and I. Huh, Evena? You won't leave. You won't give up your pardon. You're like me—you know how to hate."

Evena turned her back to Celestine in a deliberate dismissal.

Celestine pushed up along the wall, rising to a standing position. She took two stumbling steps toward Adam, but he didn't reach to steady her, instead his hand remained on his weapon.

Suddenly, she lurched toward Evena, raising her arm.

Adam saw a flash of metal, but before his sword cleared its sheath, Evena spun on her heel and swung a leg high to intercept the dagger arcing down at her.

The dagger fell, skittering across the floor. Adam bent to retrieve it, then stood back to watch. The battle was fairly weighted, now.

Celestine let loose an unearthly shriek and leapt at Evena with her fingers arched like claws.

Evena easily brushed aside her hands with a sweep of an arm, then planted her fist in the middle of Celestine's face.

The woman dropped like a rock, blood spurting from her broken nose.

Guards ran up to the door, peering inside. Evena strode past Adam and out of the cell without a word to the other women.

Adam moved to follow Evena. Over his shoulder, he said to the gathering women, "Remove Aurelia from the room, then lock this cell down. No one goes in."

Evena kept walking, past the row of high security cells, through the HS Block gate. Her back stiff and unyielding, her pace increased until she was running.

Chapter Ten

Adam ran after her.

When he caught up, he reached for her, but she shrugged his hand away. Next, he grabbed her shoulder and spun her to face him, finally halting her. He hit the button to open a portal on a nearby cell and pulled her inside, then he swung her into his arms and held tight.

Evena shoved hard at his chest. "Let me go."

Instead, Adam gripped her by the waist and lifted her off her feet, taking her the few steps to the waiting bed. He tossed her down, and she landed in a sprawl of flailing limbs.

"You bastard! I don't want this. Not now," she said, her chest heaving.

Adam ignored her words and crawled over her, holding her legs and arms down with his superior weight. She would face this!

Evena struggled, her face growing red from her exertions, but she couldn't budge him.

When she quieted beneath him, he laid his forehead on her shoulder. "Are you quite finished?"

"Only until you move," she said between gritted teeth.

Adam drew a deep breath and lifted his head. "Then we could be here for a very long time." To emphasize his point, he stretched over her, making himself comfortable by arranging his body to match her curves.

Her chin jutted out. "I've work to do."

"You've got grief to unleash," he said quietly.

She glared at him. "You want me to cry?" She acted as if he'd asked her to commit a heinous crime.

"That would be a good start."

"Well, I won't."

"Now you're acting like a stubborn child."

"Well aren't you glad you found out before you—" She gasped.

"Before I what?" he asked, wondering whether she'd been close to admitting what he already knew.

Her gaze slipped away from him. "Before you make a terrible mistake."

"Do you have so little confidence in my judgment, love?"

"Don't call me that."

"What? Love? My love?" His hands pressed hers into the mattress. "Because you are, you know."

Her expression darkened. "This is ridiculous. It doesn't matter." She renewed her struggle.

Adam's grip on her remained firm, "Don't run away."

She snorted. "I can't even breathe. "

He lifted his chest, resting on his arms. "You need to face this, Evena."

"I don't need your help. I don't need anyone." Her face crumpled.

His heart lurched. Now he wasn't so certain whether he wanted to see her break. Her tears would unman him. "It wasn't your fault."

"I'm in charge of this ship. If I'd been there..." Her eyes blurred with unshed tears.

He rolled to the side, carrying her with him, his arms surrounding her. Their faces rested on the pillow. "Let me help you." Slowly, he forced her closer.

Stubbornly, she resisted him until their chests met. For a moment, she remained rigid. Then he felt a shudder pass through her. He wrapped his arms around her, and she began to tremble.

Trembling, was followed by weeping that started softly, then grew from a well of anguish.

Adam tucked her face into his neck and held her as sobs racked her body. Gradually, they subsided, and Evena's arms wrapped around his waist as she nuzzled closer to his neck.

"It's so stupid," she whispered, her voice clogged with tears.

Adam didn't say anything, just began to stroke her back, letting her do the talking.

"Why did she go back there? Celestine nearly killed her when they were lovers. After she left, she knew Celestine had it in for her."

"Celestine gave her that scar, then?"

"Mm-hmm," she murmured against his neck.

"Aurelia likely wanted revenge. To taunt Celestine with her good fortune."

"That's so stupid. Celestine's nuts. Why would Aurelia even care what she thought?"

"Why indeed?" Knowing now was the time to push his point, nevertheless Adam hesitated. He didn't want Evena to feel cornered. There wasn't much time for him to work around her anger. Anger that would be directed at him. Adam pressed a kiss to her forehead. "We probably won't ever know."

"Adam?" Tears leaked from eyes onto the pillow.

"Yes, love."

"Are you trying in your not so subtle way to get me to admit my desire for revenge is just as stupid?"

Adam clenched his jaw. Her tears were tearing at his heart. "It's destructive love. And futile."

She closed her eyes. "It kept me alive."

"No," he said, pressing a kiss to her cheek. "You're stronger than that."

Her arms snuck around him and she pulled him closer. "Adam?" She brought her tear-stained face nearer to his.

"Yes, love."

"I can't stand it here any more. Please, don't leave me behind."

"Never," he promised, his voice rough.

Evena sighed and rested her cheek in the corner of his shoulder.

Adam rocked her from side to side, bemused. He'd never comforted another human being in his life. With Evena, it came as naturally as breathing air.

Her lips slid to his ear and she drew his lobe between her teeth.

A shiver wracked his body.

"Adam," she whispered, "I need you inside me. Now."

Eager to give her anything she wanted, and just as eager to fill her body and life, Adam quickly unbuttoned his pants and shoved them past his hips.

Evena lifted away to peel off her suit and pushed it off the bed.

They met in the middle of the bed, hands seeking each other's bodies, trading caresses and kisses.

Evena climbed over him and reached between them, grasping his cock in her hand, placing it at her portal. With a single flex of his hips he drove up, as far as he could reach, wanting to be a part of her, wanting her to acknowledge she was a part of him.

"I love you," she said and leaned down to kiss him.

He closed his eyes for a moment, savoring her words. "I love you." He pushed her hair back, bracketing her face. "I love you," he repeated.

Evena's breath caught on a sob and she began to move — slowly at first, her eyes drifting closed. Her hands clutched his shoulders, kneading. Her hips rose and fell, building friction between his cock and her steamy channel. Until the heat consumed them both.

When she cried out, she crumpled, folding over him and he held her until their hearts slowed.

For a long moment they clung to each other. Then recovering herself, Evena straightened and wiped the tears from her face. "It's too late for you to change your mind now. You're stuck with me." Her face wore a fierce frown.

He smiled and cocked an eyebrow. "Now why would I keep looking? You're a perfect fit."

She slapped his shoulder playfully. "That's right. No more testing the well with your wick."

He laughed. "What? You won't share me with five wives? I was rather hoping to start a colony all by myself."

"You'll just have to settle for the children I bear," she said, a glower wrinkling her forehead.

"Have you no pity for your sisters? Shouldn't you share?"

"It's because I care about them that I don't want them torn asunder by your — "

" — enormous cock?"

"I was going to say enormous ego!"

"And you won't ever have a hankering for a threesome again?" he asked, the devil in his smile.

"Well," she began, a blush staining her cheeks, "if I ever get a hankering it will only be a one-off thing. Occasionally." Her blush grew darker. "Maybe. But I won't share a marriage with another woman. If you want that, then you'll just have to—"

He drew her down for a kiss. "You are all I need. But if you ever want a walk on the wild side, darlin', well I'm not the man to deny you."

She shoved at his chest. "You did that on purpose."

"Of course," he grinned.

"You drive me nuts."

"It's my mission in life."

She shook her head. "I have work to do, now." She leaned down to press one last kiss against his lips. Her expression grew serious. "Thanks," she said softly, then climbed off him and quickly dressed.

Adam reached for his breeches, which were a crumpled mess around his thighs and wrestled a moment to pull them up.

When they entered the corridor, it was to find a group of Evena's guards awaiting her orders.

Adam let her go. He had his own duties to attend to, and a prison escape to arrange.

* * * * *

Evena found Adam in the cafeteria later, surrounded by a group of laughing pirates, an earphone tucked around his ear.

"Yes. Around 350 of them," he said into the microphone.

His face reddened, and his men laughed harder.

"Will you leave off, I can't hear a damned thing when you're giggling like a bunch of girls." He stalked several feet away and turned his back to finish his conversation.

Darak looked up. "Hello, Evena. He's just making the last arrangements for the shuttle. It will be here in the morning after first rising."

"Perhaps your first," Ivan said, clapping Darak's shoulder. "Old man."

The men grinned when Darak batted Ivan's arm away. "I'll give you old man." He turned back to Evena, a crooked grin on his face. "Why aren't you packing along with the rest of the women?"

Evena shrugged. "There's nothing I want here."

Adam's arm slipped around her waist. "I certainly hope you're wrong."

Evena leaned back against him and ground her buttocks against his cock. *I'm a wanton. I don't care who sees how much I love him.* "Maybe one little thing or two."

Adam growled into her ear.

"If you gentlemen will excuse us," Evena said, and walked quickly to the door, Adam shadowing her steps. Her heart beat fast and she felt a smile warm her face. *Everyone should be as happy as I am right now!*

"About that little thing," he said, as he caught up with her.

Evena giggled, then bit her lip. *I giggled!* Her pace picked up.

"Why are you in such a hurry?" he asked, amusement in his voice.

"We've only seven hours until morning. Do you want to waste a minute? Of course, perhaps you'd rather spend the time with your men."

He snagged her with his arm around her waist and pushed her up against the wall of the corridor. "Perhaps we shouldn't waste time finding a bed." His hands landed on the wall on either side of her shoulders and he leaned down to kiss her.

Evena hooked a leg around his hips and ground her pussy against his cock. "I don't care if you don't."

"Captain!"

"Yes!" Evena and Adam both shouted as Mary strode down the corridor, face dark as a thundercloud.

"Fights are breaking out in the cells."

Evena drew her gaze from Adam's lips and frowned. "What the hell do they have to fight about?"

Mary rolled her eyes. "Whose shirt is whose? Who gets which pirate?" She threw up her hands. "Everything!"

Evena lowered her leg with a sigh. "Sorry. Duty calls."

Adam's sigh was louder. "Don't be long," he growled.

Evena wrinkled her nose at him, then followed Mary down the hallway. "Think we need clubs?"

"No. But we might want them anyway. Darak's gonna find himself some trouble if he doesn't wait for me."

Evena laughed, and the two women loped down the corridor.

* * * * *

Evena made her way back to her cell several hours later, tired and cranky. Women! Thank God, after tomorrow they were Adam's headache. Her days as CB Captain were over.

The door to her cell slid open silently, and she stepped inside. Adam's gentle snore greeted her. *Well damn!*

In the dim light of early dawn, she stripped off her suit and walked over to the bed. His large body sprawled over the mattress, leaving only a small space next to the wall. She climbed over him, careful not to disturb him and lay down on her side. With her hands tucked beneath her face, she watched him as he slept.

All mine! From his dark, tangled hair to the beard stubbling his strong chin, his face was very dear to her already.

His chest rose and he murmured, and then rolled toward her, his heavy hand landing on her hip.

Evena's gaze trailed down his chest, and she couldn't resist touching what she saw. Her fingers combed the light furring, circled his velvet-skinned nipple, then trailed lower to follow the arrow of dark hair framing his sex. His burgeoning sex. She glanced up and found him watching her, a smirk tilting the corners of his mouth. "Don't stop now," he whispered.

Needing no further invitation, Evena wrapped her fingers around his cock and slid down the bed. Her heart beating loudly in her chest.

Adam's hand lifted the hair from her neck and wrapped it around his fist. "God's ballocks, woman! What the hell took you so long?"

Evena grinned, and then smacking her lips loudly, poised over his cock. "Believe me, sweetie, you don't want to know."

Adam's eyes narrowed. "So long as it wasn't another of my scurvy crew, you can stow it until after you've had breakfast." His hand pushed her face closer to his cock.

"Did I ever tell you that Rufus is a very impatient little man?"

"Will you get on with it, woman?"

Evena trailed the tip of her finger down the length of him.

His cock jerked. "Evena?" His voice rose in warning.

Evena opened her mouth and pushed the head of his cock inside, and then commenced chewing softly.

"Sweet J—! Evena!"

She laughed and licked the places she'd abused, and then slid her lips and tongue down one side and up the other. His hand tugged on her hair, but Evena remained steadfast. Torture—slow and uneasy— was the name of her game. She rose and knelt beside his hips, her lips never leaving his cock. At this angle she could sink her head over his cock and swallow a good bit of him—if she had a mind to. But she didn't.

Adam's head thrashed and his hand pulled harder on her hair. "There will be a price for this, sweetheart."

She continued her sweet torture, but a niggling doubt cast a shadow on her love play. What form would his revenge take? Evena decided to stop teasing and give him what he wanted. Besides, her belly was tightening and she wasn't sure how long she could keep this up before she had to have him inside her to assuage the kindling fire.

Her mouth opened wide as she bobbed over his cock, sucking hard. Her hands joined her play, and in concert with her mouth, enfolded him in her warm, moist heat.

Adam groaned and he planted his feet in the bed to leverage his hips, pushing up into Evena's hot little mouth. The faster her head bobbed and the harder she sucked, the closer he came to ending her play and giving her the banging she deserved. *Little witch!*

When Evena started to make groaning noises of her own, he knew she was ready. "Evena, come around to me." He let go of her hair and urged her with his hands to come over him. When her pussy poised over his mouth, he latched on to her labia and sucked and chewed and tongued, until she squirmed.

Her lips disengaged from his cock. "Adam?" Her voice rose on the last syllable.

"Mmmm, sweetheart. I could go for hours. How about you?"

"Do something! My clit—your fingers—please Adam!"

Adam smiled and reached around to pat her ass. "Revenge is sweet, huh love?"

"Bastard!" She rose, turning to take his cock inside her pussy, but he rolled her on the mattress until she lay beneath him, her legs spread wide—her cunt, his for the plundering.

"I'll teach you to tease." He realized he was poised at her nether mouth. He held himself still, but his cock twitched.

"Who is teasing whom?" she asked and rolled her hips, taking his head inside. "Looks like Rufus is in charge here." She snickered.

Adam closed his eyes. Bad move. All sensation centered on her hot, dark tunnel. Her entrance pulsed around the sensitive skin at the crown of his dick. His hips lunged forward.

Evena screamed and her legs pumped, urging him to move. Then she was shouting for him to move. "Adam! Do something!"

Adam went wild. His hips jerked, his cock leading where Adam had resisted. Pounding, hard and deep.

Evena's legs rose, and her hands gripped the backs of her thighs to bring them higher still. Anything to keep his hips unimpeded. "Give it to me, baby!"

Adam pounded faster, his balls slapping her ass. Then he loosed a growl that rumbled in his chest, as an orgasm ripped though his balls releasing a stream of steamy come deep inside Evena.

She screamed again and released her legs, darkness blending with light. Then realized she hadn't stopped yelling until the sound bounced around the walls and back.

She unclenched her eyes to see Adam leaning over her, his face stretched into a wide, cocky grin. "Good morning, love!"

Her eyes narrowed. "Eat me!"

"An invitation I can't refuse." He leaned down and kissed her lips, his tongue sweeping inside her mouth to mate with hers.

Evena pushed him away. He rolled onto his back and tucked his hands behind his head. Evena turned on her side and scooted her body as close as she could to his, her leg rising to slide over his hips to nudge his cock. "Adam?" Why was she hesitating? *Just blurt it out! Where's my backbone?*

"Yes love?"

"I want to go with you."

"I know that. I never had a doubt in my mind you'd see the sense—"

"Adam! Not that. I meant. I want to be with you when you go pirating."

Adam's complacent expression turned sour. "I won't have it. I'll not put your life in harm's way. Besides, it's bad luck to have a woman on a raid."

She rubbed his cock again, and didn't look back into eyes. Cowardly, but she didn't want to lose this argument and needed to keep her wits about her. "That's nonsense. I'm strong and smart. I'll learn fast."

"Give it up, Evena. I won't take you," his voice firm and even.

"But I know there are female pirates out there. Why there's Annie Cohen—"

"That's not the same. She was born to it. Women don't belong on aboard a pirate ship. My men wouldn't have it. And it's too distracting."

"For whom? I wouldn't be any trouble." Evena slid her hand over his stomach, and then lower to scrape her nails along his cock. "How long will you be gone?"

His cock twitched and stretched. "I could be away for months."

"And I'm supposed to be doing what in the meantime?" She grasped him at the root and squeezed. "And with whom?"

He growled, but lifted his hips to spear between the fingers clutching his cock. "I'll lock you in a bloody chastity belt with only my palm print to open the lock."

"That will guard my vagina, but I guess that wouldn't be so bad. Now that I know how enjoyable—"

"—you will not have another man anywhere near your ass. It's mine!" His hands came out from beneath his head and his arms encircled her, pulling her on top of him.

Evena rubbed her chest on his. "And my breasts have become extremely sensitive to touch. I suppose so long as he scraped me with his stubbly beard—"

"Who? You little witch!" He pulled her up his body until his cock fitted into her pussy.

"Tell the truth," she said, wriggling to take him deep inside. "You wouldn't have gotten your pirate ship out of port before you missed me."

"True enough. Fact is, I'm not sure I can stay out of your sweet cunt long enough to be a proper captain ever again."

Evena opened her thighs to straddle his hips. "So I get to go a-pirating?" she asked with a little shimmy and bounce.

"My men are going to mutiny."

Chapter Eleven

Adam congratulated himself on the satisfactory outcome of his single-minded campaign to win Evena's heart. Someday, he'd have to tell her he'd never intended to leave her aboard the New Attica. Someday soon. Before she'd decided to come with him, Adam's plan had already been set in motion. The timetable was just pushed up.

Evena's capitulation only made things easier. It hadn't really changed the outcome, but it did ease his conscience regarding his original intention to remove her from the prison — bound and gagged, if necessary. Her body's intolerance for the electro-stun would have precluded a more peaceful kidnapping.

She would soon discover the truth, anyway. His first mate, Cantor, had been busting his gut laughing over his predicament for days. Adam was sure their frequent, secret conversations, via the portable commbox he'd brought with him, had been the source of much enjoyment for the crew aboard the Intrepid.

No, Cantor wasn't known for his discretion. Adam wouldn't put it past him to use his knowledge of Evena's seduction to rile the woman, just to put a spanner in the works for Adam. Hopefully, Cantor would have his hands so full with organizing the women aboard the ship, he might forget Adam's plan for a time.

The fact was, Evena's fate had been decided, with or without her consent, the moment he'd clapped eyes on her.

Eventually, she'd concede the logic of his decision, being the sensible person she was. That is, once she got past her anger at his arrogance. He rather looked forward to the battle she would give him.

Adam watched the woman who would be his mate as she walked down the long rank of women. The line stretched down the length of the corridor and beyond. All waited patiently for transport to his ship. The many cartons of their meager belongings would be loaded last.

Evena stopped every few feet to talk to the women, reassuring them all was going according to plan.

Pride welled in his chest for the strength she'd shown over the past few hours. Early that morning she'd lead the women in a funeral ceremony as they'd launched Aurelia's silk-wrapped body into open space.

Then she'd set the women to preparing food for the prisoners in HS block who would not be traveling with them. The most dangerous women would remain on the New Attica, until the warden and her police force arrived. Evena had made sure every one of them would be as comfortable a possible until that time. Every one, that was, except Celestine. She received no food or water. Her loud curses could be heard in the next cellblock.

"You seem awfully relaxed for a man who's about to run a Dominion gauntlet, Captain," Darak said, as he drew alongside him.

"Huh," Adam grunted, never taking his eyes from Evena.

"Ivan's confirmed the window opens in ten minutes. As we speak, Cantor's readying the breaching craft. When it's clear, they'll begin ferrying the women to the ship."

"Good. I hate this waiting game. I'd like to get a good head start on the Dominion fleet."

"Aye, Captain. We'll need it. The Intrepid's not built to outrun cruisers."

"As long as we can make Arturia before they catch up to us, we'll survive."

"So, do you still intend to split up once we get there?"

"It's going to be hard enough hiding 350 women in prison-issue reclamation suits. Unless we're able to purchase or steal another ship at port, we'll have to take the women fifty at a time aboard our cruiser to the new planet."

"That could take us months. A lot could happen on Arturia before we're finished."

"I've gold enough to grease the palms of the local constabulary for a while, but I'll have to take the Raptor back out."

"I thought you were selling her." Darak's eyes widened. "Are you planning to return to piracy?"

"For a time," he replied curtly.

"What about Evena? Does she know you'll be abandoning her as soon as you get to Arturia?"

"She's coming with me."

Darak looked alarmed. "Sir, you know it's bad luck to take women on raids."

"We'll make our own luck. Besides, she wouldn't take no for an answer."

"Ooh-hoo! You're sounding hen-pecked already. I'm surprised you don't just tie her up and send her along with the other women. That was your original plan, after all."

Adam gave him a searing glance. "You're to forget that bit of folly, and that's an order, scivvy!"

Darak laughed, unimpressed with Adam's ire. "Does Cantor know yet that you're appointing him interim governor until your return? He's not going to like being grounded."

"I haven't had the pleasure, yet."

A light dawned in Darak's eyes. "Ah, you're going to make sure he and Evena are kept separate for a time." He laughed merrily. "Very nasty. But I like it."

"Cantor's a fine choice for the job."

"If you say so. Somehow, I can't picture him in charge of a company of women."

"It'll make a man of him."

"He's going to kill you."

"He can try." Adam's gaze was drawn once again to his woman. She was striding toward him, a smile on her face.

"I fear that one's going to lead you a merry chase, sir."

"God, I hope so," Adam replied emphatically. "By the way, you'll be in charge of the women left on Arturia."

Surprisingly, Darak didn't appear a bit perturbed. Then Adam watched Darak's expression grow soft when his gaze lit on Mary Grogan.

"So, have you decided to take Mary as your mate?"

Darak smiled. "To tell you the truth, I'm not so sure who did the choosing. But, aye, she's the one for me."

"The one?" Adam was well aware of Darak's proclivity for variety.

"My 'Number One.' It'd be cruel to leave so many unattached females without the love and support of a good man."

"I suppose you're going to sacrifice your manhood for the greater good?"

"You know our motto: So many women, so many cunts to plunder."

"Ships, dammit. It's ships!"

Evena's eyes narrowed as she stepped close. "Definitely going to have to find a new motto, Captain."

"Captain, huh?" He placed his arm around her waist and pulled her near.

"Only in public. Don't go getting all puffed up," she warned, with a sliding caress of his cock. "Can't have more than one aboard a ship. And since I'm a pirate-in-training, it can't be me."

"And what will you call me when we're alone?"

"Oh, I think we'll find much more interesting things to call each other."

"Master and slave?"

"Hmmm." Her eyebrows rose. "Sometimes. But we'll have to trade roles, occasionally."

"How about...husband?" He held his breath.

She looked up at him, her eyes shining. "And wife?"

"If you'll have this pirate."

Evena leaned upward to kiss his mouth.

Their tongues mated and their bodies aligned. Oblivious to their amused audience, Evena and Adam sealed their promise.

"Ahem, Captain."

Adam bussed Evena's lips one more time, before shooting Darak an annoyed glance.

Darak raised his hands in defense. "Thought you might like to know, the breaching crew's opened the portal."

A cheer arose from the women, and they surged forward to greet the newcomers climbing through the opening.

Evena sighed. "We've work to do, before we can continue this discussion."

Adam brought her hand to his mouth. "Tonight, then."

"Bring a slave's torque?"

"Will you wear it for me?"

"I was hoping to try it on Rufus."

Adam grinned. "Ah! He's a slippery fellow. Do you really think you can chain him?"

She licked her lips slowly. "I can make him my slave."

Adam felt blood converge in his loins from all parts of his body. *Damnation!* The woman would lead him by his ballocks, and he'd be a happier man for it.

Evena rubbed against his lengthening cock, then backed away. With a coy smile, she turned and walked toward the crowded docking station.

Adam shot a sideways glance at Darak, who quickly wiped the smile from his face.

"You know, Captain. It's going to take several trips before all the women are removed."

Adam's cock rose higher in his breeches. "See to it," he commanded, then walked briskly after Evena.

Darak laughed as he watched his friend and Captain grab Evena from behind. With a deft twist, Adam hoisted the struggling woman over his shoulder and headed down the hall, out of sight.

When his gaze returned to the women shuffling through the portal, he found Mary. Her eyes brimmed with humor. She favored him with a saucy wink.

As Darak strode forward to greet his mate, he wondered how quickly he could have Mary backed up to wall.

Something of his intent must have shown on his face. Her eyes narrowed, and frown creased her brow. "Oh no," she said waving her finger in his face. "This girl did not wait five years to miss this ship!"

Darak ducked, and gently rammed his shoulder into her belly. As she folded over his back, he patted her ass. "Don't worry, love. This won't take a minute."

Mary's muffled voice replied, "Take a minute? Baby, why so slow? I'm there, already!"

THE END

SLAVE OF DESIRE

Chapter One

Despite the meager light offered by the single crude fixture above the bar, Drago Chavez knew the creature in the dark, hooded cloak was a woman.

He first spied her when she elbowed her way through the crowd. She wore a long mantle, no doubt to disguise her figure. Instead, the flowing cloth clung to the enticing curve of her hips as she settled onto a barstool.

His curiosity aroused by her bold action, Drago withdrew to a murky corner where the sweet smoke from *hatta* pipes shrouded the occupants. The better to watch, while he remained unobserved.

He'd heard a ship full of escaped convicts, women from the Dominion prison, the New Attica, had arrived in Arturia's port city of Aghora. The women could be seen walking on the starship's dock, closely guarded by the pirate crew of the Intrepid. He had heard of none venturing beyond the end of the dock. And the fearsome reputation of the Intrepid's captain, Adamarik Zingh, kept Aghora's curious from approaching them.

Drago suspected he was staring at one of the escaped cons now. Only a woman tasting forbidden freedom would be so foolish as to wander into this tavern alone. The Pirate's Cove was a magnet for pirates and petty criminals who made their connections and targeted their next victims within its walls.

The woman was lucky she'd made it this far down the docks. Procurers for the brothels had circled like sharks around the Intrepid for days, waiting for a foolish woman to step beyond the boundary of Captain Zingh's protection. Drago hadn't been one of them, but seeing as the woman courted disaster anyway, he hunkered down in the shadows to see whether an opportunity would arise.

This woman was either fearless or incredibly naïve.

And as far as he could tell, broad-shouldered with wide-hips. The sturdy sort of woman Arturian men prized as breeders. If she possessed any beauty whatsoever, she'd earn a trader a pretty *dinar* at Aghora's monthly auction the next day.

She ordered ale. Although pitched low, her voice drew the attention of several men standing nearby. While there were whores aplenty inside the bar, every one of them blended with the décor — shabby, tawdry, over-used. This one's voice was youthful, hesitant, but at the same time, sultry.

Drago recognized several of the men closing around the woman who appeared oblivious to the interest she stirred. They were a dangerous lot — belligerent and stupid. Leaning toward Kaspar, he whispered, "Find Gilbert and have him bring the hovercar around. And make sure he's armed."

His assistant nodded and left the bar.

Drago decided to make his interest known to the crowd surrounding the woman and approached the bar. He clamped a hand to the shoulder of the man sitting next to her and slipped a dagger between their bodies.

The man's eyes widened when his flesh was pricked, and he gave up his seat immediately. "Didn't know this was yer seat, Chavez."

With a warning glare to the others, Drago slid onto the stool. Angry muttering sounded behind him, but he knew the men were leaderless at the moment. Not one of them would have the balls to take him on.

From the corner of his eye, he watched the woman raise her glass. When her head tilted back, light penetrated the folds of the hood, illuminating her features. He heard gasps from the men around him, and knew they'd been struck, as he was, by the beauty revealed.

Her hair was the color of Arturia's desert dunes, golden and rippling, and it complimented skin as pale and lustrous as an Earth pearl.

To hell with the local sale. If the rest of her was as enticing, she'd bring a fortune at the *Hazar's* auction — and he'd finally have his foot in the door of the more lucrative market — an opportunity that had eluded him since arriving on Arturia.

Leaning close, he said, "You're attracting attention. This isn't a safe place for a woman alone."

Her shoulders stiffened. "I'm exactly where I want to be, and I can take care of myself." She turned on her stool to face him. Regardless of the deep shadow cast by the hood, Drago was near enough now to discern her full lips pursed in a tight frown. "Besides, you're the only person who's bothered me so far."

"All right. So you have business here. What's your price?"

Her eyes narrowed to slits. "Beyond your dreams."

He deliberately swept his gaze down the front of her cloak and then shrugged. "If you've nothing to sell, what are you doing here?"

"I'm looking for transport to New Australia. I'm seeking employment in the minefields." She hesitated, her gaze searched his face. "I'll work for my passage."

Drago shook his head. "I wouldn't say that too loudly around here—you might just get your wish."

"Did I ask for your opinion?"

"Finish your drink. We're leaving."

"Huh!" She snorted. "You and who else are going to make me?"

"Hey," said one of the men, a tall fellow with yellowed teeth and a scraggly beard. "Sounds like the lady don't want nothin' to do with you."

Drago stood, straightening until he looked the man in the eye.

Yellow Teeth glanced over his shoulder to his buddies, but they all looked the other way. When he faced Drago again, he muttered, "Must be a lover's quarrel. Sorry 'bout that, mate."

Knowing the crowd would get uglier by the minute, Drago reached for the woman's arm and yanked her to her feet. When she swung, he grabbed her fist and pulled her close, his face only inches from hers. "Don't press your luck. If these men get any drunker, you'll be the evening's entertainment. So, unless you want to be spread-eagle on the bar, you'd better come with me."

She blinked, wide-eyed. "Did the captain send you after me?"

Without missing a beat, Drago nodded. "He asked me to keep an eye out for you."

The woman snorted. "I'm surprised he even noticed I left."

"How could he not? You're a beautiful woman."

"He has eyes only for Evena, now. And she's not likely to share him with me again. Not after what happened to Aurelia."

Not knowing who Evena or Aurelia were, Drago murmured, "You feel responsibility for Aurelia?"

Her expression turned grim. "Of course I do." Her voice grew brittle. "It was my duty to keep an eye on the high security cell block. She died while one of your pirate friends had me up against a wall."

While Drago digested this bit of information, he kept an eye on the door of the tavern. When Kaspar slipped back inside the doorway, he gave Drago a small nod.

Good. Everything was in place. Now, all he had to do was convince the woman to leave with him.

"I don't remember seeing you aboard the ship."

He detected a note of suspicion and wished he could discern more of her darkly shadowed features. "Finish your ale. Our friends are becoming more curious about you by the minute. I don't want to have to fight my way out of here."

"A bit on the nervous side, are you?" She straightened and fisted her hands. "I can handle myself in a brawl. Perhaps, I should escort you."

Drago smiled. The woman had a smart mouth and a bravado way out of proportion for her gender. Her courage was misplaced, but amused him just the same. "I'll let you lead the way."

"Fine." She reached for the glass, drained it, and then slapped it on the counter. "Don't let me disturb you any further. I don't need a babysitter. I can make it back on my own." She turned on her heels and strode out the door.

Nodding to Kaspar to watch their backs, Drago followed her outside.

Drago kept pace with the woman's long strides, passing warehouses and the ramshackle offices lining the street opposite the docks. The acrid aroma of engine fuel masked the less savory smells emanating from the alleys.

"Are you one of Captain Zingh's women?" Drago said, hoping to divert her attention from her surroundings.

"No." The single word was clipped.

"You sound bitter."

"I'm a woman. You'd think I'd know better than to believe that just because a man finds his bliss inside me, his heart will follow."

"Are you in love with him?"

"No. But I had hoped for some small measure of his esteem. Instead, I'm a pariah."

Drago wondered where the car was. Had Gilbert ducked into an alley to take a piss? "Perhaps you imagine it."

"No. I see the way the other women look at me. I failed in my primary duty to protect a fellow inmate."

"You made a mistake."

"I let Aurelia slip past the security gate. I wasn't watching the goddamned monitor. If I had..." She drew in a deep breath but didn't continue.

"Sounds like this woman was someplace she had no business being."

"I had responsibility for the security of that cell block. I failed." She dropped her chin. "I just never seem to learn."

"How was it your fault?"

She glanced toward him for the first time. "Look, drop it. You weren't there in the high security block when it happened. You can't know."

The cargo ship Intrepid loomed in the distance. Its large black hull glistened in the late afternoon sun.

A figure darted out from an alley. Drago recognized Kaspar as he raised a blanket to toss over the woman's head.

She dropped him like a stone with one well-aimed kick to his groin.

Kaspar rolled on the ground, cursing and clutching his genitals.

Drago winced in empathy and reached down to grab the cover.

"Bloody bastard." She straddled Kaspar's body and pounded her fists against his face. "Don't just stand there," she threw over her shoulder.

Drago sighed, and then stepped behind her and dropped the blanket over her head.

She reared up, fighting to free her arms from entanglement and butted against his chin.

Drago tasted the copper of blood. "Easy, now." He tightened his arms around her struggling body. "I won't harm you."

"Bastard," she cried, her words muffled by the fabric. "Let me go. Captain Zingh will kill you for this."

"I thought you said he didn't have any interest in you. What makes you think he'll come to your aid?"

"Because I'm a woman, and he's a bloody gentleman."

"Well, sweet girl, you're mine for now. Best get used to it."

"When hell freezes over." She wriggled partway free and drove her elbow into his stomach.

"Damned monkey! Be still, you'll only hurt yourself."

"You think I should make this easy for you?"

Drago wrapped his arms more firmly around her and squeezed tighter. "Kaspar, get up. Gil's bringing the hovercar around."

The woman continued to struggle, kicking at his shins.

"Easy, girl. We aren't going to harm you."

"Forget Captain Zingh! *I'm* going to kill you."

Drago grinned. She talked tough, but she'd be purring like a kitten once she understood her good fortune. He pressed his arms around her ribs, constricting her tighter until she stopped struggling.

The hovercar turned a corner and drove toward them. When it came to a halt, Gilbert leapt out. He spared a glance at Kaspar. "What the hell happened to him?"

Kaspar sat up and groaned, one hand still covering his crotch. "Watch out for her feet," he said, his voice strained.

"Kaspar, just get into the car," Drago said. "Gilbert, get a rope from the trunk."

While Gilbert tied her feet, Drago wound a rope around the blanket, binding the woman's arms to her sides. "That'll keep her out of trouble until we're out of the city. Let's get her stowed."

After dumping the cursing woman into the trunk, the men climbed in and drove away from the docks, through the city to the outskirts of Aghora.

Under the cover of darkness, they parked the hovercar in an abandoned barn. After instructing Gilbert and Kaspar to saddle several *llamyx* for the trek into the desert, Drago carried the woman into his makeshift office. He sat her down on a chair, and then turned on a light. "When I free you, you'll have to behave," he warned her. "You're in my territory now. There's nowhere to run."

He knelt beside her and removed his knife from the scabbard on his thigh. "I won't harm you. I'm going to cut the rope away."

Moving slowly, he sliced through the rope binding her torso and unwound it from her body. Then he pulled away the blanket. "Let's get a look at you."

He sat back on his heels and stared. Her hood had fallen to her shoulders, and despite her dishevelment or perhaps because of it, Drago admitted she was the most sensual creature he'd ever seen. Her hair was a soft, golden cloud, her lips full and rosy, her nose was slender, and her eyes were large windows into her sultry soul — sharp silvery flecks floating on deep blue pools.

"By the gods, you're a beauty."

Chin held high, she glared back, her sky-blue eyes glittering with outrage.

"I'm going to remove the rope around your feet. Then we're going to talk." He cut the last rope, and moved back a little, half expecting her to erupt in a blur of swinging fists and deadly-aimed kicks.

She did neither and stared stonily.

He sighed and sat on the edge of the desk behind him. "I wasn't lying when I told you, I mean you no harm. You're an escaped convict, aren't you? And I don't know what Captain Zingh offered you, but I gather you aren't happy."

When she didn't respond, he continued, "I don't know if you're aware, but women such as you are highly prized by Arturian men."

Her eyes narrowed. "I don't give a damn what Arturian men want. I'm leaving this planet."

He continued as if she hadn't spoken. "Arturian women vie for places in the *ha'arems*. With your beauty, you're sure to find a favorable position. Perhaps even in the *Hazar's ha'arem*."

Her brows drew together in a frown. "You're sending me to a *ha'arem*? You'd have me exchange one prison for another?"

"You don't seem to understand. Life in the *ha'arem* is desirable. You'll be pampered and petted. You'll have everything a woman could want."

"And I'll just bet you're doing this out of the goodness of your heart," she said, sarcasm dripping from her lips.

Heat painted his cheeks. "I'll earn a commission," he admitted.

"You're a slave trader?"

"I trade goods," he enunciated slowly. "Sometimes, I place people in better circumstances."

"I'll lose my freedom. How is that a better circumstance?"

Drago began to take the woman's measure. She wasn't just stubborn—she was as obstinate as a mule. He'd have to gentle this one slowly...for her own good. "Think about this, blue-eyes. Do you really believe Zingh will outrun the Dominion fleet? He'll be captured, and the women returned to the New Attica. But you won't be among them. Isn't that a better fate?"

"And if he isn't caught? How is my situation bettered?"

"You'll be a concubine, perhaps even a wife, to a powerful man. And if you use your assets wisely, you may wield tremendous influence. Your every want will be granted."

"And if all I want is freedom to leave?"

"You say that now, but someday you'll thank me. Don't fight this. I'd rather our time together be pleasant. If you force me, I'll tie you to a *llamyx* for the journey."

For a moment her lips trembled, before she thinned them to a straight line and lifted her chin. "Fuck you."

Relieved she hadn't given into tears, which would have annoyed the hell out of him, Drago replied, "Before we leave, I'll need to see what we've got to work with here—if I'm to get you into the catalog in time."

Her eyes narrowed. "You're going to list me in a catalog?"

"You'll be sold at auction. The auctioneer will want advance notice of your attributes to stir interest and attract the highest bidders."

"You're going to sell me in an auction?" Her voice rose. "I'm not an animal."

"It's the custom here."

Her face as black as an angry storm cloud, she rose from her chair. "No. Forget it. I'm not going anywhere with you. I won't cooperate."

"Sweetheart, you'll cooperate. If you don't, men will assume you're playacting and that submission is your game. Do you want some S&M freak to purchase you?"

"I'll tell them I was abducted and have no wish to be sold."

He laughed. "They won't believe you. No woman on Arturia would pass up an opportunity to catch the *Hazar's* eye."

She didn't answer, but her scowl deepened. Reddened cheeks and the stubborn set of her chin said she wasn't going to make his life easy.

Drago straightened. "Let's get started. Take off your clothes."

She folded her arms over her chest.

"You can take them off yourself, or I'll assume you prefer I do it."

"Oh yeah? You and what army?"

"Oh, I'll get them off, but they'll be in shreds. And tomorrow, you'll spend the day on the back of a *llamyx* buck naked."

Drago waited while the woman's thoughts paraded across her face. Stubborn resistance, followed by a desperate desire for escape. And finally resignation. She reached for the neck of her cloak, unfastened it, and let it slide down her body to the ground.

His gaze flickered over her lithe form, defined by the sleek, black reclamation suit that conformed to her curves. His attention was arrested by her chest. Her breasts were enormous, and while he stared the tips jutted against the fabric. His mouth grew dry, and his loins stirred and tightened.

Her expression set in stony rebellion, the woman lifted a hand to the fastener at the top of the suit, and opened it, peeling it down her body until she stood nude before him.

Drago couldn't drag his attention from her breasts, noting the unusual peach color of the aureoles that framed rosy-brown nipples.

His breath grew ragged and he realized the woman should fear his intentions. His erection pressed uncomfortably against the placket of his breeches. Although accustomed to the company of nude beauties, this one stirred him more than the others. Not willing to acknowledge his interest might be for more than a quick ride, he reluctantly forced his gaze to descend past her slightly rounded belly to the triangle of blonde hair. This was a woman a man could spend a lifetime exploring. A twinge of regret was all he allowed himself to feel. Ruthlessly pushing away that emotion, he forced himself to remember she was merely a commodity.

Reaching into his pocket, he removed the small transmitter, placed the earpiece in his left ear and pointed the microphone toward his mouth. "What's your name?"

"Calandra. Calandra Jones," she spat the words at him.

"Gentlemen," he said into the microphone, "Calandra is a natural blonde."

Chapter Two

Calandra simmered while the trader listed her attributes to his unseen audience as if she were a racehorse.

"Her hair's the color of ripening wheat" and "she possesses eyes the vivid blue of a summer sky" were only mildly embarrassing. But as he described her skin as "white as cream from a Samureen cow," her breasts as "the size of melons, with large peach-colored areoles," and her hips "broad enough to whelp a litter of Arturian pups," she began to plot his murder.

When he wet his fingertips and tugged the tips of her breasts to describe the length they reached, she decided a quick death was too good for him.

If only he had a face to match his black heart. Instead, his features were ruggedly handsome, sharply etched with danger. Dark as the devil. His brown-black hair, cut short as a Dominion soldier's, and deep olive complexion lent a sinister, yet sexy, caste to his appearance.

And he was tall. She'd always had a thing for big men. When he circled her to describe her body in minute detail, she felt small and very, very feminine.

To her dismay, his matter-of-fact comments and passionless caresses slowly turned her on. Her breasts grew heavy, and her areoles dimpled tightly. Her feminine core wound like a spring with each sweep of his gaze across her chest and hips.

When he squeezed a buttock to test the firmness, she shuddered, and her traitorous body released a trickle of feminine excitement.

"Jump up," he said, indicating the desk behind him.

She was grateful for the suggestion—her knees trembled. But once she sat on the edge, she was sure her thighs spread every bit as wide as a Samureen cow's.

He shook his head. "No, lie back."

Pride demanded she refuse, but desire proved stronger. Perhaps, he'd take her now.

When she reclined, he encouraged her to raise her legs and grip the edge of the desk with her heels. With only a light pressure at her knees, he persuaded her to spread her legs apart.

Her stomach quivered, and she smelled her own ripening arousal. The heady combination of submission and wide-open exposure—her two favorite turn-ons—was more than her body could resist.

Her eyes closed. Better to imagine another circumstance, rather than lying on a shabby desk, splayed wide for this man's clinical observations.

She didn't care, he thought her a whore. And at this moment, didn't care he trafficked in human flesh. Her flesh trembled with need.

Unfortunately, he seemed unaffected. Standing between her legs, he continued his endless recitation. "Labia are delicate folds, rosy to bright red." He raked his fingers through her hair. "The hair covering her mons is surprisingly soft, and a shade or two darker than the hair on her head."

She gasped as fingers pulled back the hood of skin that concealed her clit. "Clitoris is a bright red when aroused."

Her eyes flew open and met his gaze.

He raised a single brow.

Angry that he mocked her response, she rose up on her elbows, ready to leave her perch.

A butterfly touch flicked across the kernel of her clit. Nerves beneath the surface shot a signal to her brain and released the floodgate of her passion. She gasped when a single long finger pressed inside, and her hips rose to deepen the penetration.

He withdrew the finger and brought it to his mouth. He licked it clean. "Her dew tastes of salt and spice," he said, his voice rough, "and she releases a generous wash of pre-come."

With the same finger, he traced a path leading beyond her cunt, finally grazing the delicate mouth of her anus, and then circled it twice.

Calandra moaned, her head rolling from side to side. "Please," she whispered.

"Sorry, sweetheart. The auction house owns your response. I will only describe it."

Incredulous, Calandra cried, "You're going to leave me like this?"

He seemed amused by her strident complaint. "I'm not cruel. I don't intend to come inside you, we haven't the time, but I can give you relief."

"Damn you. You knew I was becoming aroused. Why didn't you stop?"

"I needed to see your response to describe it. Arturian males crave real passion from a woman before they become aroused. They can smell deceit. So don't ever try to fake it or hold back."

She rolled her eyes. As if she could hold back a thing. "All right, so you won't fuck me. Do something!"

He smoothed a hand down the inside of her thigh. Calandra's hips rose, inviting him into her center. He pressed a finger into her channel and circled.

Calandra lay back against the desk and rolled her hips, following the motion of his hand. Her arousal resumed its climb, curling inside her belly. Her hands sought her breasts, and she caressed nipples that were painfully stiff. "Ah...Ah," she moaned.

He shoved one of her hands aside and leaned over her breast. Opening his mouth wide, he drew the tip deep inside his mouth, his cheeks hollowing as he sucked. He shoved another two fingers into her vagina and pushed deep.

Filled with gliding fingers, and overwhelmed by the attention her sensitive breast was receiving, Calandra's thoughts shattered. Her hips pumped on his hand, her head rolling wildly. Her own fingers slid down her stomach to her clitoris and she rubbed it vigorously. *So close!* "Oh God. I need more...Please, eat me."

"Hell." He withdrew.

For a moment she thought he'd halted his lovemaking and she bit back a protest. Calandra groaned, now desperate to come. Her fingers continued to work on her swollen clit, sliding her juices over the hardened kernel. Her hips undulated, seeking to be filled.

She heard the scrape of a chair and opened her eyes to see him place the chair at the end of the desk. When he sat, his breath washed over her cunt. *Oh yes! Now! Now! Now!*

She rose on her elbows to watch as he spread the lips of her pussy. "Do it. Eat me," she commanded, her voice husky with desire.

"You're not the least bit inhibited, are you sweetheart?" He bent his head, and his tongue flickered lightly over her clit.

Her knees trembled and her pussy wept. Calandra gripped the edge of the desk, fighting a scream building in her throat.

He lapped at the moisture that seeped from her, spearing his tongue inside.

"More. I need more. Come inside me," she begged. *Fuck me, now!* But she didn't let him see just how wild she was. The bastard already knew her body too well.

Ignoring her command, he licked his way back up to her clit, then placed his lips around it and sucked hard. At the same time, he slipped three fingers into her cunt, and pressed his thumb into her asshole. He thrust his fingers in and out, faster and faster.

Finally, Calandra let herself go, her hips undulating wildly. She shouted, "Bloody hell, don't stop. Don't stop. *Deeper!*"

Then she exploded, her orgasm rising from her toes, stiffening her legs, her hips. She held her breath while her body released the coiled tension, and feminine come bathed the fingers shoved deep inside her.

Calandra slid her hand down her belly and lower, between her legs, her fingers stroking herself and his strong hand. She thanked him silently, rubbing over his knuckles, kneading the balls of his palm. He might have made her his captive, but he hadn't denied her need. Was this something she could build on? And as powerful as her arousal had been, how had he resisted taking her?

While the last tremors of passion rocked her, Calandra wondered what cruel act of fate brought her a man who matched her every fantasy, yet didn't find her equally irresistible.

How would she convince him to let her go? She couldn't give up her dream. Somehow, she must persuade him to grant her freedom to continue her journey to New Australia to begin her independent life — without responsibility for anyone but herself.

As the lethargy of passion's aftermath relaxed her body, she wondered if he could be seduced, and if her heart was strong enough to resist his sensual allure.

* * * * *

Drago pushed back his chair and stood. Turning his back, he dragged air into his lungs, willing his heart to slow its pace. With his back to her, he adjusted his cock, which rose painfully, nearly poking beyond the waistband of his breeches.

Having denied himself relief, Drago forced his mind back to business. He still had a journey into the desert to organize.

"What's your name?" Calandra called from behind him.

He glanced over his shoulder to see the woman still draped across the desk, her hands indolently caressing her breast and belly. Her features were warm and softened by her release.

He gritted his teeth before answering, "Drago Chavez."

She straightened one bent knee and let her leg drape over the edge of the desk toward the floor. Her thighs spread wider and he could see her pussy glistening with feminine cream. When she noted his attention, she smiled and rolled her thigh outwards, exposing the fullness of her plump cunt.

One hand slid low on her belly, tangled in her pubic hair, and then drifted lower. A finger dipped into her pussy and swirled inside.

Withdrawing the finger, she brought it to the crest of one pouting nipple and painted it with her dew.

Her boldness was an aphrodisiac. Arturian women were known for their subtlety and restraint. And he'd had a steady diet of restraint for two years. If he had the time, he'd want nothing more than to spend a week inside her pussy, drowning in her heat and unbridled passion. Drago's cock pulsed with the need to plunge inside her depths. His back grew rigid as he fought her siren's call.

He took a step toward her, then stopped. There wasn't time for this. She deliberately tempted him—spread wide over his desk like an offering. Her pussy open and reddened with her passion. How easy it would be to slide inside her…

Frustration made him angry enough to resist—just. He wondered what game she played now. Did she think he would set her free if she pleasured him?

"You are one stubborn man." Calandra rose from the desk. She shoved him down into the chair he'd sat in previously, and then leaned over him, her glorious breasts dangling in front of his face. "I'm not satisfied yet. You promised I would have anything a woman could want. I want you."

Drago let her lead, his will flagging now that her impressive incentives hovered over his lips.

She straddled his lap, her warm, wet cunt gliding along the rigid pole of his sex still trapped inside his breeches. With a hand cupping one breast, she traced his lips with her nipple.

Drago resisted, trying not to note the velvet areole or the pungent aroma of her arousal. But when she clasped the back of his head and directed his face toward her breast, he surrendered the last of his restraint and opened his lips wide to suck it into his mouth. The taste of her come coating the nipple exploded on his tongue and he groaned, his hands reaching for her buttocks.

Squeezing hard, he pushed and pulled her hips to slide her pussy over his cock.

"Harder, suck me harder," she said, her head falling back as she shoved her chest higher.

Lost to her boldness, he obeyed, rolling the distended nipple between his teeth, chewing gently. Then swirling his tongue around it, he suctioned. Had he really thought a week would be enough? Her breasts could feed his desire for a month!

She panted like a cat and ground her cunt down against his cock. "The other one. Bite the other one."

Releasing her tit with an audible pop, he turned his head and roughly rooted at its twin until he found the aureole, warm and soft as velvet. He tongued the end of her nipple, fluttering against it.

"Harder! You're killing me," she complained loudly.

Instead, he slowly explored her breast, sliding his lips and tongue over the mound and beneath to the tender underside, building her passion as he stoked the fire in his belly.

With an oath, she shoved his face away and climbed off his lap. Her hands ripped open his shirt and pulled it from his pants. She pushed his knees apart and knelt between them.

Drago's heart leapt to his throat and he felt the heavy, pounding need pulse in his cock.

Leaning toward him she nuzzled the side of his neck, while scraping her pointed tits across his bare chest. She licked a path downward, paused at his nipples and gently tortured them with her teeth. "This is how you do it."

129

Drago vowed he'd never again consider attention to his nipples as a mildly pleasurable form of foreplay. Red-hot current shot from his chest to his groin.

Then she reached for the front of his breeches.

Drago tried to remind himself of the job at hand—that this coupling needed to be quick. That Kaspar and Gilbert would come for them when the beasts were ready. But her hands, poised atop his straining erection, blew every coherent thought from his mind. His brain was rooted at the apex of his thighs. He had to have her—*now!*

He winced as she yanked down the slide, but relief followed immediately when finally his eager flesh rose from the opening.

Calandra didn't give him time to consider her next move. She wrapped both fists around him and bent her head to take the head of his cock into her mouth. When she slid down the length of him, his hips rose, seeking the warm glide of her tongue, until he bumped against the back of her throat.

Moaning, he combed his fingers into her cloud of blond hair to anchor her mouth where he needed it most. Her head bobbed, her mouth suctioned, her teeth grazed the length of him. Drago's cock pulsed, his stomach and thighs grew hard as rock, his balls tightened painfully and nested high in his groin as he ascended toward his climax.

Abruptly, she withdrew and stood. Drago reached for her, ready to pull her to the ground and finish it. Instead, she gripped his shoulders and planted her feet on opposite sides of the chair. Determination hardened her features as she straddled his lap and impaled herself on his cock, crying out as she descended.

Her channel was hot and tight and it spasmed when he butted against her womb. She held herself still for a long moment.

Then Drago felt a ripple caress his cock from end to root. A loud moan erupted from deep inside his chest.

She gasped and circled her hips.

Drago reached for her hips to guide her, but she resisted and lifted up slowly, stopping at the ridge circling the head of his cock, and then lowered herself fully onto him. Slowly, she pumped up and down, gradually increasing the pace, her breath coming in short, harsh gasps. Then, finally, she bounced vigorously on his lap.

"Oh...oh...oh," she cried. Her eyes screwed shut and her teeth bit her lower lip.

Drago wrapped his arms around her back and nuzzled her tits, seeking a stiffened button. Catching it between his lips, he drew it into his mouth and suctioned hard.

Her hips slowed, and her head fell back. Sensing she had relinquished control at last, Drago clasped her buttocks and lifted her off his lap. He had to have her now, hard and fast. His steel-hard cock demanded release.

Before she could protest, Drago pushed her onto the desk and draped her thighs over his shoulders. Pulling her toward him so that her buttocks extended beyond the edge, he slammed into her.

The lift of her hips to meet his next thrusts signaled her approval.

Gripping the edge of the desk, he drove into her, slowly at first, circling his hips with each thrust to rub the crisp hairs at his groin against her clit. He wanted her with him, needed her wild, abandoned passion to be as hot and painful as his was.

Soon, she wriggled beneath him. "Faster, faster!" she urged him, even as her vagina rippled and clenched, squeezing his cock.

Drago drove harder, faster, the force of his thrusts lifting her back off the desk.

When Calandra finally shrieked with her release, Drago gritted his teeth, leaned over her and pistoned his hips into her, his balls banging against her ass. With a roar, he came deep inside her.

Drago continued driving shallow thrusts as his orgasm waned, reluctant to end the encounter.

Calandra still shuddered beneath him, so he quickly wet his fingertips and rubbed her clit to prolong her release. Her head rolled from side to side.

Drago couldn't recall ever being with a woman who gave herself so unreservedly. No calculated caresses, no coy glances. No, lovely Calandra lost herself when deep into orgasm. If only he were looking for a mate...

Her face and the tops of her breasts were flushed, her eyes closed and mouth slack. When the last sweet convulsions gripping his cock slowed, he helped her lower her legs to his waist, then hefted her into his arms. Not ready to sever the connection and lose the warm glove that caressed his cock, he walked with her to the chair and sat.

She laid her head on his shoulder and pressed a kiss to his skin. He smiled. Calandra was a kitten now.

He rubbed circles on her back until her breath was less labored. He hoped she found comfort in their lovemaking and had released the tension that had made her so contentious. Now that she was gentled to his touch and past the upset of her abduction, perhaps she'd be more receptive to his plan.

"Calandra, you're a very passionate woman. I'll be sure to enter that into my report. Arturian men are well-schooled in pleasuring their mates and will appreciate a truly responsive woman."

Her back stiffened against his embrace. "Bastard! You fucked me to prove a point?"

He held her to him. "Didn't you?"

"Oooh! That's different. I'm fighting for my freedom."

"And I'm ensuring you have a better life."

"You can't make that choice for me. I won't allow it."

"You're hardly in any position to fight me."

Her eyes glistened with unshed tears, and her lips trembled. She wriggled on his lap, but instead of freeing herself, only managed to re-ignite the flame of his passion.

His cock stirred deep in her belly, lengthening until he touched her womb. Her vagina pulsed and clasped his cock tightly. Clamping the back of her head, he forced her down to accept his kiss. She tried to resist, but he rolled his hips and she moaned.

Needing her mindless and compliant again, he slid his hand around her hip, traced the crevice between her buttocks until he found the tightly furled rose of her anus. He circled it.

She moaned against his mouth.

He shoved a finger inside.

She screamed and bounced with abandon on his cock.

He sought the swell of her breast and twirled his tongue around the stem, sucking it into his mouth.

"Ohmygod!" she cried, then keened long and loud, her head falling back, her nipples stretching long, beckoning him to suckle harder.

Suddenly the door to the office flung open, slamming against the wall. Kaspar and Gilbert rushed in, weapons in their hands.

To Drago's amusement, Calandra didn't appear to notice their audience. She reached for her breasts and cupped them, squeezing the nipples between her fingers. With a start, he realized her eyes were slitted, observing the two men whose gazes were riveted to her breasts. She was playing to them. He should have felt some relief that she'd surrendered all her inhibitions—she'd need to display wantonness when she appeared before the gathering at the *Hazar's* auction.

Instead, he was angered. Perhaps, she fancied a foursome. For tonight, she'd have to settle for his cock.

"Gilbert, Kaspar. Wait outside, I'm not finished here."

"Lucky sod," Gilbert muttered.

Both men took their time letting themselves out the door. Once it closed behind them, Drago planted his feet firmly on the floor and reared up, spearing her. For this moment her sweet response was all his.

Calandra was helpless in her growing arousal. The unexpected arrival of the two younger men had sparked a fire that threatened to consume her.

The possessive tone in Drago's voice had reassured her that her campaign was finding holes in his armor.

She leaned toward him and licked his ear, and then bit the lobe sharply. "You promised my every want would be met." She continued exploring his ear.

"Have I neglected you?"

"Yes. I'm dying here."

He snorted, and his lips twisted into a grin. "How did I fail to note your nymphomania?"

She pulled back and pushed her lower lip into a pout. "You haven't given me an orgasm in the last five minutes."

"Do you care how you get it?"

She cocked her head to the side and pretended to consider his request. Truth was she liked surprises. She shook her head.

"Climb off me and get on your knees," he commanded.

Calandra liked the coarseness of his command. Loved that he was directing their loveplay now. She lifted one brow in challenge, and then rose from his lap. She faced away and knelt before him, spreading her knees wide on the floor. Open, and achingly vulnerable to his whim, she shivered when she heard his sharp intake of breath. Could he look at her gaping pussy and know how much she needed him there? Did he need to be inside her just as much?

At the rustle of clothing, she peered over her shoulder and saw him push his breeches to the floor. When he straightened, her gaze fell to his cock.

She'd played with it, caressed it with her mouth, but still she wasn't prepared for the beauty of the thick reddish-brown cock that thrust straight out from a nest of black, tightly curled hair. Her bottom and thighs quivered with anticipation.

He raised one eyebrow, mocking her attention to his dick.

Calandra bit back an angry retort. He thought she was panting for him. She'd show him who held the real power. She faced away and widened her legs, pushing her ass higher.

Steps closed in on her. Her ass shivered when instead of hands, his warm mouth pressed against her. When his tongue stabbed into the crevice between her buttocks, her pussy wept.

His tongue slid lower, spearing into her asshole briefly before lapping at her open cunt.

His torture was diabolical. Mind-stealing. Calandra lowered her forearms to the floor, and then rested her forehead against them, her belly dipping lower to tilt her hips just a little higher, hoping he'd take the hint and she wouldn't have to spell out exactly where she needed him most.

His tongue stabbed into her, then his chin rubbed against her clit, the bristle of his stubbly beard scraping deliciously along her sensitive flesh.

She arched her back, driving her hips higher. Teeth nibbled her labia, and then he withdrew. Calandra shook as strong hands grasped her ass, and Drago's cock pushed against her cunt.

Finally! With a slight wiggle of her ass, she pushed back, helping him slide into her. Then she pulsed backwards to encourage him to come deeper, and groaned when he sank all the way inside.

His hands squeezed her buttocks, lifting them, then pressed them apart. A drop of moisture fell onto her asshole, followed by a finger spreading it around the opening. A finger slipped inside her ass, followed by another.

Calandra yelled, "Yes! Bloody hell!" She rose on her arms and surged backward against him.

Drago pulled out, slammed back into her, and then out again. His hips pumped faster, his fingers swirled in circles inside her ass. The strength of his thrusts shuddered through her, until she grunted loudly with each slam of his hips.

"Faster! Oooh, faster!" she pleaded.

Drago pushed her shoulders down until her face met the cool tiles on the floor.

Calandra reached for the leg of the desk and braced herself.

Drago's thrusts quickened, his belly slapping her buttocks. Faster, deeper, harder.

Calandra's soaked pussy convulsed, twisting and clamping around Drago's cock.

With a shout, he spewed come inside her. The easy glide of his penis pushed her over the edge. She screamed in accompaniment to the sloppy wet, sucking sounds emanating from her pussy.

Drago draped over her back, gasping as he pumped one last time. "If you tell me you want more, I'll strangle you."

Calandra snorted, then laughed. "I won't be able to walk for a week."

"Then it's a good thing then that you'll be riding a *llamyx*."

Calandra wasn't reassured and cursed silently. Her campaign to win her freedom from the stubborn trader had just begun.

Chapter Three

"Darak, Calandra's missing."

Darak paused at the worried note in Mary's voice. "Perhaps she's taking in fresh air on the dock."

"I checked there already. I've had the prison guards searchin' for her the better part of the mornin'. She's gone."

"Ballocks!" he swore. "I'll have to gather a party to scour the docks further along. If she's been taken, someone will have information for a price."

Mary tugged at his sleeve, worry in her dark brown eyes. "What if she wasn't taken? What if she left of her own accord?"

Darak knew it was a possibility. Calandra had wandered the ship like a lost soul since Aurelia's death. He cupped Mary's dark face with his hand and pressed a kiss to her lips. "I promise I'll find her and bring her back."

"I'm comin' with you."

He stiffened and let his hand fall away. "That's out of the question. Adam ordered all the women to stay aboard for their own protection while he's gone. That includes you."

"I'm in charge of the women while Evena's away with Adam. It's my duty to find her."

"And it's my duty to keep you here—safe."

Mary's expression grew more mulish by the moment. "Adam and Evena are mille-leagues from here. I know if she were here, Evena would accompany the search party."

"Well, she's not." He knew his suggestion would fall on stubborn ears, but he had to try. "Perhaps, you should wait until they contact us to gain permission."

"You sorry S.O.B. You know damn well they're not goin' to contact us with the Dominion on their ass. Besides, they have problems enough tryin' to draw the fleet away from this planet. You have to make the decision."

"And I have. You're staying."

"You'll need me if you find her."

Darak sighed. Mary was right. Calandra trusted Mary more than anyone. If she decided to get stubborn, or worse, to hide from them, he would need Mary to draw Calandra out. "You'll follow my orders?"

Mary nodded — too quickly. "Of course."

Darak wanted to refuse her, to protect her from harm in the rough pirate's port. He sighed. "Dammit, Mary. Can't you just once err on the side of caution?"

Mary grinned, triumph gleaming from her brown eyes. "You won't be sorry."

He pulled her into his arms. "I already am." Darak combed his fingers through Mary's short, course hair, and then tugged gently to raise her face to meet his kiss. He supposed it was better to keep his dark warrior where he could protect her. She'd never willingly remain behind. Besides, he couldn't bear to let her any farther than arm's-reach away.

* * * * *

Calandra shifted her bottom, attempting to ease the sting of the saddle sores she was sure were raising on her inner thighs. Never mind a layer of thick fat naturally cushioned the *llamyx's* wide back, or that its white coat was soft as goose down.

The fact that her pussy was still swollen from her vigorous coupling with her captor complicated matters. When she slid forward to ease the sting on her backside, her pussy took the brunt of the swaying motion, reminding her of the sweet pounding her tender flesh had taken the night before. She still couldn't believe he'd hustled her onto the *llamyx* so soon after their mind-blowing sex. The man was made of steel.

Add to her sore tush and swollen cunt the fact that the sun had beat down on her head the whole morning long, and her list of complaints grew longer by the minute.

And she hadn't been shy about voicing disapproval for Drago's treatment. Her last complaint had resulted in Drago urging his mount to a gallop to escape her. Calandra's glee at his annoyance sustained her most of the morning.

He'd returned to thrust a long black robe at her. While she'd been secretly thankful he'd insisted she wear the long, hooded *kahfet*, she'd resisted accepting it—until he'd threatened to remove the remainder of her clothes if she didn't.

Although she knew he hadn't insisted out of kindness, she'd come to appreciate the garment's protection from the sun's harsh rays. She was being churlish because he was just protecting his investment.

A sunburn would mar her pale skin.

Drago's kindness had been motivated by greed. That knowledge was a bitter pill for her to swallow.

The previous evening while she had lain on the floor recovering from the most glorious orgasm she'd ever experienced, he had completed the transmission of her attributes to the auction house. He'd even had the gall to describe her orgasms as "great rolling spasms, easily and frequently attained."

At the time she'd been angry. But if she admitted the truth, the concept of a society where men shared intelligence regarding a woman's sexual response didn't offend her. She was curious. Perhaps this was a place that truly valued an experienced and uninhibited woman.

Not that she was persuaded to give up her dream. The thought of depending on anyone other than herself, or worse, anyone depending on her, left her cold. When people depended on her, they died.

The object of her rancor rode at the head of their small procession. She didn't want to notice how dark his skin looked against the white *kahfet* he wore. The drape of the fabric only hinted at the powerful muscle that cloaked his broad frame. If she let herself recall how the muscles of his thighs had rippled, or the tensile strength of his arms as he'd anchored her thighs when he'd plunged inside her, she'd be more miserable than she already was.

Here was a man a woman could cleave to—if she had a mind to settle for just one. But Calandra didn't need entanglements. All she wanted was transportation to New Australia where she could live life on her own terms—without any man weighing her down.

Calandra kicked the sides of her beast to spur it faster. Her mount was old and plodding and couldn't maintain the pace of Drago's younger *llamyx*. She suspected he'd given her the aged creature to ensure their conversations would be short and few.

Since fucking her senseless, Drago had paid her little attention. If she hadn't found his gaze lingering on her body from time to time, she would have believed he was completely unmoved by her presence.

He hadn't touched her since pulling her roughly to her feet, and throwing her clothes into her arms the night before. He'd strode out of the room without looking back, instructing his two assistants, Gilbert and Kaspar, to ensure she dressed. He'd shouted over his shoulder, "Don't let her delay us any longer."

Unaccountably, she'd been hurt by his callous treatment. Not that she'd expected him to bask with her in the afterglow.

Today, she was grumpy and sore, and badly in need of a bath.

"So why didn't we just bring your hovercar?" she asked as she pulled "Grandma" alongside his beast.

Drago flashed her an irritated glance. "The engines stir up too much dust. The particles are so fine they work their way into an engine's intake despite filtering."

"But riding animals is so primitive. Why not a skycraft?"

"You and Lumina aren't bonding?"

She admired how neatly he changed the subject. "No. She keeps turning around to smile at me, but I get the feeling that doesn't necessarily mean she likes me."

The corners of his lips curled. "She smiles before she feeds."

"Oh." The last thing she wanted to do was show weakness in front of this man, but her bottom was screaming for relief. "When are we stopping?"

"When we reach the Nagara oasis. We'll sleep beneath the stars tonight."

"Does oasis mean water?"

"Yes."

"As in, enough to wash with?"

"Enough to swim in if you like."

She quit pretending to be nonchalant. "Please tell me we're close."

"We're close."

"Really?"

He smiled, squinting at the rising sun. "Yes, we can't travel in the midday heat." He spurred his *llamyx* and the beast leapt forward.

He was escaping her presence again. She wondered if he was irritated with her questions, or if perhaps, he was as uncomfortably aware of her as she was of him.

Calandra pulled the *kahfet* away from her reclamation suit. If it grew much warmer, she wouldn't be able to breathe. The black R-suit, which was designed to wick moisture from the skin in the temperature-controlled environment of a prison ship, did nothing to shield her body from the heat of the desert. The suit felt glued to her skin now. And without a R-suit-evacuator handy, the moisture collecting in the suit grew heavier by the moment.

She shielded her eyes with a hand and gazed across the peaks of red-gold sand. The oasis wasn't in sight. But she knew that beyond any one of these dunes could lay a surprise—a rocky shelf overlooking the steep sides of a canyon—or a green oasis.

Calandra planned to swim in the pond until her skin pruned—or until Drago pulled her from the water. He'd pay attention to her then. And every inch of his masculinity would answer to her command.

Perhaps she couldn't convince him to release her, but she could make him regret abandoning her to the mercy of an Arturian slave owner.

"What makes you smile, mistress?" Kaspar's Arturian singsong voice interrupted Calandra's wayward thoughts.

Calandra shot a glance at Kaspar. "Nothing."

Apparently, he'd recovered from her blows from the previous evening—and he was suffering far less than she was after a night atop a *llamyx*.

Kaspar yawned. "Not to worry, mistress. Drago brings you to Nagara. You may rest there. He'll not make you travel during the heat of the day."

Calandra didn't appreciate the reminder of her discomfort. The long, black *kahfet* was becoming more stifling as the sun rose higher. The heat drummed down on her covered head. She'd begun to perspire so heavily her head swam and spots appeared before her eyes.

She unstrapped the water bag from her pommel and lifted it to squirt a long stream of tepid water into her mouth.

"Look, mistress!"

Calandra lowered the bag and stared across the dunes. Despite the wavering heat, she noted a ridge rising above the sand. At its foot, a glimmer of sunshine reflected off the surface of a pool of water.

Calandra kicked the sides of her beast. Lumina didn't need any further encouragement. The smell of water was the only incentive she needed to break into a gallop. Calandra held on for dear life, but didn't discourage the beast. She was just as eager to reach the oasis.

* * * * *

When Calandra passed him on her way to the pool, Drago expected she would fling herself down beside the water to drink her fill, and perhaps wash her exposed skin with handfuls of water. The pool offered little privacy. When night fell, he planned to accompany her at her bath.

But at the water's edge, Calandra leapt from the back of her steed and stripped.

Drago halted, ensuring the men behind him also stopped. The *kafhet* landed at her feet, and the reclamation suit puddled on top. Pink buttocks jiggled as she ran into the water.

"*Ahfalla!*" Kaspar exclaimed. "She will make us very rich men."

Drago shot him a searing glance, but Kaspar's gaze remained pinned to the woman. Drago turned at Calandra's glad cry. She ducked beneath the water, then rose and shook her head like a dog, shedding water in an arc and causing her breasts to bob on the surface of the water.

The woman had no inhibitions—or she was deliberately taunting them.

"Kaspar, see to the animals. Take them to the far end of the pond to drink. Gilbert, you'll prepare the camp." He kneed his mount and rode straight for the woman.

Drago intended only to drink at the water's edge. He was there to ensure her safety. No more. But the woman played like a water fox, turning to dive beneath the surface, exposing her buttocks and long, water-slick legs. Then she swam on her back, her arms slicing the surface, her chest rising above the water with each stroke. Crested nipples broke the surface to point toward the sun.

Frustration fisted his hands. The woman was flaunting herself. Daring him to join her. Or perhaps hoping all of the men would strip and cavort with her.

As he stepped toward the water's edge, Calandra stood and laughed. "Join me. The water's blessedly cool." To prove her point, she cupped her breasts and angled her body to display her tightly beaded areoles. "See?"

Oh, he saw. He also noticed his two assistants hovering next to him, staring at her breasts—again. Had the woman no sense of propriety?

"Kaspar! Gilbert!"

The two men glanced at him then shrugged, smiling sheepishly.

"She appears happy," Kaspar said.

Drago glared, then looked pointedly at the *llamyx* lapping at the water.

Gilbert mumbled, "We was just looking."

"Well, you've work to do—for which I pay you well."

"Come on Kaspar, let's take the beasts behind those rocks over there," Gilbert said.

Drago's gaze narrowed. The men would be watching Calandra from behind those rocks. Damn her hide.

Calandra was a big girl and appeared to have made her own choice in the matter. And his men were big boys—they could watch or not. If the lady didn't appear to care, then neither would he.

He bunched his *kahfet* in his hands and lifted it over his head. Then stripped the rest of his clothing from his body.

Calandra watched avidly, her hands still on her breasts, caressing them now.

Drago strode into the water, heading straight for the woman who'd been driving him crazy since he'd first spied her in the Pirate's Cove. The closer he drew, the faster her chest rose and fell. Cool water lapped over his balls, drawing them painfully taut. His dick swayed on the surface, then lifted as he stepped deeper into the water.

When he stood before her, Calandra's hands left her breasts to disappear beneath the water. Her fingers closed around his cock, and she pulled him toward her, guiding him straight into her pussy.

From the cool water of the pool into her hot, wet channel, his rigid flesh sank inside gratefully. But Drago fisted his hands on his hips, determined she would take full responsibility.

She raised a leg and draped it around his waist, while her hands sought purchase on his shoulders. With an undulating roll of her hips, she took him deeper inside, her bush-hair grinding against his groin.

How she tempted him! Her lush breasts and hips invited a man to linger. Her fearless seduction of *him*, her master, challenged the male conqueror inside him to wrest control.

She leaned back, exposing her breasts to his gaze, and let her hair trail into the water. She watched him through slitted lids, and he knew she saw his rising passion in the tightness of his jaw and heat that stained his cheeks. With a small smile, she lifted her other leg and wrapped it around his hips. Then, slowly, she pushed with her hands against his shoulders to lift and fall upon his cock.

Drago closed his eyes. Each stroke of her vagina exposed his cock to the chill of the pool before plunging again into her heat. Cold, hot. Cold, hot. Faster and faster.

Drago's hands clutched her buttocks, and his fingers splayed wide over the soft flesh—pressing her cheeks together and apart with each stroke. His body tuned to her response. Her jagged breaths told him she neared the precipice.

He opened his eyes to watch her completion. Her journey there never failed to fascinate him—she was wild for it and she never withheld a single moan or shudder. She gave herself fully. He wished for the same lack of restraint.

Calandra's head flung back in abandon. Her mouth slackened and her tits jiggled with each jerk of her hips. He bent his neck to suckle a nipple and teethe the rigid point, encouraging her to come.

Calandra cried out and let go of his shoulders, sliding backward into the water to float on its surface, her arms spread wide. She looked like a water nymph, gliding back and forth of the surface. Her expression was pure, tortured bliss.

Eager to join her, Drago dragged up her legs, one at a time, to his shoulders, then slammed hard into her, pumping his hips while her hair swirled in the water.

As the ripples of her orgasm slid along his cock, she arched in the water, her breasts thrust high, and screamed.

Drago rammed his dick into her hot, convulsing pussy and shot come deep inside her, emptying himself into her.

When Calandra spluttered, he realized he'd pushed her below the surface. He pulled her quickly into his arms.

Her arms snaked around his neck and she lifted her mouth to his.

He clutched her hair, holding her head still for his assault on her lips. He ate them, chewing gently then lapping afterwards to soothe.

Calandra moaned and swept her tongue inside his mouth. Taking control, she suctioned his mouth, while she pressed her body closer to his.

Drago felt his flaccid penis slip from her warm channel and groaned. Calandra's mouth curved into a smile, and Drago felt the quiver of another growing erection. Never had a woman inspired such a swift recovery!

He nudged his cock against her hip. Calandra twisted her hips to trap his eager flesh between her thighs.

Dragging his mouth from hers, he said, "So soon?"

"Not up for it?" she asked, with a bump of her hips against his.

His cock nudged deeper between her thighs. "I think he's starting to prune."

"Mmmm," she moaned. "He is feeling a little wilted. Maybe he needs sunlight."

A scraping sound from the rocks beyond the edge of the pool drew Drago's gaze. His eyes narrowed, and pebbles rolled down the rock nearest them to plop into the water.

"We have an audience."

Calandra's brows rose. "Oh?"

Her innocent tone raised his suspicions. "They've watched from the beginning, haven't they?"

"Were you too distracted to notice?"

Drago growled. "You like an audience, don't you?"

"I prefer one partner—one male partner. Someone I can trust with my body. Someone who will make sure I don't go too far. Sometimes I like a woman and a man. But when other people watch..." She shrugged and glanced up, her expression almost shy. "I can't help it—the experience is enhanced. It makes me really, really hot."

Drago's ripening cock speared into the soft fur between her legs. "How hot?"

She grinned then—a siren's smile. "Fuck me at the water's edge, and I'll show you."

Chapter Four

She was hot as a laser. Drago followed her to the shallow edge of the pool. She faced toward Kaspar and Gilbert hiding in the rocks.

When the water lapped at her ankles, she fell to her knees in the sand and scooped a handful of water, raising it to her breasts for it to stream down her belly into the water-darkened hair between her legs. Her hand stroked across her breasts, down her belly, then her fingers dove between her legs. With her face raised to the sun, her tongue circled her lips.

Impatient to participate, Drago dropped to his knees behind her, and wrapped his arms around her belly.

With his lips pressed to the side of her neck, he cupped her breasts in his hands, lifting them, kneading them and gently twisting the burgeoning nipples until Calandra writhed in his arms.

Her hands reached behind to grasp his head, lifting her breasts higher still.

Drago urged her with his hands to spread her knees wide, and skimmed his palm down her soft belly to cup her quivering pussy. At first, he rubbed his palm over it, petting her.

"Please, stick your fingers inside me," she said loudly.

Reminded of the watchers, Drago smothered a growl. With one hand he stretched her labia wide, exposing them to the air and the other men's gazes.

"Pinch my clit."

He obliged her, repeatedly plucking the swollen nub, then he sank two fingers into her pussy while he continued to scrape his thumb across her clitoris.

Calandra's hands dropped to her breasts. Watching her over her shoulder, Drago's dick hardened as she tugged her nipples until they stretched to tight points, reddening from her harsh treatment. Her belly quivered beneath his touch.

Suddenly, she pushed his hands away and turned to urge him to lie half in the water, half on the hot sand. Positioning herself beside him, she leaned over his groin and grasped his penis, guiding it to her mouth.

Drago forgot the voyeurs and pumped upward, deeper into her mouth, past her hot tongue to the back of her throat.

She murmured and bobbed her head over his cock, lubricating the length of him. Then with her hands twisting on his cock and her mouth devouring the tender head, she suctioned hard, her cheeks drawing until he feared he'd explode.

Drago fisted a hand in her hair and pressed her mouth deeper over his cock. She continued to suck, more noisily now, slurping and moaning, the vibration shooting sensation all the way to his toes. "Christ, stop! Calandra!"

She cupped his balls and kneaded, grunting now as she took him deeper into throat, her teeth scraping deliciously along his cock.

"Calandra, end it!"

"Mmmm," she moaned, then slowly withdrew, lapping around the head of his cock, dipping the point of her tongue into the sensitive eye, drawing a bead of pre-come.

"A pearl," she murmured, then licked it off. Her tongue fluttered over the head, butterfly laps that teased around the circumference. Drago's hips lifted of their own volition, driving his cock into her mouth.

Calandra pulled away and flicked the head with her fingers. "Bad boy."

"Calandra?" Drago's voice strangled when she mouthed his balls, caressing them with long glides of her tongue, and sucking them into the cavern of her mouth. "Enough torture. It's time to fuck."

Calandra laughed, and then straddled his belly. "Who's in charge here?"

Drago groaned when Calandra wriggled her hips, seeking his cock. When she found it, she slid her wet pussy lips over his straining flesh.

"Stop teasing, or I'll take over," he warned.

"You can try." She pushed her pussy onto the head of his cock, and then teased him again with a swirl of her hips.

He gripped her ass to keep her from moving and slammed upwards into her, repeatedly. Sweat beaded on her forehead and trickled down her chest. Calandra's breasts jiggled with each relentless spearing. Unable to resist for long, he rose on his elbows and latched onto one of the nipples with his lips.

Then Calandra took over, rising and falling on his cock. Her efforts growing jerkier as her arousal heightened, finally, she sank but didn't rise again.

He released her nipple. "Tell me what you need, baby."

Her thighs trembled around his hips. "I need you behind me."

Drago helped her climb off. She faced away and spread her legs wide for him. "You know what I want. Fuck me in the ass."

Drago grasped her buttocks, parting them. At Calandra's sharp intake of breath, Drago decided a little torture of his own was in order. He leaned over her to tongue her clit, stabbing into her, lapping the creamy honey.

Her ass wiggled. "Please, now. Fuck me, now."

Drago liked the ragged edge of her voice as she begged. He bit her cheeks gently. She quivered and her shoulders sank, raising her buttocks higher. Drago tongued her cunt-lips, drawing them into his mouth to nibble. Then he licked from her clit toward her anus, skipping over the rose to continue along the crease.

Calandra was panting now, her breath coming in jagged sobs.

"Tell me what you want," he said and fluttered his tongue around her asshole.

"You! I want you!" she gasped.

His tongue pressed briefly between the tightly furled lips. "Not specific enough. Tell me, baby."

"In my ass! I want your cock in my ass!"

Drago dropped spittle over her nether mouth and smeared it with his thumb. With his hand, he guided himself between her cheeks, riding between them in a long stroke.

"For fuck's sake, do you need a goddamn map?"

Drago laughed. Calandra's frustration only heightened his arousal. He placed the head of his cock against her anus and pressed inward. When the ring of muscle closed around the head of his cock, he paused.

"Don't stop now!"

He swatted her behind. "Stop whining."

"Do that again."

"You like spankings?"

"No. I don't know. Spank me or fuck me—just make up your mind." She tried to rear back to take him deeper, but Drago backed up with her. He pinched each of her buttocks.

"Ouch!" Then, "Do that again."

Instead, Drago pressed inside her, slowly driving forward, until his belly met her ass. She was so damn hot, exquisitely tight. He withdrew partway.

Her groan ended on a sob.

"Am I hurting you?"

"Yes. Don't stop."

Slowly, he pushed inside again. Calandra's legs trembled, and Drago snaked an arm around her belly to brace her for what was to come. "Ready, baby?"

"Just give it to me. Hard!"

He did. Stabbing inward, pulling out--to slam inside her again— pumping his hips and trying to prolong the sweet agony. But she was too tight, too hot—a glove that massaged his dick until it was harder, and his balls tighter than they'd ever been. His fingers curved into her hips and pumped so hard she grunted loudly with each stroke.

Suddenly, his balls exploded, and his cock pumped a geyser of come into Calandra's ass. Her screech and answering lunge backward heralded her own orgasm.

While his body continued spurting and her vagina rippled along his cock, Drago pulled her up into his arms.

Still connected, Calandra sat in the cradle of his hips and dragged air into her starved lungs. "Do you think they're still watching?"

"*Afhalla!*" echoed from beyond the rocks.

* * * * *

Calandra rubbed her arms and huddled closer to the fire. Drago had barely said a word to her throughout their meager dinner, and he'd chosen to sit with the fire between them. As the flames banked, his broad frame was limned by shadow and fire. The exposed skin of his face, hands, and neck glowed in the reflection of the fire. His large body was a black shadow against the night.

Kaspar and Gilbert had long ago retired to their tent and warm bedrolls. Calandra had stubbornly held out, not wanting to admit her fatigue. Drago needed to see her, acknowledge her. Her will and desires would not be discounted. She was running out of time.

Foolishly, she'd refused to don her water-heavy reclamation suit. The *kahfet* was all that stood between her and the cool night air. "It's hard to believe I was roasting like a chicken on a spit today."

Across the fire from her, Drago's features grew harder, craggier in the firelight. "It's the desert."

She snorted. He'd been ill tempered ever since they'd made love at the pool. With every terse response, her heart sank further. At this rate, she'd never convince him to release her. "Geez, you're grumpy. What did I do to earn this?"

Drago's jaw tensed. "Why should I believe you aren't like every other woman on this planet?"

Calandra's gaze swung to his face. Was he reconsidering? "Because it's true. I don't want to be taken care of." She raised her chin. "I can look after myself."

If anything, Drago's dark gaze hardened. "We'll be leaving at midnight. You'd better get some rest."

She exhaled. *Don't push him now--he's wavering!* "Yeah, can't have me looking like a hag at the auction, can we? Might lose your commission." She sounded like a bitch, but her frustration was winning the war over her emotions.

Drago raised the wine bag to his lips and squirted red liquid into his mouth.

Calandra licked her lips. He'd taste heavenly just about now.

He lowered the bag. "What were you incarcerated for?"

The question startled her. Calandra rarely allowed herself to travel that painful road. "Manslaughter," she replied curtly, hoping he'd take the hint and drop the subject.

"Tell me about it." Apparently, he wasn't very intuitive.

"Is this something you need for your report?"

His dark gaze didn't waver from her face. "No. I'm just curious how a woman like you could wind up in a badass place like the New Attica. It's a maximum security ship."

"A woman like me?"

"Yes. You're soft and womanly. Built for loving and bearing children. You don't seem tough enough to make it in a place like that."

Her heart twisted. Once upon a time, she'd wanted those "womanly" things for herself. "I'm plenty tough. I was a guard in the prison—selected because I could whip most of the convicts' asses."

His knowing glance told her he was thinking how easily he'd overpowered her.

She narrowed her eyes in warning. "You got lucky."

"Poor Calandra. The place must have done a number on you."

Unable to meet his stare, she glanced away. "You're wrong. I did a number on myself."

"So what happened?"

Calandra blinked at the moisture that flooded her eyes. She'd run from those memories for too long. "I was driving. Had a little too much to drink. I lost control of my hovercar."

"You hit someone?"

She shook her head. "No. My sister was in the car, sitting beside me. When I hit the tree, she went through the windshield. I couldn't get out to help her." Calandra sniffed, and then cleared her throat. "They told me she died on impact. God, I hope so."

She hadn't heard him move, but suddenly he was beside her, his arms wrapping around her. Calandra resisted the urge to melt within his embrace. She didn't deserve his comfort.

"Still, it seems rather harsh..." The hair at her temples stirred with each word. "...them sending you to that particular prison."

Calandra's breath caught on a sob. "They were making an example of me. And I didn't fight it."

"Your family didn't fight for you?"

"She was all the family I had." The dam burst and tears streaked down her face.

Drago pressed her head into the curve of his neck.

Greedy for the stolen comfort, Calandra relaxed within the circle of his arms. As she wiped the tears from her cheeks with the back of her hand, she asked, "What about you? How did you come to Arturia? You're from Earth too, aren't you?"

"Yes, but that was a long time ago. Funny as it may sound, I was a Dominion soldier."

Startled, she pulled away to look into his face. "You're kidding, right? The corps motto is 'once a soldier always a soldier'."

"That's usually the way it works."

"What happened to you?"

His arms fell away from her. "It didn't work for me." And his tone told her he didn't want to talk about it anymore.

With questions swirling in her mind, Calandra decided to press. Something in his past shaped his opinion of women, maybe this was it. "Look, it's not fair. I got all naked."

His brows rose.

"Well, I told you my story. It's only right you should share yours."

Not looking the least bit pleased, he blew out a gust of air and glared at her. "Like I said, I was a soldier. I'd reached the rank of Over-sergeant in the Insurgents Corps."

Calandra stiffened. Insurgent teams had a wicked reputation for their no-nonsense, often violent, enforcement of Dominion policies.

Drago's mouth curved in a mirthless smile. "Yeah. I was one of them, and damn good at my job. I was trained in guerilla and urban tactics and had several campaigns under my belt. I had my own team."

His gaze left her face and he stared at the fire, his brows drawing together in a frown. "We had a mission to clean out a group of radical anarchists from a planet the Dominion wanted to transform into a mining cooperative. Several dignitaries from the mining consortium were with us aboard the ship. A chance for Dominion Enforcement to prove to them how well we could secure a world.

"Our intelligence indicated that there was a single, enclave. From our recon photos we put together a battle plan. It was pretty routine—a sweep to capture anarchists. We had orders to kill if they resisted.

"On the ground, we soon discovered the anarchists were nothing more than a farming community—with a communal house and outbuildings—and a school.

"We investigated using stealth tactics. The people hadn't a clue we were watching. I transmitted our findings to my commander still aboard the ship and requested permission to make contact. I expected our mission would relocate the civilians." His jaw tightened and anger flushed his cheeks.

Calandra knew what was coming and the dread knotted her stomach. His remorse lay heavy in his voice and the slump of his shoulders, but she waited silently for him to resume the telling, knowing instinctively that he needed to lay the wound bare before he could heal.

"The order was given to eradicate the squatters." His gaze rose to hers. "I had trained to be a soldier since I was a boy — was conditioned to accept orders without question. But that day, I refused. Before I knew it, another team was on the ground." His words grew clipped. "I was arrested. The *mission* was completed. And I was charged with treason."

"Treason is punishable with death," she said, gently encouraging him to continue. "How did you escape punishment?"

"Word got out among the Corps. I still had friends. It was suggested to the court that my death would provide a martyr to future enemies of the Dominion. In the end, they stripped me of Dominion citizenship and released me on Arturia — as far from Earth as they could manage — without anything I'd worked to accumulate over the years."

That explained his single-minded drive to turn a profit — but she still didn't understand what had shaped his opinion of women.

"Drago, for what it's worth from an ex-con," she said, knowing her sympathy shone from her eyes and that he didn't want it, "you did the right thing."

He snorted. "Yeah."

Knowing she'd pressed as far as she would get for the evening, Calandra rose. "I guess we should turn in."

"Your bed's already prepared. You go ahead."

"You're not joining me?" Her heart skipped a beat. Tonight was her last night to make him change his mind.

"I wouldn't sleep."

"Who said anything about sleeping?" Going for broke, she turned on her heels and walked toward the tent, exaggerating the sway of her hips.

When she reached the canvas lean-to, she looked over her shoulder. He hadn't moved. She bit her lip, and then glanced toward the tent where Kaspar and Gilbert slept. "Guess I'll have to look for company elsewhere."

Drago's gaze narrowed and he rose to his feet. As he stomped toward her, Calandra felt a frisson of alarm and thought perhaps she'd gone too far. She'd goaded a wounded bear.

When he was almost upon her, she ducked beneath the flap of the tent. He followed, stalking her until her back met the canvas at the far side of the tent.

"I was kidding, all right?"

Drago's hard-eyed gaze swept over her. "You'd better not be wearing that damned reclamation suit."

She didn't move, but the hard edge of his voice produced a thrill that shook her to the core, producing a trickle of come that slithered down her thighs. *He's mine now!* "I'm not wearing a thing."

"Take the robe off," he said, his voice roughening to a growl.

Her nipples tightened instantly.

"Now!"

Calandra untied the knot at the neck of her *kahfet*, then inched the fabric up her legs. Her gaze darted to his face. *How far do I push before he explodes?* Oh, and how she wanted his explosive fire.

His nostrils flared and she wondered if he could smell her arousal.

She gathered more of the material and pulled it up to her waist, exposing the triangle of hair at the apex of her thighs. She pressed her legs together and wriggled as she lifted the *kahfet* to her breasts.

Hot color stained his cheeks, and his chest rose and fell rapidly. "Woman!"

That was all the warning she got, before his hands grasped her bare hips and pulled her toward the cradle of his thighs. His erection, still clothed in his breeches, pressed against her belly.

Instinctively her hips curled to fit her mound more tightly against his cock. Her nipples scraped the *kahfet*, and she wriggled to pull it over her head, but the fabric tangled with her arms. She was blinded and bound. "Help me!"

Drago's belly pulsed with his laughter. "I don't think so, you're at my mercy now."

"Oooh!" She fought, but the *kahfet* twisted more tightly around her arms. "Let me touch you! Free me!"

Instead, his shoulder butted against her belly and she was lifted off her feet. She kicked, but he swatted her bare bottom. "None of that now. You don't want to maim me. Not when you're about to get what you asked for."

"Who says I don't want to maim? Let me loose! Ah—"

He flipped her and she landed on a layer of blankets. Breathless, she twisted her legs to roll off the bed, not ready to let him win the game. But he was quicker than she, and his hands grasped her ankles.

Panting and helpless now, she waited for his next move. She gasped when warm liquid spilled onto her belly, and she recognized the aroma of the wine they'd shared at dinner. His hands pushed her legs apart, and the narrow pallet dipped between them. Then his warm, raspy tongue lapped at the wine, causing her abdomen to quiver.

She didn't wait for him to urge her to raise her knees. Up they rose, and then splayed wide—an invitation he couldn't miss.

His hands skimmed beneath her buttocks to raise them. He was right where she'd wanted him all along.

A gust of warm breath blew over her pussy, opened wide for his assault. Instead of his tongue, his nose, cheeks, and chin rubbed around her cunt, his two-day old beard scraping deliciously across her tender flesh.

She squirmed trying to lure him to her aching clit. "Your sense of direction is abysmal."

"And you've the patience of a gnat." His tongue speared into her vagina.

"Ooh! That's better."

"That was just an appetizer." His tongue stabbed next at her belly button, then licked upward to the underside of her breasts, his torso resting heavily between her legs.

Disappointed he'd decided to tease her, she nonetheless arched her back, hoping to lure him to an achingly turgid nipple. "You're missing the point."

He bit underside of the mound. "You're not in charge this time."

"You're a very nasty man."

"Baby, you don't know the half of it." Finally, his mouth latched onto a nipple, and he suctioned, drawing the tip between his teeth to torture it.

A red-hot flame of desire shot from her breast to her groin. "The other one's feeling neglected."

He released her nipple. "Like I said before, you aren't in charge." Suddenly his weight lifted from her.

"No. Don't stop." Calandra's hips rose to follow him, but his hands were on her ankles again. "Don't you dare start over."

"Don't give me any ideas."

She wished she could see his face. "Are you teaching me a lesson?"

"Are you learning anything?"

"I don't know, but if I'm quiet will you fuck me?"

"Give the girl a star."

Calandra bit her lip and waited.

His hands guided her ankles up until they met the top of his hard shoulders. Then they smoothed down her legs and circled beneath her buttocks, lifting them into the air. Calandra waited, anticipating the thrust of his cock into her already drenched pussy. She pressed her lips tightly together to suppress the scream that was rising to the back of her throat.

"Good girl," Drago said, his voice soft and soothing. But still he didn't enter her. Instead, his hands squeezed her buttocks.

Sweat broke on her forehead and chest, but still she held her tongue while silently swearing at the bastard. *This had better be worth the wait or you'll be sorry!*

The smooth broad head of his cock butted against her cunt, then withdrew.

Calandra shook her head. *The sorry son-of-a-bitch!*

His cock poked at her again, sinking an inch inside her before pulling free. "Baby, you're so wet. Aching for it, are you?"

No fucking kidding! Her shoulders writhed and she felt the fabric loosen.

Another dive into her cunt, and this time he circled his hips. Her pussy made a sucking sound when he pulled out.

Her hands sought the hem of the *kahfet* and she started to pull it upwards past her mouth, her nose, then and her eyes. Her gaze found him, but he was staring at her pussy as if it held the secrets to the universe. Then he lunged forward, sheathing himself to the hilt inside her.

Calandra screamed, and his eyes rose to her face. Her arms were still entangled, but she no longer cared. He withdrew and rammed into her again. She unclasped her ankles from where they had risen to clutch the back of his neck, and let them fall open, her legs straight, her toes pointed, giving him her trust and full access to the cradle of her sex.

Drago's hands held her in place as he pumped his hips, grinding into her at the end of each thrust. So deep inside her she swore she'd be able to taste his come at the back of her throat.

He pistoned, faster and faster, until Calandra forgot the ban against making noise and whimpered with each stroke. "Oooh! I'm close! I'm gonna come!"

Drago's features hardened, reddening with his approaching orgasm. His mouth stretched into a grimace. "I'm there! Come with me!"

A strangled scream tore from her throat as the first wave broke. Distantly, she heard his shout, but the pounding continued as her vagina convulsed and squeezed, until the pulsing rhythm slowed. Drago's hips stroked inward one last time before coming to rest inside her.

She wrapped her legs around his waist, pulling him toward her until he lay across her, his chest heaving. A last tug at the fabric and her hands were free. She rubbed them in circles on his back offering comfort after the storm.

As his breath evened, Calandra relaxed as well. In only two nights and one day, she'd managed to fall irrevocably in love with the man. Her dream of making it on her own in New Australia didn't seem as urgent or fulfilling now.

Neither was her old fear as compelling. If a woman had a man like Drago, self-reliant and strong, she needn't worry about him depending on her. If she screwed up again, she wouldn't hurt him.

But how would she make him see they belonged together.

Chapter Five

"So, are you gonna talk now?" Mary leaned as close to the yellow-toothed man as she could stand. His breath reeked of sour ale and poor dental hygiene.

"I told you, I don't know nothin'." In the meager light of the Arturian moons, his wild gaze sought an escape from his current predicament—tied to a drainpipe in a deserted alley—and buck-naked.

But in this part of Aghora, no one would come to his rescue, no matter how loud he screamed.

Mary squeezed her hand, tightening her grip around his bared balls. "Are you real sure about that?"

"Perhaps a more refined approach will achieve our goals, love," Darak said dryly.

Mary grunted in disgust, not bothering to look back at her lover. So far Darak hadn't been any help. "You really think I should go easy with this maggot on humanity?" She squeezed much harder now and smiled. The smelly man squealed with pain. She tried not to think about how hard she'd have to scrub her hands after touching his sweaty nads.

Luring him away from his table at the Pirate's Cove had been disgustingly simple. One flirty glance and a come-hither crook of her finger, and she bet he'd almost come in his breeches. As soon as they'd entered the alley, he'd dropped trou in under a second flat, ready to give her what he thought she wanted. Too bad getting him to answer a few simple questions hadn't been as easy.

She released his balls and straightened, her smile disappearing. "Enough with trying to be nice. Darak, hand me the electro-stun."

Darak's muffled laughter told Mary he was enjoying this a little too much. She shot him a searing glance and held out her hand.

With the lift of one eyebrow, Darak surrendered his weapon. Silently he asked with his eyes, *Do you really want to take it this far?*

Mary's lips thinned with determination. Her friend's life was at stake—she'd take this fight to the edge of the known universe.

She turned and faced Yellow-Teeth, the electro-stun held up in her hand.

His eyes widened until the whites framed the irises. "No! I swear. I don't know nothin'!" He tried to jerk away, but the ropes held him fast.

Mary smirked, her lip curling as she pushed the electro-stun under his scrotum. "Really?"

Darak's large hand landed on her shoulder. "Perhaps he doesn't understand the fundamentals of the electro-stun. He doesn't look very bright."

Mary knew Darak wanted her to slow the pace of their interrogation to let the little worm have time to stew on his alternatives. "What's not to understand? I can make him a eunuch in under a second."

The man's dick twitched and his balls shriveled closer to his groin. "Please. Please, no."

Darak's hand squeezed Mary's shoulder. "Perhaps our friend here has never been on the receiving end of an electro-stun's blast." Darak looked down at the frightened man. "What is your name by the way?"

Yellow-Teeth's wide eyes rolled toward Darak. "Tom...Tom Plant."

"Nice to make your acquaintance, Tom."

Tom answered him with a grimace that twisted his mouth and exposed his rotted teeth.

"Tom, have you ever used an electro-stun?"

"No. Too bloody expensive."

"Well, the unit Mary's pressing into your balls has five levels of charge it can deliver," Darak said, his voice as calm as an elementary schoolteacher's describing the theory of relativity. "The charge is a combination of heat and electronic pulse. When on low and pressed to certain clusters of nerves beneath the skin, it can produce temporary paralysis. At level three its heat charge does more damage, burning the nerves and skin, while the shock can knock a man off his feet. Mary's got it set to five at the moment." Darak's eyebrow arched and he smiled slowly.

Tom's eyes widened. He glanced down at Mary's hand, which held the gun to his groin. "What...what does five do?"

Mary glanced back at Darak's face. She wanted to know too.

"Where it's aimed now? I'd say after you regain consciousness, you'll discover the skin surrounding the entry wound will be melted. You'll probably lose your balls altogether, but if you're lucky, your penis will still be attached, although you'll only be able to piss through it."

Mary turned back to Tom. "So are you ready to talk, now?"

"Please don't take me balls!" Tom whimpered.

"I think our friend Tom here," Darak pointed to the now trembling man, "might be more willing to tell us what we know if you put the gun away, Mary."

"Yes. Yes. I'll talk," Tom said quickly.

Mary scowled and pulled the gun from beneath Tom's balls. She'd enjoyed playing good-bad interrogator with Darak. "If you lie to me, I'll be able to tell."

"I won't. I won't. I promise you."

"So tell us what you know about the blonde woman," Darak demanded.

"She came to the Pirate's Cove a couple of nights ago. She was lookin' for passage to New Australia, but Chavez got to her first."

"Who's this Chavez?" Mary inquired quickly.

"Ex-Dominion soldier. A mean bastard—he's why I wouldn't tell you nothin' afore. He's a trader now."

"So what happened to her then?" Darak asked.

"They talked a bit. Not too friendly, you understand, and then they left."

"Together?" Mary asked.

"Yes. I swear."

"Is that all you know?"

Tom's gaze darted away for second. "Yeah."

He wasn't telling them everything he knew.

Mary sucked in an angry breath and pressed the electro-stun to his forehead. "I wonder what kind of damage the gun would do here."

"No. No. I remember now. I got up to leave right after them, and just so happened to be goin' the same way. I seen them walkin' north, along the docks. Toward your ship. Then all of a sudden Chavez and another guy attacked her. They stuffed her into a hovercar."

"Tom, you seem an intelligent fellow," Darak said. "Where do you think they might have taken her?"

"Chavez deals with the auction houses. Word on the street says he hit the big time with the blonde woman. She's going to the *Hazar's* auction. You know, her bein' a prime piece and all."

Mary growled and started toward Tom, intent on teaching him manners.

Darak's hard arm circled her waist, halting her. "Wait, love. Tom here has given us the information we needed. Save your anger for Chavez."

Mary relaxed against his arm. "What next?"

"We hire a skycraft to take us wherever this auction is."

"You'll not get within a league of his palace compound," Tom said.

Darak turned toward Tom. "And why is that?"

"The *Hazar's* security fence can't be breached. Not from the ground or air."

"How do you know this?"

"Every thief on Arturia has dreamed of gettin' within those walls. Not a one has lived to tell the tale."

"Tom, you've been a very helpful fellow," Darak said.

"Will you release me now?" Tom followed his words with a toadying little smile.

"Mary?" Darak's blue eyes twinkled beneath arched brows.

Mary's eyes narrowed—she couldn't forgive Tom for not assisting her friend. "I think Tom needs an airing."

"Well, Tom, there you have it. Mary's letting you keep all your parts. I'd say you were one lucky fellow."

"But, you can't leave me like this," Tom whined, struggling again.

"We'll send a message round to the local constabulary before we leave Aghora." Darak held out his hand to Mary.

She slapped the electro-stun against his palm and then turned on her heels and stomped toward the street.

Darak's steps sounded behind her. Once she turned the corner, his hand circled her waist. "I didn't know I'd chosen such a bloodthirsty mate."

Mary turned and shoved him against the wall. "Being bad makes me horny." She loved the fact that they shared the same height. She leaned forward, her mouth slamming onto his, and then drew his lower lip between hers.

Darak's groan earned him a lap of her tongue—skimming inside his mouth, and then withdrawing. His hands closed over her hips and pulled her close, until her breasts smashed against his chest and his burgeoning erection was burrowed in the cleft between her thighs.

Mary smiled against his lips, and then raised her hand—the one that had held Tom Plant's balls—toward Darak's brown mane of hair.

Darak's lips curved beneath hers and one of his hands manacled her wrist. "Not until you've disinfected that hand, my darling."

"I didn't realize you were so particular."

Darak laughed. "I still can't believe you grabbed that rodent's balls."

"Lover, why waste time? I believe in going straight for a man's priorities."

Darak bussed her lips, and then sighed. "Wish we had time for you to go for mine, but we're quickly running out of that commodity." He leaned his forehead against hers. "The shuttle will be back in two days, ready to take the last of the women to our new home. If we don't find her quickly, we may have to leave her behind."

Mary wanted to protest, but he was right. The longer they stayed on Arturia, the more chance the Dominion fleet would hear of their presence. At most, they had a couple days to rescue Calandra.

* * * * *

Without the reclamation suit beneath her robe, Calandra appeared more comfortable the second day of their journey to the city of Raban and the *Hazar's* palace. But as the Arturian sun rose higher in the sky, Drago could see Calandra's despair grow in the deepening shadows beneath her eyes.

Before they'd fallen asleep the previous night, Drago had pulled her into his arms, savoring the plump curves pressing against him. With her cheek soft against his chest and his hand sifting through her hair, she'd nearly been lulled to sleep. He'd tried once more to describe the life that awaited her within the pampered walls of the *ha'arem*.

She'd gasped and then turned her back to him. "Are you trying to convince me or yourself that you're doing the right thing?" Her voice cracked from her tears.

He couldn't answer her for a long time. Her back remained rigid, and he knew she didn't sleep. How could he make her see he was only trying to give her what she deserved—a better life? "There are only two kinds of women I've known in my life. Fellow soldiers and women who service men. The soldiers I've fucked were looking for physical release, just as I was. For us, it was physical training, nothing more."

Calandra's head shifted on her pillow. She was listening.

"The other kind sought my protection, or sought what my status as a soldier could bring them. I understood this transaction. I had use of their bodies and provided for them."

Calandra turned to face him. Her face was beautiful in the silver moonlight, even though her eyes glistened with newly shed tears. "Can't I stay with you?"

Drago's throat closed against a painful burning. He shook his head sadly.

"What is it with you? Why do you think any woman is going to choose an aimless existence with lots of *things* over you?"

"Because it's true."

Calandra shook her head. "Some girl did this to you," she said with a slight quaver in her voice. "And you're going to make me pay for it."

"I'm not making you pay for anything. Don't you get it? This isn't a punishment? You will be taken care of. I want a better life for you Calandra."

"Who made you think that the best you could give a woman was 'better circumstances'?"

Drago started to shake his head in denial, but the entreaty in her clear blues eyes convinced him she deserved the truth. "Before my arrest, I had a woman I kept. She was lovely—dark-haired with creamy skin. She said she loved me. And I thought once I was on my feet I would make her my wife." He shrugged, feeling foolish for his naiveté.

"After I was released here, she followed. I hadn't any prospects— only my soldier's training. I was hired by the auction house in Aghora as a security officer. I was barely making ends meet. And we were fighting constantly. One day, she came to the auction house to speak to me. The man who owned it approached her and offered to place her in the sale. She accepted and didn't tell me.

"When I discovered where she'd been placed, I snuck into her *ha'arem* and offered to help her escape. She laughed at me. Said she had everything she'd ever wanted. Why would she want me?"

"She never loved you, Drago."

"I know. But then, what is love? I've never experienced it, except through her words. And it wasn't strong enough to survive through the tough times."

"I'm strong enough," Calandra said, reaching to cup his face.

"Well I'm not," he said flatly, pushing her hand away.

"How can you sell me?" she asked, tears in her eyes.

Like a coward, he'd closed his eyes against her accusing look. He didn't open them again until her breath had slowed and deepened in sleep. Why hadn't he said yes, she could stay with him? Why didn't he believe he could make their relationship work?

He'd had misgivings about selling her since the first time he'd pressed himself deep inside her. Nothing about her reactions rang true with his preconceptions about how she should have behaved. Instead of cowering, she'd been bold. Rather than be seduced, she'd seduced him—boldly, lushly, unforgettably. When she'd been unable to resist his caresses during his inspection, she hadn't simply submitted to her desires.

Instead, Calandra had pushed him into the chair and mounted him. She'd taken him and continued to do so, until he no longer believed she would be happy in the confines of a restrictive Arturian household. She was far too uninhibited and highly sexed to wait on any man's whim.

She wouldn't be influenced by the riches showered on her. She wasn't like the powerful women who led their masters subtly toward their goals. Calandra didn't have a subtle bone in her body. Not that she wasn't smart enough to learn the games of the *ha'arem*. But Drago knew her spirit wouldn't survive.

Her wild, mercurial nature would be muted. He couldn't bear the thought of her spirit diminished or enslaved.

But what could he do now? The contract was agreed. If he changed his mind, the doors to untold riches would forever be closed. Besides, would Calandra really be any better off in New Australia? She'd likely end up as a pleasure-giver at some roughneck camp. And he couldn't keep her with him. Without a stake, he had nothing to offer, not wealth — not even a heart.

Chapter Six

The next night, Drago continued to fight his doubts. He had a contract, albeit a verbal one, to deliver Calandra to the auction house. If he failed, he'd never have the opportunity to present another offering again.

Would that be so bad? For the first time he wondered if he needed a new career. This one was beginning to make his head ache.

Dawn was breaking over the horizon, coloring the dunes in shades of rose and pink. The colors would forever remind him of Calandra's pink mouth and rosy cunt. Damn, the woman filled his thoughts!

The object of his lust rode just ahead of him, her shoulders slumped with fatigue and a good measure of dejection, he was sure. And he was the cause. Just another reminder why he should never let any woman depend on him for her happiness.

"Drago!" Kaspar's excited shout came from beyond the next rise.

Drago spurred his *llamyx*, passing Calandra and Gilbert. When he drew up alongside Kaspar, he followed the younger man's gaze. A long caravan wound slowly around the desert trail that led from Raban, and they'd already spotted Drago and Kaspar.

"It's my uncle's caravan," Kaspar said, his voice holding suspicion. "He did not stay for the sale and festivities. He will try to take your woman."

Drago had met the wily Kabal on several occasions. He agreed this meeting was not a coincidence. "We'll keep her close. He won't do anything in the open. Just don't drink first from his cups."

Calandra caught up to him, and stared at the approaching men. "Trouble?"

"Maybe. Stick with me, no matter what."

Her chin rose. "Why? Aren't they just men? I don't think things could get any worse for me, do you?"

Drago cursed. "Fine. Kabal's fifty years old and he'll want to test the goods."

Her back stiffened, but her expression remained stubborn. "I assume you mean me. How's that any different from what you've been doing?"

Because I care about your pleasure! He swallowed his anger and turned his attention back to two riders who broke from the caravan.

Drago kneed his mount and rode out to greet them.

Kabal pulled back on his reins and grinned widely. "Hello, Drago Chavez!"

"Hello, Kabal."

"Aren't you far from Aghora? You will miss the city auction."

Knowing full well Kabal was aware of his special offering, Drago bit back an impatient retort and instead smiled back. "I have business with Mogi, the *Hazar's* auctioneer."

"Your offering must indeed be rare. I congratulate you."

"Thank you. We have a long journey, as do you. I'll not impose," Drago said, knowing it wasn't likely his little group would get away quite so easily.

Kabal's oily smile stretched wider. "But you must join me for the morning meal. I insist. Soon enough the sun will beat down on our heads and we will sleep."

Already there were signs from his caravan that they were setting up camp for the day. A large white bundle was being rolled onto the sand—a tent. Drago couldn't refuse his invitation now. Kabal was too well entrenched with the *Hazar's* business interests to risk offending him.

From behind him, he heard the others approach.

Kabal's avid gaze sharpened. He'd found Calandra.

* * * * *

Calandra followed the woman wearing a dark kahfet into the white, billowing tent. As she stepped through the threshold, her eyes didn't immediately adjust to the shadows. Despite the oppressive heat within the tent, the dimness made the air seem cooler.

The woman grasped her arm and pulled her toward the back of the long tent. Calandra's footsteps were muffled by the carpets beneath her feet.

She'd watched earlier while rolls and rolls of the brightly hued carpets were carried inside by Kabal's servants. Obviously, his comfort was paramount.

Slowly, her sight adjusted and she saw Kabal and Drago seated on the floor, bolster cushions at their backs, with trays of food before them. Small black phosphor-pots were set around the room bathing the men's skin in a gentle golden glow.

Both men had removed their *kahfets* and their shirts, and their chests glistened. Women hovered nearby to fill their cups and offer them tidbits from the trays.

Calandra's blood boiled. She'd been "refreshed" with a visit to the necessary, and offered a shower within a blind constructed for the comfort and privacy of the other women accompanying Kabal. Now she knew why. The women were all naked.

No way was she going to strip to serve the two men reclining like potentates against their pillows.

"Come join us, Calandra Jones," Kabal beckoned her with a wave of his hand. He patted the space beside him. Although past his prime, Kabal wasn't unhandsome. The distinguished gray that silvered his temples and the dark moustache above his lip, complimented the rakish twinkle of his brown eyes. His body was trim and his legs were long. Without his clothing, she imagined he'd still be pleasing to a feminine eye.

Instead of taking his suggestion, she skirted the trays and dropped down beside Drago, leveling a killing glare at him.

His glance held a warning, but Calandra decided to ignore him and reached for slice of fruit on the tray nearest her.

"Uh uh!" Kabal tsked. "You will eat what your master provides you."

Calandra dropped the fruit and folded her hands in her lap. She'd rather starve than ask Drago to feed her.

"Perhaps you would be more comfortable if you removed your robe," Kabal suggested, his voice silky.

Calandra gave him a saccharine smile. "I'm fine for now. Thanks."

The woman who had accompanied her inside stood next to Kabal and drew her robe up her body and dropped it to the ground. Naked, she lay on the carpet on her back before the older trader.

Calandra shot Drago a questioning glance, but the smirk that tilted the corners of his lips only raised her blood pressure.

Kabal reached for a bunch of blue grapes and settled them on the woman's abdomen. One by one, he pinched them off and offered them to her, her mouth opening obediently to receive the fruit.

Calandra's hunger made a gurgling sound in her belly.

Drago slowly lifted a ball of meat from a tray and popped it in his mouth. He didn't look her way even once, but Calandra knew he toyed with her. The look of rapture on his face was too exaggerated for her to believe.

When another woman knelt beside him, he offered her a meatball and her mouth closed over his fingers to lick away the sauce.

Kabal laughed quietly. His interested gaze had never left Calandra and Drago, she realized.

The challenge had been laid down. Wanting to wipe away his grin, she reached for the hem of her *kahfet* and stripped it over her head.

Drago stiffened, but fed her the next tasty morsel. When the same fingers entered her mouth, she bit him.

This time Kabal's laughter boomed. "Such a treasure!"

"I hope you know what game we're playing," Drago murmured.

It was the sauce that was her undoing, she said to herself, and licked his fingers, soothing away the little hurt she had inflicted.

Drago's gaze narrowed, but his body told her how she pleased him. His cock slowly tented the front of his breeches.

A devil of mischief took its seat upon her shoulder. Calandra couldn't resist the sexy challenge. She reclined on the carpet on her side and propped her head upon her hand. Then she opened her mouth and waited.

Drago slid a piece of fruit between her lips, careful to release it before her teeth closed around it. It was sweet and juicy and she let its juice drip from the corner of her mouth.

His finger caught the trickle and brought it to his mouth. With her act of submission, she'd caught him. His cock stirred and lengthened further. She could tell—it was level with her gaze.

Calandra opened her mouth again. This time he dipped his finger into a pot of creamy joghurt, and he brought it to her mouth and painted her lips with the sweat cream.

Her tongue swirled around her mouth, licking the white cream, and Drago growled deep in his throat. A warning, perhaps? She'd never been one to heed caution.

She dipped her fingers into the pot and slowly brought her hand to her breast. She glanced at him from beneath the fan of her eyelashes and painted her areoles. His stare never left her as she circled her tits. The column of his throat moved as he gulped.

You're mine! She rolled onto her back. Her smile dared him to take what was offered.

"Witch!" his voice rasped. Drago shifted and sank on his knees before her, his mouth closing over the nearest nipple. His tongue circled to take her offering and then his lips tugged the tips until they crested. When he'd swept the last trace of cream from her breast, he shifted and took the next nipple.

Calandra opened her eyes and saw Kabal's avid gaze upon her glistening breast. She covered it with her hand, but Drago's mouth was doing wicked things to the other nipple, and she rubbed herself, unable to resist the seduction of Drago's mouth and the naughty lure of her audience. Her knees rose and parted.

Kabal stood up to circle the trays of food and knelt beside her hips. He lifted the pot and poured a dollop of the sweetened joghurt over her open cunt. "Drago, you must feast." He invited his guest to taste her with a wave of his hand.

Drago's expression was hard, his cheeks reddened with anger and desire. She read retribution in his gaze, but she was so aroused by the thought of his "feasting" before their watchers that she didn't care. Her fingers combed his short-cropped hair and tugged his head lower to her pussy.

He groaned rubbed his face in her cream.

Calandra mewled like a kitten and pumped her hips. "Please, lick my cream."

Drago lapped at her, his tongue gliding over her slit to lick her cunt clean.

"Your advertisement didn't do your offering justice," Kabal murmured.

Drago's head lifted and he scowled at Kabal. "She is *my* offering."

Kabal inclined his head, acknowledging his claim. "Will you leave her needing?"

Drago's gaze narrowed and his nostrils flared. His hands went for the placket at the front of his breeches and opened it. His cock sprang out and the women murmured in appreciation. Calandra was just as appreciative of his firm, reddened penis and opened her thighs wide in invitation.

Drago knelt between her legs and slid his hands beneath her hips to lift her from the floor. He centered his cock on her cunt and drove into her, straight to her core.

Calandra gasped as he filled her. This might be the last time she enjoyed his taking. For once, she wished their audience would leave them. She would have liked this last time to be strictly theirs. And she wished she could slow the pace of her growing arousal to savor it and commit the details to her memory.

But her body clamored for release. She straightened her legs, pointing her toes, and let them fall as wide apart as she could bear, giving him full access to the cradle of her thighs. She needed him to come inside her as deep as he could reach.

Drago's strong hands clutched her buttocks and thrust in and out, traces of the joghurt and her body's own creamy invitation glazing his cock. Faster and faster, he pounded against her pussy. She sobbed and moaned and writhed on the carpet.

She ignored the murmurs around her, ignored Kabal's excited gaze, and her own recriminations to her heart. This was their last time. Tonight, she'd belong to another man.

Drago paused the movement of his hips, and she moaned in protest.

"Baby, hold onto me," Drago said, lowering himself over her.

She wound her legs tightly around his back and her hands gripped his shoulders, her nails digging into his skin.

"Yes! Just like that," he whispered. Then he flexed his hips in and out, his thrusts more shallow and grinding.

Her body quivered and she circled her hips on his cock, increasing the hot friction between their groins.

His breath hissed inward. "I'm gonna explode," he said, from between clenched jaws.

Her hands reached for his face and she lifted her head and kissed him, telling him wordlessly that she needed his explosion and she was as ready as he was.

His hips drove hers hard against the carpet, no longer rhythmic — jerking, pounding faster, until her back arched off the floor and she cried out.

Her orgasm ripped through her, curling her toes, her inner muscles gripping his shaft in a long rippling caress. Drago uttered an oath and thrust once more before his release bathed her womb with his sweet cream.

When her last shudders quieted, Drago smoothed the hair from her face and kissed her tenderly. Her eyes teared. He was saying goodbye.

Kabal stood up. "I will send a message to Mogi. This one is a flame. She will earn you and my nephew a fortune."

✻ ✻ ✻ ✻ ✻

Drago sought the sun in its arc toward the east. They'd reach Raban before it set below the horizon. Despite Kabal's insistence, Drago had pushed to continue their journey during the heat of the day. He didn't trust Kabal. He might still try to take Calandra.

After putting several leagues between them, he'd stopped briefly at a watering hole to rest the animals and give Calandra relief from the heat. She'd been quiet since their sex sharing.

Drago told himself he preferred it this way. He needed the distance. He had no control over his body when she was near enough to reach out and touch. Her soft breasts and sensual allure made him forget his purpose.

When he was inside her, he forgot himself.

In Kabal's tent, all it had taken for her to bring him to his knees was for her to part her own. He'd slid into her warmth and felt cherished and a part of her. That had never happened before. It scared the shit out of him.

Even now with her fully clothed and riding at a distance from him, he felt connected.

The cowl of her robe rested on her shoulders and the sun glinted on her burnished blond hair. He longed to run his fingers through her hair and put that look on her face—the one that told him she felt the connection, too. In the throes of passion, she reached for him, clinging like she'd never let go. And he wanted that. He wanted her. Forever.

Glancing at Calandra, he pulled back on his reins. They had to turn around. *Now.* "Calandra," he called out to her.

But she didn't turn at his voice. Her shoulders were rigid, her muscles taut. Her stare remained fixed straight ahead.

"Calandra!" He spurred his mount to catch her. As he drew alongside, he followed her gaze toward the crest of a dune. Figures on horseback galloped down the side, leaving deep gashes in their path.

Horses! Only the *Hazar* himself could afford the creatures. Mogi had sent an escort. Probably at Kabal's suggestion.

Drago cursed. It was too late for him to change his mind now. Calandra was lost to him.

The guard, dressed in the famed golden livery of the palace, came to a halt in front of Calandra. Reluctantly, Drago spurred his *llamyx* to approach them. He became aware of the men's avid scrutiny of Calandra who rode at his side. The hood of her *kahfet* rested at the back of her neck, her red-gold hair falling about her shoulders in soft waves. He knew what they saw—luminous hair, eyes the color of a stormy sky, and a softly curved body a man would sell his soul to possess.

Drago shook with the intensity of his rage. He longed to put his mount between the men and his woman. But he didn't resist when Calandra's reins were lifted from her hands and she was led away.

* * * * *

Calandra didn't turn to see if Drago followed. She knew without being told that their relationship, whatever it had been, was now over.

The men on horseback had come for her. When the man nearest had respectfully asked for her reins, she'd felt the subtle shift of ownership. She was no longer Drago's woman.

With the passing of her reins, so went Calandra's last hope of reprieve. She would live in a *ha'arem* for the rest of her life. Despite the heat radiating from the surface of the sand, Calandra felt a cold shiver of despair touch her spine.

Men rode on either side of her. Since her *llamyx* was a larger creature than any horse, she had a slight advantage of height. It was a small thing, but she felt better for it.

When she'd first spied the riders on the horizon, fear had dried her mouth. Their uniform appearance and clothing had only emphasized the power of *Hazar*. They were all of a similar build—dark, leanly made, tall. Their hair was black, straight, and tied back from their faces.

Her escorts were clothed in gold robes that were belted with black cords. The ends were braided and dangled down the sides of their muscular horses. Black, round-toed boots peeked from beneath the hems of their white trousers. The rich clothing, spotlessly maintained, screamed the *Hazar's* wealth.

She looked to her left. "Are we very far from the palace?"

The man glanced back up at her, before quickly lowering his eyes. "We will reach the outer gate of Raban in a very few minutes, Mistress."

"Tell me. What will the auction be like? Is it held near the palace?"

"You will be housed with the rest of the offerings in the auction house that lies within the palace compound." When he finished his quick explanation, he faced forward once more, a pointed message that conversation was not invited.

Calandra sighed. Not two weeks ago, she'd have been delighted to be surrounded by so many dark and handsome men. Three years aboard a prison ship full of women should have honed a hard-edged hunger for all things male. Not that she had been celibate all those years. She'd frequently worked off her frustrations with many of her sisters in bondage.

But nothing had filled the hollow part of her heart that yearned for a man to wrap her arms and legs around. And nothing ever matched the sexual excitement of a full-blooded cock driving her to orgasm.

So why was she missing one cock in particular?

Unable to resist, she glanced over her shoulder to find Drago. Their gazes collided. Fascinated, she saw a wash of heat flood his cheeks. His nostrils flared like an animal seeking the scent of his mate.

While her *llamyx* rocked from side to side, Calandra became achingly aware that nothing but the *kahfet* lay between her and Drago's gaze. She wet her lips and discovered her breath was shallow. She struggled to draw a deeper breath, but nearly strangled when Drago rubbed a hand across his chest. Too well, she knew his sinew and muscle, clothed in dark-furred satin, and how it tasted. She longed to tongue his flat brown nipples into tightly beaded peaks—

"Mistress, we are entering the outer wall of Raban."

Calandra blinked and her thoughts dragged away from her fantasy. Her gaze rose to Drago's face. Instead of the knowing smirk she expected, his mouth was thinned into a strained smile. His gaze held regret.

Drago regretful? Calandra frowned at him. *Aren't you a little too late?*

She faced forward, but found she didn't see a wall, just another endless expanse of sand.

Ahead, one of the guards held up a small black box. He pointed it in front of him. The air rippled like the surface of a pond. A huge gate appeared, its translucent bars swinging open on unseen hinges. Her escort, now formed into a column, moved through it.

Calandra passed the gate and discovered it to be the entrance to the city of Raban. She turned in her saddle, looking behind her, and saw the bars of the gate weren't clear from this side, rather they were made of black iron and attached to a whitewashed wall. She glanced at Drago and saw he also appeared surprised. Obviously, a cloaking force shield protected the outer wall of the Raban. Cloaking devices were unheard of outside of the newest Dominion war ships.

As the procession proceeded to the heart of the city, Calandra glanced around her in amazement. No hovercars moved along the roads. No laser-lit mega-marts advertised goods for sale. The buildings appeared to be made of a mortar mixture consisting mostly of sand, for where walls were bare of whitewash, they were the same red-gold color of the dunes outside the city.

For as far as she could see, the city was empty of a single pre-fab building which were composed of the plasti-metal composite that most of the known universe purchased from Dominion stores.

Even more surprising was the marked absence of any evidence of technology. Animals pulled wheeled carts, and mothers carried children in their arms. The streets were cobbled with sandstone.

Suddenly, her *llamyx* came to a halt outside another large walled structure with a golden gate. It had to be the *Hazar's* palace. The wall rose high above any of the city's other dwellings; large, costly blocks of white sandstone piled precisely one on top of the other, without mortar. On close inspection, the gates appeared to be made of solid, molded gold. Guards wearing the same distinctive livery of her escort stood to either side of the gate.

As the gate creaked open, her party spilled through the opening. A man appeared at her side with a step stool, but he didn't offer to assist her. She supposed he wasn't permitted to touch her and climbed down from her *llamyx* unaided.

Once she stood on the cobblestoned ground, she noted she was in a large courtyard with several impressive structures made of the same white stone nestled against the outer wall of the compound. The center of the compound was dominated by what could only be the palace itself. The most astounding feature was the large wooden door at the top of a flight of steps. A door so wide, six *llamyx* could have entered side by side.

It was a tall white stone structure with turquoise facings surrounding every window and a dome crowning the top that appeared painted in gold leaf. A large palace made of roughly hewn stone, dominated the center of the enclosure.

The sound of the gate creaking closed alarmed her. She looked around, wanting to assure herself that Drago remained near by. Her throat went dry when she saw him on the opposite side of the golden gate.

Chapter Seven

Drago stumbled into his room, and cursed as his foot slammed against the bed. When he didn't find the phospher-pot where he thought he'd left it next to his bed, he cursed again. He toed off his boots in the dark, one at a time, and then wrestled with his shirt to get it past his head.

Reminded of Calandra's difficulties with her *kahfet,* he sat on the edge of the mattress and swallowed past the bitter lump that lodged in his throat. He sighed and skimmed the shirt the rest of the way off, then sat staring into the darkness.

After paying off Gilbert and Kaspar for their share of her capture, he'd tried to drown his memories in enough ale to allow him to sleep just one night without regret. Since leaving Calandra at the palace gate, his mind had raced trying to find a way to get her back. The pocketful of gold he'd earned wasn't nearly enough to buy him access to the exclusive sale, let alone enter a bid.

He flopped back onto the mattress, then immediately regretted moving so swiftly. His stomach lurched, and the room spun. Still, he hadn't drunk nearly enough to drown his guilt.

Or to mask the aroma of warm goat and manure that emanated from the other side of the wall. Due to his excellent advertisement of Calandra, the auction had drawn buyers from all over Arturia. The only vacancy he'd found was a room attached to a stable. His stomach burbled and he knew he was going to be sick.

A scrape sounding from the floor next to his bed was all the warning he got before something heavy fell over him, immobilizing him. As Drago struggled against the weight that settled over his legs and arms, a male voice broke in, "Darling, I think you have his attention."

Suddenly, yellow-green phospher-light illuminated the room. Drago found himself face-to-face with a very large, very angry woman—if the fierce scowl that pulled her black brows together was any indication.

Drago forced a nonchalant grin. "How may I be of service to you, ma'am?"

"You son-of-a-bitch," the dark Amazon screeched, then rammed her fist into his bare belly.

As Drago struggled to catch his breath, he realized he was in real trouble. He'd bet all the gold in his pocket that he was staring at one of Calandra's friends. Another escaped convict who looked ready to commit murder.

"Mary dear," the male voice said, "have you blown off enough steam yet? We need to get down to business."

The woman atop Drago growled. "Five minutes. Just give me five minutes."

Drago grimaced, expecting more of the woman's powerhouse blows, and knowing it would be foolish to deflect them.

Her scowl grew darker, but she shifted.

His arms were freed. Not knowing if the man held a weapon, Drago kept his arms at his sides.

Straddling him still, the woman sat back, preparing to climb off. She halted suddenly, her eyes narrowing, and then delivered another breath-stealing blow to his abdomen. "There's more of that where that came from," she warned. Finally, she climbed off the bed, leaving Drago to grit his teeth against the pain and nausea.

When she straightened, she looked over her shoulder at the man holding the phosper-pot. "Give me one good reason why I shouldn't just—"

"Mary, I'm very proud of your restraint," the dark-haired man said with an amused drawl. "I wasn't sure you had it in you."

Mary's hands fisted on her hips. "Darak, don't you go tryin' to sweet talk me. I'm still gonna have a go at him. I just want him to be able talk out of that pretty mouth before I break his jaw!"

Drago lurched to the side of the bed.

"Look out!" Mary yelled.

Drago held up an arm to keep her back as he bent over and emptied the contents of his stomach onto the floor.

* * * * *

"Time for us to prepare for the auction, Cal-*andrrra*."

The trilling of the r's in her name jerked Calandra from her sleep, reminding her she was in Arturian territory and lying on a sumptuous, velvet-covered mattress. And most depressing, Drago wasn't going to rescue her.

She pried her eyes open and found a young woman with a sweet smile standing next to the bed. With long sable hair and large brown eyes, there was no question of the girl's pure Arturian heritage.

Fahgwat, Calandra remembered. Her roommate. And another of today's "offerings".

"How can you be so happy this early in the morning?" Calandra asked, knowing she sounded churlish.

"The sun shines brightly and now that you are awake, a lavish meal will be delivered to our room." The woman's sing-song voice, as sweetly soft and girlish as its owner, made Calandra feel guilty for being grumpy.

She rubbed a hand over her eyes and sat up. It wasn't the girl's fault she didn't appreciate the velvet and gilt opulence of their cage. "Fahgwat, your name must not have a comparable translation in the Universal Language dictionary. I've never heard it before."

Fahgwat's face beamed with pleasure. "My father named me for a flower that grows between rocks near my village."

"Must be lovely," Calandra said dryly.

"Oh, it is. *Fahgwati* are small flowers with slender purple leaves — almost the same color as the *gahna* I am to wear today." Fahgwat spun away to lift two lengths of sheer fabric from the upholstered bench at the foot of the bed.

"You brought that with you?" Calandra asked.

"No, it was a gift from Mogi. He wished us to be properly attired for the event."

At the mention of the auctioneer's name, Calandra bristled. The small, rotund man had taken one look at her the previous evening and gasped in dismay. "She is sun-burned! And look at those freckles — this is a disaster!"

Mogi had continued his diatribe until Calandra had smiled sweetly. "And my hair hasn't seen a stylist in three years. Since I'm such a disappointment, I'll leave. Can I catch a transport to New Australia from here?"

Mogi's avid gaze settled on hers, and his thick lips stretched into a wide smile. "Such fire I see in your eyes. Silly girl, I will transform you into a perfect little flame."

Calandra's bravado gave way to panic. "And if I tell you I don't clean up any better?"

His expression turned nasty and threatening. "You must trust me in all things—and obey. You will thank me later."

Calandra hadn't thanked him yet. She'd been glad for the bath, but would have preferred to do the honors herself.

Instead, five women had attended to every detail of her appearance. After they had held her down to remove every bit of body hair with a floral-scented cream, Calandra hadn't bothered to resist the exquisite attention to her hands and feet or the haircut. But the soak in the bathing pool with all five scouring her flesh to remove desert dust and the upper layer of her epidermis had left her skin feeling raw and flushed.

But still, she hadn't resisted. Until now. Fahgwat held up a flame-colored *gahna*. "I'm not wearing that handkerchief—it's transparent!"

Fahgwat looked disappointed in her reaction and lay the outfit down. "But the red will be so beautiful with your golden hair."

"No fucking way."

"That is the same thing the black girl said when she was brought in. Doesn't she know her good fortune?"

Calandra's heart stopped. Black women weren't a common sight in Arturia.

"A black woman is here?"

"She is a goddess! And not black at all," Fahgwat said excitedly. "Her skin is the color of roasted coffee beans. She is tall as any of the *Hazar's* personal guard. And her arms are tree trunks."

Mary! She'd been kidnapped too. Calandra's heart sank. "Fahgwat, can you take me to her?"

"We must dress first. If Mogi finds you outside this room without your *gahna*--"

"All right, all right." Calandra held out her hand for the outfit. "Just how are you supposed to wear this thing?"

* * * * *

As Faghwat led her down a long gilt and red marble hallway, Calandra tugged the edges of the sheer fabric strips that bisected her breasts. Although common attire for the offerings, Calandra doubted the designer had taken a woman of her proportions into consideration.

At least Fahgwat's top covered the small globes of her breasts. Her purple strips appeared demure despite the transparency that revealed the dark circles surrounding her small nipples.

Calandra's on the other hand covered *only* her areoles. With the bulk of her breasts bare, she felt flabby and grotesque, despite the many admiring glances she received from the guards they passed.

She tried not to think of what was revealed of the lower half of her body. The *gahna* was comprised of two pieces of fabric. One part fashioned into bands that covered her nipples and was tied in the back. The other was a large square that wrapped around the hips and was pinned with a gold brooch at one side, leaving the length of one leg bare.

Again, Calandra's square was the same size as Fahgwat's. The extra cloth draped in folds to shadow Fahgwat's denuded mons. On Calandra's wide hips, however, it was stretched taut. "I may as well be naked," she grumbled.

"The dark one is in the bathing chamber." Faghwat pushed open the door and Calandra entered to find a crowd of women, dressed in groomers' white tunics, circling a long wooden table. Stretched across its surface was a naked Mary Grogan.

Calandra approached, her heart beating loudly, wondering what sort of reception her old security force teammate would give her. After all, she had been responsible for one of their fellow prisoner's death.

Mary's gaze landed on Calandra. "C, do you know what they wanna do to me?" she asked incredulously.

So relieved there was no censure in her gaze, Calandra's eyes welled and she bit the inside of her lip to stop from smiling.

The groomers appeared fascinated with Mary's dark hair and skin, for they touched her—everywhere.

One of the groomers brushed her fingers through the thick hair that covered Mary's mound. "It is wiry, like a Spiny-Mole."

Another tested the texture. "We will have to trim it before we can use the smoothing cream."

Mary glowered at Calandra. "He'd better be worth it."

"The *Hazar* will be very pleased," said a woman holding shears to the thatch of pubic hair.

"Who?" mouthed Calandra.

"That muscle-headed fool who brought you here," Mary hissed.

"That worm! Ooh, what I wouldn't give to get my hands on his—"

"You got it bad girl." Mary shook her head, pity in her expression.

"You've got it all wrong," Calandra hotly denied. "But how did you meet him?"

"Let's just say my fists had a meeting with his mind. By the way, he says he's sorry." With the sound of scissors snipping away, Mary continued, "I just don't know what you see in him. That is, besides his having a butt that could crack a walnut."

"Who said I saw anything in him?" Calandra realized the groomers' ears were perked to their conversation because all other conversations had ebbed.

"You wouldn't have stepped a foot outside the Pirate's Cove with him if you hadn't been interested."

"She has a point there," said the woman applying the hair-removing cream to Mary's armpits.

"He tricked me!"

The one with the scissors paused. "You mean you *let* him trick you."

"He took me against my will!" Calandra protested loudly.

"Against your will?" Mary snorted. "C, you sure about that? That man doesn't act like you two only had a kidnapping between you."

Calandra looked around the room for support, but every face held conviction. Angry that no one believed her, Calandra snapped, "Enjoy your bath!" and then exited the room.

Behind her she heard, "Perhaps it is just as well she will have a new master."

* * * * *

After Calandra walked off her pique, she regretted losing her temper with Mary, and over the slave trader! But by the time she had returned to the bathing chamber, her friend was gone. She'd hoped for a few moments alone to say goodbye. The chances of their ever seeing each other again past the sale were small. And she still didn't know how Mary had come here or if more of their "sisters in time" had been captured as well.

Just like she'd never get the chance to say goodbye to Drago. Why she should care eluded her. But he'd said he was sorry. It didn't change a thing about her circumstances, but it was a balm to her wounded heart.

Seated in chair in a long line of chairs facing a mirrored wall, Calandra waited with the other offerings to be called to the stage and wondered where Mary was. As groomers raced from one woman to the next, combing and applying light applications of makeup, the sounds of music and the low rumble of masculine voices sounded from the other side of the wall.

Wishing her reflection luck, Calandra was as ready as she would ever be, but she kept an eye trained on the door for Mary's entrance.

"Are you ready, little flame? The sale starts momentarily," Mogi said, as his reflection stepped beside hers in the mirror.

Little flame? Calandra restrained a laugh—the top of the man's head didn't reach her shoulder. "Is there still time for me to make that shuttle to the minefields?"

He ignored her half-hearted attempt at humor. "Would you care for something to drink?" he asked, laying his hands on her shoulders and gazing at her reflection in the mirror.

"Does it contain alcohol?" Calandra asked in a brusque tone. She didn't like the little toad. With an apologetic shrug, she reminded herself that as the proprietor of the auction house, he had a lot of influence over her fate. "Sorry, Mogi. I'm a little nervous."

Mogi smiled, his expression condescending. "I will see to your drink in a moment. Just remember what I told you earlier. There will be men in this audience who will purchase a surly girl for the more vulgar entertainments."

Calandra shuddered at the thought of an S&M house procuring her services for customers. "Just tell me again what I have to do to attract someone looking for a concubine."

Mogi patted her cheek approvingly. "Be yourself. Play with the audience." His hand dropped to her breast and he lifted its weight in his palm. "Let them see your inner passion."

Calandra willed herself to accept his touch. "How will anyone see my inner passion when I'm only walking across a stage?"

Mogi closed his hand around her breast and squeezed it painfully hard. "Perhaps I didn't describe the process fully."

As she held his gaze, she pried his fingers away. "What did you leave out?"

Ruddy color washed over his cheeks and his eyes glittered with excitement. "Women who wish to promote themselves prove their passion to the audience."

"Do you mean I have to screw one of them?" Calandra's voice rose.

"No, no," he said with a reptilian smile. "The men are not permitted to have intercourse with the offerings. They may place their hands on you to test for firmness or the texture of your skin and hair."

Calandra felt the heat of outrage rising to her cheeks. "You expect me to submit to strangers? I don't like being touched, unless I invite it."

"It is up to you, my dear. They cannot molest you—but you can touch yourself. If you are clever, you will keep them so mesmerized, they will not think to touch you."

"I've never performed solo like that before an audience. I don't think I can," she said flatly.

Mogi's smile disappeared and revealed the desert asp behind his smarmy mask. "But you will."

She lowered her eyes and prayed for control of her temper. "I'm afraid," she said, hoping to fool the man with a little feminine reluctance.

"Ah...now there is a problem I can solve." Mogi held up a hand and snapped his fingers.

A groomer approached with a glass filled with a frothy pink concoction.

"As you wished. A little cocktail with Arturian wine. This will relax you and help you be yourself. Let the drink take the edge off your fear." He pushed the drink into her hands.

After a glance around the room to assure herself others were partaking of the drink, she tipped the glass into her mouth. It tasted like strawberries and hard candy. "This is nice." Calandra took another gulp. "What's it called?"

"The Passionmaker." Appearing satisfied she was enjoying her drink, he said, "I must see to the comfort of the other offerings." He tapped her nose with his finger. "Passion will earn you a kinder fate. I predict you will be the diamond of the sale. Now, if you will excuse me."

Calandra watched him as he left and took another drink. The foam melted in her mouth, tingling as the bubbles popped. She swirled it on her tongue for a moment before tilting her head to let it slide down her throat. From her mouth to her belly, warmth spread over her and she relaxed deep into her chair.

Behind her, she heard Mogi calling the first girl to the stage in the next room. She tried to imagine what would happen when her turn came with a hundred or so male gazes stripping her as she walked along the runway, into their midst. Would they really try to touch her?

Sighing, she crossed her legs and kicked her foot slightly, back and forth, while she watched the other offerings as they dressed. They were lovely, and for the most part, Arturian. In various stages of undress, they giggled and joined in animated conversations, while they slid their *gahna* around slender hips. Small, ripe breasts were harnessed in fabrics the colors of the rainbow. Calandra noted their pebbled nipples, and her foot swung faster. The tip of her tongue itched deliciously, and she rubbed it against her upper teeth.

The fabric that banded her own breasts seemed suddenly too constricting, and her nipples strained outward. What's with this? *My breasts are budding too, and I'm not excited to be here!* She pressed a hand to one breast and kneaded it, but the contact didn't soothe.

Then she realized the motion of her foot was sliding her inner thighs together, generating a heat that rose to her core. Her hips flexed of their own volition. She shifted in her seat, bit back a moan, and then repeated the motion to grind her crotch against the nubby upholstery beneath her. Moisture pooled between her legs.

"Bloody hell, I'm getting turned on!" Distressed her body would betray her now, Calandra felt a rising panic clamoring as heat spread to every nerve ending.

A dark hand landed on her arm, and Mary's voice broke through the red haze of her rising passion. "I sure as hell hope you didn't drink that go-juice, girl!"

Chapter Eight

Calandra stared at Mary, who stood behind her in the mirror. Mary's areoles were small with hard tips that sprang against the yellow fabric that covered her breasts. Calandra's mouth watered, imagining her tongue flicking the distended points.

What the hell? Even when they'd helped each other out in prison, she'd never lusted after Mary. She shook her head to clear the image. "Go-juice? You mean that pink drink? I think it's making me sick."

"It will definitely be poisonous to your will-power," Mary said. "I held it in my mouth for a second. Soon as it burned, I knew what it was and spit it out. Had something like it on Moldan once."

Only half listening, Calandra noted the lower half of Mary's garment didn't conceal the shadow of her newly mown pussy.

Mary snapped her fingers in front of her face. "Wake up, C! It's an aphrodisiac. Mogi gives it to the girls who might cause him trouble."

Calandra's hand crept into the slit of her skirt. "That bastard!" She palmed her moist pussy and shuddered. "Christ, I need to come."

Desire was so keen it twisted her belly. She opened her eyes and saw that her face was flushed, and her lips swollen where she had tugged them between her teeth.

Unable to bear the pressure any longer, she spread her legs wide, pulling the fabric back to expose her cunt. Not caring who watched, her fingers went to work, a thumb flicking her clitoris, two fingers disappearing into her opening. She sobbed as the pressure to climax caused her body to quake.

Mary's hands reached around her to cup her breasts. "I know it hurts. Let me help. You've gotta come, baby girl, before we can talk." Mary's fingers plucked her aching nipples.

Calandra reached her free hand behind her and pulled Mary's head down, capturing her full lips for a kiss. Her tongue slid into Mary's open mouth, then circled inside her teeth, rubbing her tongue on the edges. With her hips pumping against her fingers and their mouths grinding together, Calandra reached for completion, keening loudly in her throat.

Then it burst over her, a cool wash of relief that left her gasping for air.

Mary hugged her shoulders. "Almost like the old days, hmmm?"

Calandra smiled weakly. "We helped each other through some hard-up times."

She jerked at a giggle that sounded nearby. A glance down the row of seats told her she'd become the center of attention. She glowered at the women. "If I ever get my hands on that little toad—"

"Sweetie, I hate to tell you this, but you only have a few minutes before it starts up again. It's not over yet."

"What do you mean it's not over?" Horror crept into her voice. She couldn't control these storms.

"That aphrodisiac can last several hours. We need to talk while you're still thinking with your brain."

Calandra lifted a hand to Mary's face, palming her cheek. "I was hoping we'd have time to say goodbye."

Mary leaned close to whisper in Calandra's ear. "Look, I have no intention of being any man's concubine. Darak and I are here to rescue you."

It took a moment for Calandra to realize what Mary had said. Her nose had caught the scent of Mary's musky perfume. "You're here because of me? You weren't captured?" she asked, keeping her voice low.

"No, Darak and I convinced that boyfriend of yours to help us."

Drago's face, suffused with heat as he bent over her body at the oasis, came instantly to mind. But why was she torturing herself with memories of someone who didn't care enough to let her set her own path? "Who?"

Mary rolled her eyes. "Try tellin' me you haven't been ballin' an ex-Dominion soldier with devil eyes."

Calandra blushed. "Why would Drago help you? And he's not my boyfriend."

Mary mocked her with raised eyebrows.

"In fact, he's dead as far as I'm concerned!" Calandra clamped a hand to her breast. It budded instantly. Soon, she'd be mindless again.

"Well, he's actually the one who came up with this plan. He brought me to Mogi and told him I was just one of a hundred women he could bring to auction. It was the only way we could get through the gates."

"And you trusted him not to leave you here?" Calandra's breath came faster as a shiver of awareness lifted the hair on the back of her neck.

Mary crossed her arms over her chest. "Darak won't let him double-cross me."

Calandra tried really hard to ignore the want clamoring at her sweet-spots. "So how's this rescue supposed to work?" she whispered.

Mogi materialized at her side. "Calandra, you are on now."

Mary blew out a breath. "Somehow, I'll find you later."

When Mogi grasped her arm to pull her from the chair, Calandra panicked. Mogi was the last man in the known universe she wanted to have sex with, but at that moment she wanted nothing more than to rub her aching breasts against his chest. Get her on a stage with a horde of men, and there was no telling what she might beg them to do. "I can't do this."

She dug her fingers into the base of the chair and refused to budge.

Voices beyond the wall grew louder. "They are growing restless. We haven't time for this." Mogi's gaze shifted from Calandra to her friend. "Go together then," he said. "I'll offer you as a pair."

Not wanting to lose the opportunity to stay with her friend, Calandra rose from her chair and gave a wobbly smile to Mary who looked triumphant.

Mogi let go of her arm. "Follow me."

"Mary, maybe you can tell me what you wanted in between gropes," she quipped.

Mary walked close behind her and whispered, "We have to be good together so we'll be bought as a pair by the same man."

Calandra didn't understand why, but wanted to do everything in her power keep them together. With her last friend by her side, Calandra followed Mogi down the short corridor to a door.

Mogi paused there and looked over his shoulder. "Once you are on the stage, Cal-*andrrra*, you will show the gentlemen what they came to see."

She cursed her passion-soaked brain. "What do you mean?"

"You will remove your *gahna*."

"I'm wearing little enough as it is. Why should I strip? I won't do it."

"But you will." Mogi smiled slyly. "You won't be able to stop yourself from rubbing your body on the carpet like a cat. You'll beg the men nearest you for release."

He opened the door and stood aside for them to enter. Calandra waited behind a red curtain on the stage. The rumble of voices on the other side had subsided. She could feel their excitement. It fed her own excitement, even as it terrified her.

Mogi pushed her forward. "Go! To the center! They await you."

Calandra glanced at Mary, who nodded, then pushed aside the curtain. The only light in the room was provided by candles burning from gold lamps suspended above a small stage and a carpeted runway that seemed to stretch forever through a sea of upturned male faces. The sweet odors of burning incense and smoke from a few *hatta* pipes perfumed the air.

"My good gentlemen," Mogi's voice enveloped the room, unnaturally loud, "for your pleasure tonight, I offer a pair of Earthlings. Let's show them how happy we are to see them, then perhaps the blonde will let go of the curtain."

Startled, Calandra realized she had a death grip on the velvet and dropped it. Cheers erupted from the crowd.

"Let's get this over with." Mary shoved gently at her back.

Calandra stepped across the blood-red carpeted floor toward the center of the audience.

"As you can see, Calandra is everything we advertised. Imagine her long, soft cloud of golden hair spread on your pillow, or those gargantuan breasts—yours to fondle whenever you desire..."

"You gotta be kidding me," Mary said from behind her.

Despite Calandra's mind screaming for her to resist, her hips swayed widely from side-to-side. Her breasts swelled with each slip-slide of her thighs, and the air warmed with expectation. By the end of the night, one of these men would own her—*and* her body screamed—fuck her. And the thought didn't repulse her.

"Now, let's turn to the offering that was added as a supplement to your catalog. Mary is a rare black pearl. What man wouldn't want a child of a woman such as this? Note the muscled flank, the sculpted arms. And mating will be all the more pleasurable for the full, lush lips that will..."

"If he says 'suck chrome from a hovercar bumper,' I'm gonna twist him like a pretzel," Mary said, her voice venomous.

The heat climbing across her skin caused Calandra to snap. "Put a sock in it, Mary. Now's not the time to blow up. That pink poison's doing its thing again." The end of the runway held a round platform and she halted in the center.

Mary stepped up beside her. "I wonder what's supposed to happen now?"

At that moment with passion licking at her genitals, Calandra understood Mogi's instructions through the fog of the Passionmaker clouding her mind. Her hands were already shifting the bands of fabric that bound her breasts, exposing her nipples. Freed from constraint, she sighed deeply. Her nipples extended in an instant.

"Oh brother, here we go again," Mary grumbled.

"They are indeed the color of ripe peaches!" one male voice exclaimed.

"She could suckle a herd of *llamyx* from such breasts!"

From one moment to the next, the roar of conversation rose around Calandra and Mary.

Calandra didn't care. More than her breasts were dying for exposure. "I can't stand it!" She reached for the clasp at her side and removed it. The skirt fell to the floor.

Instantly hands reached for her thighs, caressing her legs, trailing upward. She leaned down to them, allowing them to caress her breasts.

Mary jerked her out of the men's reach, and Calandra fell to the center of the circle. Once more, desire was an agony, burning her pussy and drawing her tits to tightly beaded points. Remembering Mogi's prediction, Calandra cursed—and rubbed her body on the carpet like a cat in heat.

Mary knelt beside her and took Calandra's hands, placing one on her breast and the other on her mons. "Keep yourself busy while I undress—and stay in the middle of the circle!"

Obediently, Calandra kneaded a breast while her fingers rubbed her clitoris vigorously, her legs splayed wide. When Mary dropped the last piece of her *gahna*, Calandra nearly wept with relief. Mary opened her arms to her and that was all the invitation Calandra needed. She sat up, wound her arms around the other woman's back and bent her head to take a nipple deep inside her mouth.

As Calandra suctioned, Mary's nipple stretched impossibly long. She switched to the other breast and tongued the crest before drawing on it, encouraging it to grow with gentle tugs. Then she leaned back in Mary's arms to watch the glistening, purple-brown buds that resembled the long stamens of flowers.

Mary pulled her closer, encouraging Calandra with her hands to climb onto her thigh.

Sweat broke over her, and she ground down hard, riding it. "It's not enough," she moaned.

"You like it when someone else watches you come, don't you C?"

"Yes. I want it so bad. Am I bad, Mary? For needing this so much?"

"No, baby girl. The drug takes what's natural for you and twists it. I won't blame you. Let me help." Mary sat on the floor and spread her legs. Calandra scooted in between, her back to Mary's stomach. "Spread your legs wide, baby girl. Just relax. I'll do all the work."

Calandra let her head fall back against Mary's shoulder and stared out at the audience. Avid faces stared at her open core, and the men screamed suggestions to Mary.

Red laser-lit paddles were held high by a few of the men, and Calandra realized the bidding had begun.

Mary cupped her breasts, then glided her hands lightly around the globes and circled the tips. Then she raised one hand and traced Calandra's lips with her fingers.

Calandra stuck out her tongue to lick the long fingers along the sides, and then she sucked them into her mouth. Her mind leapt to the night in the shabby office when she'd taken Drago's cock into her mouth. She'd drawn, pulled, swirled her tongue along the sides, suctioned hard on the smooth head. She repeated the motions now, pretending she was far away from this stage with her head buried in the lap of her lover.

When Mary withdrew her fingers, Calandra was brought abruptly back and moaned a protest.

With her fingertips wet from Calandra's mouth, Mary rubbed the tips of Calandra's nipples—soft, teasing slides that weren't nearly enough. "Harder, please."

Then Mary grasped the tips and rolled them between her fingers. Again, Calandra's frustration became an urgent heartbeat pounding in her clit. She brought her hands to her pussy intent on masturbating herself, but Mary pushed them onto her knees, murmuring in her ear, "Look in front of you now. Those are our guys."

Calandra opened her eyes and her gaze slammed into Drago's. He was dressed in a *kahfet* of fine silk that shimmered in the candlelight. The hood was drawn over his hair, but his face was illumined by the candlelight. She gasped at the anger that flushed his cheeks and carved his face into the hard edges of a stony mask.

"You betrayed me!" she screamed in her mind.

Despite her anger, Calandra's heart opened to him. The roar of the crowd faded away, and Calandra let Mary's hands become Drago's. She covered the hands with her own and pushed them down her belly. She raised her knees, planting her feet firmly to lift her buttocks from the floor and leaned hard into the body behind her for support. As his hands grazed the open mouth of her cunt, Calandra's gaze never left Drago's face.

One hand spread her labia wide and pulled up to expose her clitoris. The other smoothed over the soft, bare outer lips, then circled inside them, darting a finger into her vagina, then withdrawing to rub cream on her clit.

Calandra's heart beat faster and moisture wept from her cunt.

Lubricated now, a thumb massaged the hard nub, and a finger pushed into her again. Her channel was so hot, a ripple starting deep in her belly twisted on the finger, pulling it further inside. Her lover inserted another finger, and Calandra moaned, circling her hips, feeling the spring wind tighter inside her belly.

Gasping, moaning, Calandra started to come apart. Her hips jerked and a tear leaked down her cheek. The fingers shoved inside her thrust harder, faster. Calandra held Drago's gaze as, at last, she orgasmed, splintering into a thousand pieces of light.

When the tremors grew farther between, Calandra noted that Drago's face was ashen, his gaze hollow.

Shamed by the weakness inside her that responded to the drug, and the passion that was enhanced while Drago watched, Calandra's heart broke. She was an idiot. He'd never cared about her. Was here only under duress. He'd gotten his fistful of gold. If his expression said that he held regrets, she hoped guilt ate a hole in his gut for a long, long time.

Calm, cold anger welled inside her chest. *Too late for remorse, Drago! You're the bastard who put me on this stage.*

Mary whispered in her ear, "I don't know what this means, but I think we better get off this stage."

Calandra pulled her gaze from Drago and finally noticed the dozens of red-lit paddles held in the air.

"Such a response! I am pleased you all covet my discovery," Mogi said, his voice enhanced by the microphone in the ring he held to his mouth and transmitted to speakers in the ceiling. "But I am afraid I must remove this talented pair from the sale."

"What the f—" Mary disentangled her limbs and rose and rose from the floor.

Protests from the men grew to an angry howl and they pushed toward the stage. Calandra feared a riot would break out. She stood on wobbly legs, desperately seeking Drago in the crowd. When she didn't find him, she turned back to Mogi.

"Let us have order," he shouted, his face lit with excitement. "These girls are no longer available. The *Hazar* himself has selected them to serve him as his concubines."

Calandra turned to Mary.

"Shit!" Mary cursed loudly.

"This is good, isn't it? We'll be together. And the guys know where we are."

"No, C. This is the worst thing that could have happened. They'll never get past the *Hazar's* security."

Chapter Nine

Drago and Darak shared a look of dismay. The *Hazar* claiming the women offered a twist they might not be able to overcome.

Drago was still trying to put aside the shock of witnessing Calandra's endless orgasm. Did she even want rescuing?

Darak grasped the material at Drago's neck with his fists and pulled it tight. "Offering Mary was your bright idea," he hissed. "Were you just trying to get rid of us one at a time?"

Drago held up his hands. He wasn't going to resist. He knew he'd made a serious miscalculation and didn't blame Darak for suspecting his motives.

Darak thrust him away. "Damn you! If Mary's lost, I'll kill you."

Drago rubbed his neck. "Darak," he said, his voice pitched low, "if we leave the compound when the sale closes, it will be next to impossible for us to get past the gates again."

Darak stared at him, most likely deciding whether to risk listening to him again. "Are you saying we should find a place to hide?"

"Yes. Now, while the sale is still in progress."

His expression doubtful, Darak asked, "Won't security know as soon as the rest of the buyers leave that the two of us weren't among them. They'd keep a headcount, wouldn't they?"

"But we didn't come through the front gate, did we? Mogi brought us in the service entrance. So unless Mogi takes a personal interest in seeing us leave, we'll remain unnoticed."

"But how do we get out of this room without the guards knowing?"

Drago glanced at the exits. Both were watched. His attention returned to the stage. Mogi was once again extolling the virtues of a beauty that strutted to the center stage. All eyes greedily followed her progress.

Drago grabbed Darak's sleeve. "Follow me."

Skirting the edge of the crowd, they slowly made their way to the side of the larger stage where Mogi and all of the women had first appeared. "There's got to be a door behind that curtain."

"Do you think we're going to climb onto the stage in front of everyone here and just walk through it?"

Drago gritted his teeth. Darak's negativity was getting on every last one of his nerves. "If you have a better idea, let's hear it."

Darak glowered back at him. "If you get us thrown in the *Hazar's* dungeon, I'll make it a point to really enjoy killing you."

"He doesn't have a dungeon."

"Well, that's something anyway. Probably just means we'll head straight to the gallows."

Drago nodded, then maneuvered close to the side of the stage. The young offering had just reached the circle in the midst of the men. With the crowd staring at the woman and Mogi's gaze intent upon the rising excitement of the crowd, Drago ran up three steps and slipped behind the curtain, Darak at his heels. In the darkness, he felt along the wall until he found a door, then passed through it into a deserted hallway.

He came to another door and peered into a large room. There was clothing strewn over chairs and a long mirrored wall, but no one inside. A door on the far side of the room beckoned him. "Darak, let's try this way."

He heard a gasp and turned toward it. A young woman was huddled in a corner, her large brown eyes wide with fright.

"Hello there," Drago said, and hunkered down in front of her. "We won't harm you. We're looking for friends of ours." He held out a hand to her. "Let me help you up."

The woman shook her head. "I'm hoping Mogi forgets about me. I'm not ready to go out there."

Drago dropped his hand.

Darak nudged hem. "We haven't time for this. We have to hide. Mogi will be looking for this one in a few minutes."

Drago ignored his testy partner and continued to smile at the girl. "What is your name?"

"Fahgwat."

Drago suppressed a wince. "The name must mean something very pretty."

A little smile tipped the corners of her mouth. "I'm named for a flower."

"Well, Little Flower, perhaps you can help us. We are looking for two women who were sold earlier, Calandra and Mary."

Fahgwat's eyes rounded. "They were already taken to the *Hazar's ha'arem*. You will not be allowed to see them."

"Can you tell me the direction to this *ha'arem*?"

Fahgwat blinked. "Are you the trader who has broken her heart?"

Drago rocked back on his heels. "She may be angry at me, but I haven't wounded her that way."

The young woman nodded sagely. "You are both denying your hearts."

"Come on, Drago," Darak said. "We have to go."

Drago looked into Fahgwat's eyes. "Little Flower, is this what you truly want from your life?"

"This is all I know. I am frightened now, but Mogi tells me that is to be expected."

"If you had the chance for a life elsewhere, where you could choose your own mate, would you be happier?"

She bit her lip and giggled. "Would the men take their clothes off and perform for me on a stage?"

Drago grinned. "I bet they would."

"Then I would most certainly want to see that."

Drago held out his hand. "Then come with us."

This time she took it and let him pull her to her feet. "The *ha'arem* is very well guarded. How will you get inside?"

"Yeah," Darak said. "I'd like to hear this too. You're going to get us both castrated."

"We aren't going into the *ha'arem* unless you have a death wish, Darak. We'll wait until the women are in the *Hazar's* quarters."

"But his rooms are on the highest floor of his palace. I've seen him in the window." Faghwat tugged on his hand. "Unless you sprout wings, you will never make it inside."

"We'll need rope," Darak said.

"The stables, then?" Once again, Drago looked to Fahgwat.

She shook her head. "Just what sort of plan did you two have?"

"Little Flower, we're playing it by ear."

✳ ✳ ✳ ✳ ✳

"The *Hazar* was much impressed by the report of your performance." The head concubine, Delia, stepped out of the water and waited while servants patted her skin dry.

Calandra settled her arms atop the cool white tile rimming the pool, and let her head fall back on her shoulders. After the tension of non-stop arousal, her body was weakened and she needed sleep. "Can we stay here a little longer?" Calandra asked.

Delia raised one haughty eyebrow. "Of course not. We must hurry to get you prepared. He is most impatient to enjoy you."

When Delia turned to accept a robe, Mary made a face at Calandra. Calandra smothered a giggle and reached for a towel.

Delia was a tight-ass. Tall and slender, her back was impossibly straight. At their first meeting, she'd lifted her chin and stared down her long, aquiline nose as if something very rotten were beneath her feet.

Not that she'd been unkind. Mary and Calandra had been led naked by guards straight from the auction house to the *ha'arem's* doors, where Delia had greeted them and brought them immediately to a bathing pool.

Still suffering from the throes of the Passionmaker, Calandra had nearly wept with relief when Delia had produced a glass containing the antidote. Then Delia had surprised them by joining them in the bath. Of course, she'd only joined them to in order to lay down the rules of the house.

"Then the *Hazar* was at the auction?" Mary asked.

"Oh no. He rarely leaves the palace." Delia shrugged into a robe. "Usurpers lay in wait outside our doors. No, his guards keep watch for him at the auction. They let him know when something special comes along."

"What's so damn special about us?" Mary asked, her tone disgruntled.

"Our master's taste normally runs toward younger fare," Delia said with a sniff. "But reports of your unusual appearance and, shall we

198

say, *rapport*, intrigued him." Her smile didn't reach her eyes. "I'm sure he'll grow bored once he's sated his taste for your exotic flesh."

After they were dried, Mary and Calandra were led into another room, also covered in sterile white tile and were invited to sit in plush, peacock blue chairs. Four women, all dressed in baggy white *gahnas*, stood in a row as they passed.

"You will follow the directions of the servants," Delia said, as she drifted toward the door. "If you cause them any trouble, you will only be wasting your precious energy. Am I clear?"

Not knowing what to expect, Calandra nodded, happy to see the last of the older woman as she left.

"There's no hair left for them to take," Mary said. "I wonder what other tortures they have in store for us."

One servant placed a silver tray on the table between the two chairs. Devices that resembled inoculation wands lay in a bed of white linen. Calandra and Mary shared an uneasy look, and then a servant stood in front of Calandra and lifted her left breast in one hand. With the other hand she picked up the wand and brought it to the nipple.

Calandra dug her fingers into the arms of the chair. "What the hell?"

Faster than the words left her mouth, a small gold ring was inserted through the base of her nipple. The procedure had been entirely painless. When the right breast was pierced, Calandra let out a relieved breath. "That wasn't so bad." She glanced at Mary.

If looks could cause harm, the scowl that Mary delivered to the two working over her small breasts would have incinerated them where they stood.

Calandra jerked her gaze back to find a fine gold chain, interwoven with blue sapphires, clipped between her nipples. It was long and sagged to her lap.

"Please stand, mistress."

When hands pushed her legs apart, Calandra let go a horrified, "I don't think so." She tried to close her legs, but surprisingly strong arms wrapped around her hips and held her in place.

As she watched, her labia were spread with rough fingers, and her clitoris was squeezed. Then a third ring was inserted through her clit and attached to the chain. When she was released, she collapsed onto her chair, grateful to be off her wobbly legs.

"No fucking way." Mary's angry voice echoed loudly in the room. All four servants were lifted from their feet when she raised her arms.

"Mary," Calandra broke in, "They'll just bring more people in here. Beside it didn't hurt."

Mary snarled, and then fisted her hands on her hips. The servants quickly pierced her clit and attached a gold chain, beaded with lustrous brown topaz. "It's a good thing you don't love that trader—'cause if I ever see him again, I'll kill him."

"Mistresses," one of the servants said, "you are to follow me to the next chamber."

The next room held several lounge chairs upholstered in red leather. The servant indicated that Mary and Calandra should climb onto them, and then left the room as two more women entered carrying baskets.

After buffing their already manicured nails, the women dressed their hair, braiding Calandra's with beads of precious blue stones, and sliding diamonds on pins into Mary's short hair. Then they were asked to stand, and perfumed cream was applied to their bodies.

"Enough! He grows impatient," Delia said from the door. "Come with me."

Calandra took a deep breath and followed Delia from the room. They were lead up an ornately carved staircase to the upper level of the building, then along a corridor with arched windows that looked out over the city of Raban.

"I'm kind of getting used to being naked all the time," Calandra whispered to Mary.

"Yeah, but why is it that everyone else gets clothes?"

Calandra shrugged.

"What you want to bet he's old enough to be our grandfather?" Mary hissed. "With a wrinkled prick."

Calandra giggled. "At least he wouldn't be able to do us much harm with it. Besides we're so well oiled, he'll probably slide right off."

"Let's hope he does his thing quick. I'm gonna close my eyes and pretend Darak is the one pumping on me."

"I'd rather see what's coming at me." Calandra cleared her throat. "What do you think they'd do to us if we refused to have sex with him?"

"We're not going to find out. We'll just hope the guys find us soon. Darak told me to do what I had to until he rescues me."

Calandra remembered Drago's furious face. If she were his woman, she didn't think he would be as forgiving. Besides after seeing her at the sale, he probably thought she was having the time of her life.

They approached a dark double door with guards posted to either side. Delia nodded to them and shoved open the doors. Calandra sucked in her breath at the wealth evident in the furnishings within the room. Golden marble floors were strewn with thick Samureen carpets. To her right, dark brown leather sofas framed a bathing pool and the lights of Raban flickered beyond more arched windows. On the walls, still paintings and living holograms framed in gold, provided violent splashes of color against the beige walls.

To the left was a massive bed with ebony tree-trunk posts at each corner and creamy gauze draping to the floor—concealing what lay within the bed.

Delia stood before the bed and clasped her hands together, bowing at the waist. "Sire, I bring your new concubines."

"Open the curtains, Delia," a richly melodic voice ordered.

Delia pulled a cord at one end of the bed and the curtains rose revealing deep red and gold pillows and a dark comforter. As the shadows were dispelled, Calandra's heart beat faster.

In the center of the bed lay the most exquisitely formed man Calandra had ever seen. Dark like all Arturians, his features were sharply drawn, his slanted eyes catlike, his body lean and glistening with oil that even from a distance smelled of forests and hot sex. Her gaze swept his muscled, hairless chest, past his flat, defined belly, and then widened when it reached the juncture of his thighs.

Gold chains formed a harness that circled his hips. A gold pouch encased his balls, but his penis which rose from the center of the harness, was unadorned—by itself, a precious jewel. A shade darker than his bronze skin, it was smooth and crested with a thick purple head. And it was enormous.

An unexpected thrill ran down Calandra's back.

A guilty glance toward her friend confirmed that Mary's gaze had also been arrested by the *Hazar's* impressive manhood. "Well, at least it's not wrinkly!"

Chapter Ten

Laughter, deeply masculine, reverberated in the large room. "Delia, you may leave us. I don't believe they have weapons concealed on their bodies."

Delia bowed again, then turned to walk to the door. The glance she shot the women as she passed was malevolent.

"Don't worry about her." The *Hazar* sat at the edge of the bed, and then stood. "Perhaps if you please me, I will give you charge of the *ha'arem*." His smile, which stretched two perfectly symmetrical lips, revealed straight, white teeth.

On bare feet, he padded silently toward them. "Without clothes, one cannot tell who is slave and master."

Despite his handsome exterior, Calandra's skin prickled when his gaze raked over her.

He stopped in front of Mary. Because they shared the same height, they stared straight into each other's eyes. His hand rose to her breast and cupped it. With his thumb, he rubbed her nipple. "I've heard wondrous tales of about these breasts." He swung abruptly to Calandra. "I would know whether my men exaggerated." When Calandra didn't move, he voice grew cold, "Stimulate them!"

Calandra jerked, then reached for Mary's breasts. She rubbed and plucked, but they did not peak.

"Get the jar on the right!" He pointed toward a small wooden table next to his bed. On top of it were two stoppered jars, one with a pink liquid inside, the one on the right was clear.

Calandra brought the clear jar back with her and removed the stopper. Pouring a small amount into her palm, she placed the jar on the rug next to her feet.

"Don't be miserly. Use more."

Calandra added more, until the oil threatened to overspill her palm.

"Rub part of it onto her breasts and the rest onto her pussy."

As Calandra obeyed, the *Hazar* circled them, touching them, randomly sampling their textures and curves. Mary's nipples blossomed, stretching to long, thin points.

His fingers reached for them and rolled them.

Mary's breath hissed out.

"Can't bear to be touched, can you?" the *Hazar* drawled, his expression gloating. "The sensation is exquisite, no?"

When Calandra bent to rub the oil around Mary's cunt, the man circled and cupped Calandra's buttocks and squeezed. Her heart stilled and she darted a wary glance over her shoulder, but he simply smiled at her.

"Now you," he said, looking at Mary. "Do the same for your friend."

As soon as the oil warmed by Mary's hands spread over Calandra's breasts, blood rushed straight to her nipples. "Oh no. Not again."

He circled again, and as Mary knelt to apply oil to Calandra's cunt, he stepped close to Mary. If she turned her cheek, her mouth would graze his penis. "It's lovely, isn't it? It's called activator oil—an unexciting name for something so delicious."

He looked into Calandra's eyes. "Not mind-stealing, like the drink you were given before. It simply draws heat to your genitals." He nudged Mary's face with this penis. "Now, rub it all over my cock. Wondrous things happen when it reacts with friction. You will see, when my cock is driving into you."

Mary poured a copious amount in her hands, then stroked him from the base of his penis to the purpling head.

"Harder. Squeeze me harder." He pushed himself, in and out, between her hands. "Enough!" he said, and pulled away. "We will eat first." He turned from them and walked to the sofas, plucking grapes from a bunch on a low table. "Sit on either side of me."

Feeling like an automaton, Calandra followed him to the sofa and sat on one end.

His eyes narrowed, and she scooted closer.

Mary was about to take her seat, when he held up a hand. "No. I would have you fondle your friend."

Mary stepped around him and sat on the opposite side of Calandra, angling her body toward her. She placed a hand on Calandra's breast, and then stared defiantly at the *Hazar*.

"Don't be stupid. Arouse her."

Calandra stared out at the night sky through the open arches, wishing herself a million miles from the palace. A shadow momentarily blotted the lights of the city below. "We do what we must," she murmured, her mind racing.

Mary kissed her lips and her mouth skimmed along Calandra's jaw. Calandra let her head fall back against the couch, and Mary took advantage to slide down her neck before pausing over her nipples.

Despite the angry glittering eyes she knew were watching from outside, Calandra couldn't resist the thrill when Mary tongued the new golden loop adorning the crest.

When the *Hazar* leaned toward her to gently tug the chain between her breasts, Calandra moaned and a flutter of arousal awakened in her pussy. His lips latched onto her other breast and suckled loudly. While he was thus occupied, Calandra pulled on Mary's short hair until she raised her head, and then darted a furtive glance toward the window.

Outside Darak swung from a rope. He signaled that they should move to the bed, and then swung out of view.

"Sire, wouldn't the bed be comfortable for our play?" Mary asked.

His mouth lifted from Calandra's breast. "When I am ready. This breast deserves attention." Again, his lips latched onto the breast, widening to suck more of the tender flesh inside his mouth. His hand slid down the curved contour of Calandra's belly and cupped her pussy, rubbing back and forth.

A pulsing heat curled deep in her belly. Calandra gasped when something cold and wet was pressed inside her vagina. She looked down and saw him insert a second grape.

Rising from the sofa, he moved in front of Calandra and grasped her knees, shoving them apart.

Calandra's heart leapt at the strength of his hands as he positioned her buttocks at the edge of the sofa and spread her legs wider.

Then he knelt and draped her legs over his shoulders. With his fingers, he parted her smooth, pink cunt lips and bent his head toward the juncture of her thighs.

Calandra nearly bucked off the sofa when his tongue licked the delicate folds of her inner lips. The activator oil had sensitized the flesh, and the soft friction of his tongue increased the sensual heat.

While he lapped, he moaned, and the sound vibrated against her flesh. With Mary's mouth on her breast, and the *Hazar's* mouth torturing her cunt, all thoughts of the men dangling outside the room fled.

The *Hazar's* tongue dipped inside her and rolled, capturing a grape. He looked up into her eyes and chewed once, then pulled Mary's head toward him. With a kiss, he transferred the fruit to her mouth, and Mary sucked on the fruit before swallowing it.

Calandra was given no respite when he buried his tongue inside her a second time to search for the next grape. Unable to control her arousal, her hips pumped against his mouth and his groaning grew louder.

With one last attempt at keeping her mind on the rescue she said, "Please...the bed!"

Ignoring her plea, his lips found her clitoris, and he fluttered the hard tip of his tongue against it, then lifted the ring and tugged it gently.

She squirmed and bucked, but couldn't dislodge him from his intent.

Thus began a cycle of loving torture as he circled her clit with the flat of his tongue, then stabbed into her vagina and tugged the ring again. Over and over again, he suckled and parried, until her mind reeled and her belly shook with building excitement.

Calandra lost herself in his mastery, vaguely aware of Mary pleasuring her breasts. The pressure built until the dam burst in splinters of silvery light, and Calandra cried out.

The *Hazar* pressed closed lips to her cunt, then her belly. "Well done!" He licked his lips and grinned. "Your passion is sweet."

Coming back to herself, Calandra's face burned. Again, Drago had a ringside view of her orgasm in another's arms. She'd seen his face dart out from behind the blue window casing — but too quickly to gauge his reaction.

"Come!" The *Hazar's* voice drew her back. "There is no place for embarrassment here. Your passion pleases me."

Calandra offered him a small smile. "What can we do to please you, sire?"

He sat on the sofa and stretched his arms along the tops of the cushions. "I would have you both pleasure me with your mouths, but do not forget each other's as you work."

Mary and Calandra shared an exasperated glance. It might be morning before they convinced him to take them to his bed. Whatever the men had planned, the women knew tonight would be their only chance of escape.

Together Mary and Calandra, operating from opposite sides, kissed and licked their way from his head to his hips.

Not content to simply enjoy their efforts, the *Hazar* often pulled their heads up to savor their lips in deep, tongue-writhing kisses.

Calandra found his breath minty, and his perfect lips were soft, yet firm. His kisses stole her breath.

Had her heart not already found its mate, the man might have tempted her to stay.

Again, reaching his hips, Calandra tongued the chains surrounding his hips and stopped. "How do we remove these chains?"

"The chains meet beneath my penis," he said, grasping his cock in his hand to pull it high, exposing the pouch and the golden clasp. "The clasp will release them, and you can slide it away."

Calandra touched his penis for the first time and it pulsed. Indulging her curiosity, she wrapped her fingers around it, dislodging his hand.

His laughter curled around her. She had pleased him with her daring.

Warm velvet skin gloved a pure steel rod. Pushing it up, Calandra looked beneath to find the clasp. When Mary drew the chains away, Calandra noted his balls were brown, and the sacs hairless. She stroked them with a finger.

The *Hazar's* breath hitched and his hand grasped her hair and pulled her face toward his groin.

Resigned that there wasn't any way around it, Calandra bent to lick his balls, capturing one in her mouth and sucking it rhythmically.

Above her Mary's hand grasped his cock. Then she licked around the long shaft, while twisting her hands and riding it up and down.

Remembering that they should play with each other too, Calandra joined Mary, her tongue swirling along his dick, occasionally mating with Mary's before resuming its path.

The *Hazar's* chest rose and fell, his breath coming harder now. Fisting hands in their hair, he guided their tongues where he wanted. Finally, he pressed the head of his cock against Mary's lips.

Not needing instruction, Mary sank her mouth over his cock, again and again. Calandra did her part to encourage the *Hazar* to come by sucking on his balls and gliding her fisted hands around the base of his cock.

His hips lifted and lowered, and he groaned loudly as he neared the end. Calandra gently teethed the sacs and he came, spewing come like a fountain around Mary's face.

When he roused, he looked at them and laughed. "Come, we must clean your face my black pearl." He stood and offered them his hands to pull them up.

Finally, making their way to his bed, Calandra chanced looking over her shoulder at the open window. There was no sign of Darak or Drago.

* * * * *

In the darkness high above the courtyard, Drago adjusted the rope seat of his harness. Despite the constricting ropes, his cock was engorged.

Damn Calandra! And damn the *Hazar*! Just minutes ago, he'd seen her face contorted in passion and heard her cries as she'd orgasmed against the ruler's mouth. "Do you suppose they even want rescuing now?" he asked Darak who had no such problem with his seat.

Darak grimaced and whispered, "With all the women he has, he must know a thousand ways to please them. But my Mary likes having her own way."

"Wish I could say the same of Calandra. Why the hell is it taking them so long to get him away from the windows?"

"It's probably just as well they drain him dry first. He won't have the energy to call the guards."

The muted voices within the room moved away. Darak pushed his feet against the wall and bounced next to the window. Peering around the edge, he muttered, "About bloody time."

Drago maneuvered himself next to the opposite side of the window and saw the women climbing into the large poster bed with the *Hazar*. With the curtains rolled up, the men had a fine view of the three people rolling in the bed.

"My golden angel, kiss me," he heard the *Hazar* say. A moment later he heard, "Bring your hips to my face and let me suck you, while I pleasure your friend."

Peering around the corner, Drago watched Calandra place her knees on either side of the man's face, and saw her bite her lips against a ragged gasp when he must have licked her tender flesh. Angry that the other man could arouse her, and frustrated because she was there because of him, Drago could only watch as she bent to take the other man's cock into her mouth and bobbed her head over it.

Mary spread her legs and his hand disappeared between them. The moans that followed testified to the skill of the *Hazar* as both women lost themselves in passion.

Drago cursed under his breath, jealousy eating at his guts, even as his cock stabbed at his breeches. Watching the women from the darkness, knowing they couldn't see him, was arousing him.

Darak waved for his attention, and then climbed through the window, dropping silently to the floor. Drago followed, crawling past the sofas still redolent with arousal.

Nearing the bed, he and Darak came to their feet and crouched low as they approached. When he reached the foot of the bed, he ducked beneath the edge. Waiting for Darak, he darted a glance onto the bed and his gaze slammed into Calandra's as her hands caressed the *Hazar's* cock.

Her mouth fell open and she froze—but only for a moment before her abdomen lifted and dipped, and she let loose a long, low moan. With her eyes wide with distress, her body appeared helpless to halt its response.

Drago put one finger to his lips to remind her to be quiet, then slipped around the side of the bed.

Suddenly, the *Hazar* slapped Calandra's ass and pushed her legs to the side. "If you are intending to murder me, at least have courtesy enough to let me enjoy my last trip to paradise."

Drago leapt onto the bed and shoved the women from the *Hazar's* body, while Darak placed a laser-stun to his throat.

"Damn!" Darak said, pressing the gun harder against his skin. "Now that I'm here, I'm not sure I don't want to use this on you."

Mary pressed herself to Darak's back and wrapped her arms around him. "Baby, are you jealous? Let's not have the whole planet on our asses. Besides, he didn't do us any harm."

"I take it you know these women?" the dry tone of the *Hazar's* voice rankled Drago's nerves.

"This is my man," Mary said, squeezing Darak.

The *Hazar* nodded to Darak. "Forgive me if I cannot say with honesty that it is a pleasure to meet you." His gaze turned to Drago. "Are you here for the blonde?"

"Her name is Calandra," Drago ground out. "And I've come to liberate her."

"He's not my man." Calandra's voice pulled his gaze to her. "He sold me to Mogi." Hurt and defiance warred in her expression.

"Did you find a wealthier buyer?" the *Hazar* asked.

Drago's gaze didn't leave hers. "I decided she wasn't for sale."

The *Hazar* swept a clinical glance over Calandra. "She is a bit overblown, but exceptionally passionate. I can understand you changing your mind."

"I don't need your understanding or your permission," Drago said, feeling his body tighten against the storm of anger that threatened to break all over the *Hazar*. "Ladies, find something to wear."

"Look in the chest against the wall. I have some riding clothes that might do." At Drago's start of surprise the *Hazar* lifted a brow. "This is the best entertainment I've had in a while."

Mary dropped off the bed and padded toward the chest.

When Calandra didn't move, Drago said, "Get something on or I'll carry you naked from here."

"Perhaps I don't need rescuing," she said and crossed her arms over her breasts. "After all, what girl wouldn't want all the *Hazar* has to offer."

Noting her glance at the *Hazar's* impressive erection, Drago's eyes narrowed. "I know you aren't talking about his great wealth, you don't need money, right?"

Calandra's chin tilted up. "You're right about that."

"So it must be his lovemaking."

Flags of wild color burned her cheeks. "You should know. You watched."

Remembering her face, flushed with the release the *Hazar* had given her, Drago cursed as his cock crowded his breeches, again.

The *Hazar* chuckled and his mouth stretched in a knowing smile.

"Just get some damn clothes on," Drago ordered.

"No," she said, her expression mutinous. "You are the last man in the galaxy I'd go anywhere with."

"Is that right?" Drago reached above him and tore down a gauzy curtain.

Calandra's face paled. "I don't know what you think you're going to do, but if you touch me, I'll scream murder."

A hand clamped over her mouth and a strong embrace immobilized her. "Sorry, baby girl. But you have got to watch that temper!" Mary said.

The *Hazar's* chuckles grew louder.

Darak rolled his eyes and tapped the laser-stun to the potentate's neck. The current jerked his body.

"Darak, you didn't kill him did you?" Mary asked, her expression only mildly curious.

"No. Unfortunately, he's still breathing and aware of everything we say."

"Baby, are you jealous," Mary asked, a wicked smile stretching across her face.

"Fuck, yeah!"

Drago wasted no more time and wrapped a struggling Calandra in the fabric, careful to enclose her arms next to her body. "Can't have you pulling my hair out, love. Don't give me a reason to gag you, too."

The scalding glance she gave him could have taken strips off his flesh. He bussed her lips with a kiss, draped her over his shoulder and headed to the window.

"You are not taking me down that wall," she wriggled against his shoulder.

With a smack to her backside, Drago reached out for the rope dangling outside the window and attached it the harness around his waist.

"Ohmygod! You're out of your mind! If you drop me—"

"Sweetheart, do you really think I'd let you fall? If I were you, I'd worry more about what I'm going to do when I get you on the ground."

Calandra wriggled again, furious at Drago's tone. What right did he have to act the jealous lover? He was responsible for her being here in the first place. She'd only been making the best of a bad situation.

However, his threat tantalized her. Already stimulated by the activator oil and the wicked things the *Hazar* had been doing to her pussy, her body was further inflamed by the tight fabric that held her arms immobile and chafed her aroused nipples.

Drago slapped her ass again and Calandra's cunt oozed with excitement. Her buttocks squirmed.

"Like that, do you?" Drago's deep murmur curled her toes. He climbed onto the window ledge and turned to face the room.

Suddenly, she was suspended high above the shadowed courtyard below. As Drago began to lower them, step by step, she squeezed her eyes shut and held her breath.

Only when his feet touched the ground, did she breathe easy again. He laid her gently on the cobblestones and removed his harness, attaching it to the rope for Darak to pull back up.

Then his attention returned to her.

Moonlight and the lampglow from inside the palace illuminated his taut features. He knelt beside her and unwound the gauze from her body. When her arms were free, Calandra palmed her aching breasts and rubbed to ease the ache.

Drago's breath hitched and his hand went to the waist of his breeches. He shoved them down, freeing his erection. Wordlessly, Calandra opened her thighs and he sank to his knees between them.

Without preamble, he hooked his arms beneath her thighs, lifting her hips from the ground and thrust straight into her core. "Damn you," he muttered, but his hips glided his penis in and out of her dew-slicked channel. "Is this for me? Or are you still aroused by his lovemaking?"

"Does it matter?" She grunted as he pounded away at her cunt. The activator oil and her own desire combined to create a heat that was quickly bringing her to the brink another mind-blowing orgasm.

If his labored breath was any indication, he wasn't far behind her. Drago had been as seduced by watching her make love with the *Hazar* as she had been knowing his angry gaze had watched her every move. Her hands plucked at the rings in her nipples, tugging the chain attached to her clit.

She forgot about the cool stone beneath her back and the sounds of Mary and Darak as they climbed down the wall above her. Only Drago's powerful thrusts mattered. His cock, gliding in and out, became her focus. She'd thought she'd never know this joy again.

When the first ripple of completion gripped her vagina, her hips grew rigid and she bit her lips to stifle the scream that would have erupted. Drago's back arched and he drove his cock deep inside her and her body clasped him tightly, milking his seed.

He dropped her legs and covered her with his body, his lips seeking hers. Calandra wound her arms tightly around his neck and vowed to never let him go.

Chapter Eleven

Aboard the Intrepid once again, Calandra paced the floor of the small cabin she'd been assigned by Darak, while he and the remainder of the pirate crew prepared the shuttle for its final trip to their new planet. Having been ordered to remain inside, she hadn't seen Drago since he'd dumped her on the skycraft along with Mary, Darak, and Fahgwat, and disappeared into the night outside the walled city of Raban.

Further, she hadn't a clue where to look for him should she have the urge to find him — not that anything that insane would ever happen. After they'd made love in the courtyard, he'd withdrawn from her, leaving her confused and hurt. He'd had his pleasure, then promptly abandoned her again.

The portal slid open, and she turned expecting Mary or Darak. Instead, Drago stepped through. Dressed in a black shirt that tied at his throat and black leather pants, he looked dark and dangerous.

"What are you doing here?" she asked, and lifted her chin. No way was he going to know that her heart had leapt from her chest and was lodged securely in her throat.

He swept her with a look that started at her eyes and paused in all the tormented spots on its way to her feet, which peeked out from beneath the hem of her *kahfet*. "Just making sure you get on that flight. Can't have you roaming around inflicting chaos on an unsuspecting public."

"Oooh!" She scowled. "They should be really, really afraid. Big, bad me might eat them all up." Calandra blushed instantly.

He opened his mouth to speak, then shook his head. "Uh uh. Nope. Not going there. We'd trade insults, until one of us gets so mad we lock lips to get the other to shut up."

Wearing nothing but the silken *kahfet* Drago had given her as she boarded the skycraft between her resolve and his hot bod, Calandra licked her lips. "We're not locking lips."

"Right, no lips. You've got a shuttle to catch." He took a step toward her.

"And you had to tell me this in person?"

"Thing is, I thought you might need...help."

She raised an eyebrow. Funny, he looked a little nervous. She crossed her arms beneath her chest, molding the *kahfet* to her breasts and pushing them up so that he couldn't help but notice her nipples, straining at the fabric. She hoped his cock would strangle in his tight pants.

His gaze dropped immediately to her chest.

Calandra cleared her throat.

His eyes lifted, and he smiled crookedly. "Well, seeing as how you and Mary were anointed with activator oil...and you can't be very..."

"...comfortable?" She pouted her lips.

Interestingly, his attention seemed to be arrested with her every little move.

Her eyes narrowed, while her mind considered her course. The man needed a little lesson.

She licked her lips again. "Well, now that you mention it, I have this itch..."

His breath hitched, and he stepped closer. "Anything I can do?"

Calandra tilted her face to look up at him. "Maybe. But I'll still hate you."

He leaned toward her a little smile curving the corners of his lips. "I understand. I'm a bastard."

Calandra took her courage in her hands and shoved at his chest, pushing him back. "Dammit Drago, you left me again. Without an explanation. Do you know how that felt?"

"Baby, I'm sorry. But I had to cover our tracks to lead the *Hazar's* guard away from us."

"Why didn't you just tell me that?"

"Because I had to get away from you. "

Calandra gasped, her anger forgotten. Her heart was tearing in two.

"No." He took a step toward her, but Calandra retreated. "It's not what you think."

"It's probably exactly what I think," she said, fighting tears. "You got your rocks off and that was all you wanted!"

His face darkened with anger and he took another step toward her.

Her back met the cabin wall. There was no room to escape his intent. His hands rose to brace himself on the wall behind her, trapping her between his muscled arms. His broad shoulders and chest crowded her, reminding her of his strength. He was close enough now that she knew he'd bathed, his scent was fresh and masculine. Calandra fought her body's natural urge to soften and strain toward him.

It was just the activator oil, she told herself, that heated her loins and tightened her nipples, painfully. "Ah hell, I'm so horny I can't stand it." She gasped when she realized she'd said it aloud.

There was triumph and relief in his gaze as he shoved her against the cabin wall.

His lips slammed into hers and the kiss left her witless—otherwise, there was no explanation for how she ended up with the *kahfet* bunched around her waist and her legs hugging his.

"Thing is...," he said while fumbling beneath her for the opening to his breeches, "I can't figure out why I'm here—why I couldn't just take the first transport out of here." His eyes closed when he found success and his cock sprang free.

Calandra sucked her breath in when he pushed inside her. "Tell me why you think you had to be here."

"I had to see you."

She persisted despite the heat that curled in her belly. "Why?"

"You're different." He speared into her, lifting her along the wall.

"Not good enough, Chavez." She wound her arms around his neck and flicked his ear with her tongue. "There's a lot you're asking me to overlook."

He flexed his hips. "Oh?" he asked, sounding as though he'd lost his train of thought.

She bit his earlobe. "Slave trader...ex-soldier."

"I'm sorry now, about the first. The second one I'm not proud of."

"You're expecting me to accept a lot on blind faith."

His hips twisted and rolled. "Your point?"

Calandra moaned into his ear. "If you haven't noticed, I'm letting you have your way with me. Is there a good reason why I should?"

"Christ, isn't this enough?" he rasped. "I'm here."

"A vibrator could be here—why should I be more excited to see you?"

"Because I'm fond of you?" Drago's face pleaded for her to end the questioning.

Too much was at stake—her future and her heart. She had to be merciless. Squeezing her legs tightly around his waist, she halted his motion. "Why Drago? Why are you here?"

The arms braced on the wall on either side of her trembled. "Because I love your smart mouth. I love your toughness. I ache just looking at you—and I won't share you, Calandra!" His voice deepened. "Never again."

"Is there anything else you love?" she asked softly, hope bringing tears that threatened to spill onto her cheeks.

He closed his eyes. "You, Calandra. I love you."

Calandra placed her palm against his cheek. "Why is that so hard for you to say?"

His dark, haunted eyes opened and stared into hers. "Because I let down those I love."

Hearing the echo of her own fear, Calandra realized she was no longer a prisoner of it. "We all make mistakes, Drago. We hurt people we love. At the end of your life, wouldn't you rather have regrets you've shared with someone, than regret never risking your heart?"

"All I know is I won't let you go."

Her heart thrilled to his promise. "To the new world?"

He leaned his forehead against hers. "No. I won't let you go away from me. That is..."

She waited. "You have to say it Drago."

Frustration stained his cheeks red. "Fuck, Calandra. I'm not any good at this."

"Let me be the judge. Just tell me Drago. I deserve this."

His brows drew together. "I won't let you go—if you will have me." He looked mad as hell. "There! I said it."

She pretended nonchalance, although her heart was humming. "Hmmm, I don't know, Drago. My friends and I are going to a new world. Are you willing to accompany us?"

"Darak has already offered me a job. Someone must trade our resources for the things we will need to build the colony."

"So you have a new job. What's in this for me?"

His hands lowered to her buttocks. "My body will be yours to command," he said, his voice purring.

"You are such a man! Do you have any idea how conceited you sound? You want me to enter an exclusive relationship with you based on sex?"

His hands flexed on her flesh. The poor man was getting impatient. "Sounds good to me."

Breathless excitement wound a tight coil in her belly. She was through with talking, too. "Guess I'll need to take a test drive, to see whether I'm getting a good deal."

"All engines are firing, love. Ready for liftoff?"

She leaned forward and pressed her lips to his, and then swept her tongue inside while suctioning on his mouth. Relaxing her legs, she gave Drago room to maneuver.

He wasted no time. Clutching her buttocks, he lifted her then drove her down on his cock, grinding the curly hair at his groin against her clit. Then he lifted her again.

Traces of the activator oil reacted with the burning friction. Calandra gasped, parting their lips. "I'll want a lifetime guarantee Drago."

"I'll throw in children," he said, his voice harsh, his breath ragged. "Do we have a bargain?"

"Yes! Oh, fuck me, Drago!"

"Your command is my desire." He pushed her down his cock again.

Calandra needed to be closer to his him. While he worked her hips, she struggled to raise the *kahfet* over head.

"Damn!" Drago said, his hips halting their tantalizing movement.

Calandra dropped the robe to the floor and gave him a questioning glance. His gaze was glued to her breasts, and she realized this was his first up-close experience with her new jewelry. She brought her hands to her breasts, her palms curving beneath them to raise them higher. Shifting her shoulders, she lifted a nipple to his mouth.

"You have the prettiest tits. Sure, I won't hurt you?" His breath feathered the engorged tip.

"Never again," she vowed. In the future, she'd keep his talented mouth and cock too busy.

He opened his mouth, and she pressed herself inside. His mouth closed over her breast and suctioned, tugging the ring rhythmically.

Her fingernails dug into his shoulders and she wished he were naked as she was. She wanted her skin on his.

Drago ground his hips into hers, faster, harder, with a little twist that left her gasping.

Calandra's world rocked. An orgasm to beat all orgasms curled her toes, shuddered through her thighs, centering in her vagina to ripple and clench around his cock. With a cry she writhed upon him, barely noting when his hoarse shout heralded his own release.

When the storm passed, she found her head upon his shoulder and his arms wrapped tightly around her back.

"Do we have a bargain?" he asked again, his warm breath next to her ear.

She lifted her head to gaze into his eyes. "I love you Drago."

His mouth stretched in a wide smile, then his gaze dropped to her breasts. "I can't believe these are all mine. Don't take those rings out."

She slapped his shoulder. "Pig!"

The swish of the portal sliding open drew their attention. Mary stood in the door and rolled her eyes. "Girlfriend, haven't you had enough?"

"Never," Calandra said, tightening her legs around Drago.

"Darak asked me to find out what was taking you so long, Drago. All he told you to do was bring her down to the shuttle."

"We're coming now," he said, with a wicked smile.

Mary snorted. "Well, if you're gonna walk around stuck to each other like that, you might get a few stares."

Drago laughed, then helped Calandra bring her feet to the floor. She swayed for a moment and his arm steadied her. Together, they followed Mary out into the corridor.

"There's so much territory left to explore," Drago said, reaching down to swipe the *kahfet* from the floor.

Calandra slapped his arm. "Are you saying I'm fat?" She quickly drew the garment over her head.

"Course not. Do you think I have a death wish?"

From ahead, Mary chuckled. "We aren't going to make it to the docking station, are we? Darak's gonna be pissed."

"I haven't even had a chance to play with your new jewelry," Drago said. "I could attach a leash and lead you anywhere."

Calandra grasped Drago's hand and pulled to make him walk faster. "Just make sure our seats are together, Mary."

"Man oh man," Mary said, "this is gonna be the longest flight in history."

Drago laughed, a deliciously low rumble, then his hand landed on Calandra's buttocks. He squeezed.

Calandra gave him sideways glance. "What are you thinking?"

"We only need one seat," he murmured. "That shroud you're wearing will hide a host of indiscretions."

"Or we could find a closet." She bunched the material of her *kahfet* in her hands and lifted it slowly past her knees.

Drago's steps faltered.

"Beat you there," she said, tearing away and racing down the corridor to the shuttle, the sound of a lurid curse and heavy steps following her.

Just as she turned the corner, she heard Mary mutter, "You two are gonna populate the new world all by yourselves."

Calandra fervently hoped so. Babies, and all the loving that would produce them, would help keep the shadows from Drago's heart. She had his number now. The man might have a rock-hard body and a face that didn't give away much, but she'd scratched his surface and found a warm, wanting soul.

Her master didn't know it now, but she'd enslaved his heart.

About the author:

Delilah Devlin dated a Samoan, a Venezuelan, a Turk, a Cuban, and was engaged to a Greek before marrying her Irishman. She's lived in Saudi Arabia, Germany, and Ireland, but calls Texas home for now. Ever a risk taker, she lived in the Saudi Peninsula during the Gulf War, thwarted an attempted abduction by white slave traders, and survived her children's juvenile delinquency.

Creating alter egos for herself in the pages of her books enables her to live new adventures. Since discovering the sinful pleasure of erotica, she writes to satisfy her need for variety--it keeps her from running away with the Indian working in the cubicle beside her!

Delilah Devlin welcomes mail from readers. You can write to her c/o Ellora's Cave Publishing at 1337 Commerce Drive, Suite 13, Stow OH 44224.

Also by Delilah Devlin:

Why an electronic book?

We live in the Information Age—an exciting time in the history of human civilization in which technology rules supreme and continues to progress in leaps and bounds every minute of every hour of every day. For a multitude of reasons, more and more avid literary fans are opting to purchase e-books instead of paperbacks. The question to those not yet initiated to the world of electronic reading is simply: *why?*

1. *Price.* An electronic title at Ellora's Cave Publishing runs anywhere from 40-75% less than the cover price of the <u>exact same title</u> in paperback format. Why? Cold mathematics. It is less expensive to publish an e-book than it is to publish a paperback, so the savings are passed along to the consumer.

2. *Space.* Running out of room to house your paperback books? That is one worry you will never have with electronic novels. For a low one-time cost, you can purchase a handheld computer designed specifically for e-reading purposes. Many e-readers are larger than the average handheld, giving you plenty of screen room. Better yet, hundreds of titles can be stored within your new library—a single microchip. (Please note that Ellora's Cave does not endorse any specific brands. You can check our website at www.ellorascave.com for customer recommendations we make available to new consumers.)

3. *Mobility.* Because your new library now consists of only a microchip, your entire cache of books can be taken with you wherever you go.

4. *Personal preferences are accounted for.* Are the words you are currently reading too small? Too large? Too...**ANNOYING**? Paperback books cannot be modified according to personal preferences, but e-books can.

5. *Innovation.* The way you read a book is not the only advancement the Information Age has gifted the literary community with. There is also the factor of what you can read. Ellora's Cave Publishing will be introducing a new line of interactive titles that are available in e-book format only.

6. *Instant gratification.* Is it the middle of the night and all the bookstores are closed? Are you tired of waiting days—sometimes weeks—for online and offline bookstores to ship the novels you bought? Ellora's Cave Publishing sells instantaneous downloads 24 hours a day, 7 days a week, 365 days a year. Our e-book delivery system is 100% automated, meaning your order is filled as soon as you pay for it.

Those are a few of the top reasons why electronic novels are displacing paperbacks for many an avid reader. As always, Ellora's Cave Publishing welcomes your questions and comments. We invite you to email us at service@ellorascave.com or write to us directly at: 1337 Commerce Drive, Suite 13, Stow OH 44224.

Ellora's Cave Titles In Available in Print

Title	Author	Price	ISBN
A Grand Passion	Samantha Winston	$10.99	184360888X
A Hero's Welcome	Lauren Agony	$8.99	184360566X
A Mutual Favor	Ann Jacobs	$10.99	1843605546
A Taste For Passion	Patrice Michelle	$9.99	1843605694
A Taste For Revenge	Patrice Michelle	$11.49	1419950037
Arda: The Sailmaster's Woman	Annie Windsor	$10.99	1843607379
Atlantean's Quest I: The Arrival	Jordan Summers	$10.99	1843605686
Blood Of The Rose	Anya Bast	$12.49	1843609290
Bound Hearts: Submission & Seduction	Lora Leigh	$10.49	1843609452
Captive Dreams	Angela Knight Diane Whiteside	$14.99	1843605015
Dangerous Desires	Julia Templeton	$12.49	1843609053
Dark Dreams	Dominique Adair Margaret Carter Kit Tunstall	$14.50	1843603934
Darkeen Dynasty: Raeder's Woman	Angelina Evans	$10.99	1843609479
Death Row: The Trilogy	Jaid Black	$12.99	1843606585
Deep is the Night: Dark Fire	Denise A. Agnew	$15.99	1843605635
Dream Lover	Cassie Walder	$13.99	1843605619
Dream Shadow	Mary Wine	$12.99	1843609304
Ellora's Cavemen: Tale from the Temple I	Sahara Kelly Ravyn Wilde Doreen DeSalvo Kate Douglas Lani Aames Lora Leigh	$15.99	1843608138

Ellora's Cave Titles In Available in Print

Ellora's Cavemen: Tale of the Temple II	Tielle St. Clare Alicia Sparks Patrice Michelle J.C. Wilder R. Casteel Angela Knight	$15.99	1843609282
Ellora's Cavemen: Tales from the Temple III	Sherri L. King Cheyenne McCray Mary Wine Delilah Devlin Anya Bast Diana Hunter	$15.99	1419951181
Enchained	Jaid Black Joey Hill Ann Jacobs	$13.49	1843605228
Equinox	Annie Windsor Vonna Harper Katherine Kingston	$16.99	184360745X
Fantasy Fix	Christine Warren	$12.49	1843605627
Fetish	Sherri L. King	$10.99	1843608103
French Quarter	Lacey Alexander	$10.99	1419950118
Full Bodied Charmer	Marilyn Lee	$10.99	1843604493
Happy Birthday Baby	Lynn LaFleur	$12.49	184360891X
Holding The Cards	Joey W. Hill	$10.99	1843604000
Hook, Wine & Tinker	Mardi Ballou	$10.99	1843608901
Hunters: The Beginning	Shiloh Walker	$12.99	1843609010
Icy Hot	B.J. McCall	$11.99	1843604019
Jacob's Faith	Lora Leigh	$12.49	1843607484
Jennie In A Bottle	Titania Ladley	$10.49	1419950053
Law and Disorder: Moving Violation	Lora Leigh & Veronica Chadwick	$10.99	1843609509
Lawyers In Love: The Defenders	Ann Jacobs	$16.49	1843607468
Legend of the Leopard	Melani Blazer	$12.99	1843609436
Lover's Talisman	Ashleigh Raine	$13.99	1843605589
Lucavarious	Stephanie Burke	$15.49	1843604469

Ellora's Cave Titles In Available in Print

Title	Author(s)	Price	ISBN
Lucy's Double Diamonds	Ruby Storm	$10.49	1419950029
Lunewulf 2: In Her Blood	Lori O'Clare	$10.99	1843608987
Madam Charlie	Sahara Kelly	$12.49	1843605724
Manaconda	Sherri L. King Lora Leigh Jaid Black	$10.99	1843609320
Marly's Choice	Lora Leigh	$14.99	1843606143
Menage a Magick	Lora Leigh	$8.49	1843606186
Merlin's Kiss	Stephanie Burke	$15.99	1843606216
Mesmerized	Sahara Kelly Ashleigh Raine Jaci Burton	$14.99	1843604965
Mistress of Table Rock	R. Casteel	$12.99	1843605716
Moon Lust: Bitten	Sherri L. King	$10.99	1843604078
Oath Of Challenge: Conquering Kate	Marly Chance	$11.99	097243772X
Party Favors	Jennifer Dunne Dominique Adair Madeleine Oh	$13.99	1843606542
Passion and Ecstasy	Ruby Storm Bella Andre	$15.49	1843607417
Passion in Paradise 1: Paradise Awakening	Jaci Burton	$9.99	1843606127
Pirate's Desire	Delilah Devlin	$11.99	1843608960
Power Exchange	Madeleine Oh	$14.99	1843605708
Primal Heat	Sherri L. King Lorie O'Clare Jaci Burton Lora Leigh	$10.99	1843607409
Promises Linger	Sarah McCarty	$16.99	141995010X
Ravenous	Sherri L. King	$10.99	184360535X
Red Leopard	Tracy Cooper-Posey	$14.99	1843607476
Redemption	Shelby Morgen	$15.99	1843606208
Secret Submission	Diana Hunter	$12.49	1843608111
Seraphine Chronicles 1: Forbidden	Cheyenne McCray	$10.99	1843605600

Ellora's Cave Titles In Available in Print

Sex Magic	Jennifer Dunne	$15.49	1843605678
Slave Planet	J. W. McKenna	$10.99	1843604027
StarQuest	Kate Douglas	$16.49	1843607956
Swept Off Her Feet	Camille Anthony	$13.99	1843605597
Symphony In Rapture	Rachel Bo	$10.99	1843608936
Table For Four	Diana Hunter	$10.99	1843609525
Tales of the Beau Monde	Sahara Kelly	$10.99	1419950002
Taneika: Daughter of the Wolf	R. Casteel	$12.49	1843609339
Tempting the Beast: Feline Breeds 1	Lora Leigh	$15.49	1843607247
The Academy	Elizabeth Stewart	$12.99	1843605643
The Crimson Rose	R. Casteel	$12.49	1843608049
The Gypsy Lovers	Sahara Kelly	$12.99	1843609533
The Possession	Jaid Black	$10.99	0972437762
The Price Of Pleasure	Joanna Wylde	$11.99	1843604477
The Slayer	Stephanie Burke	$14.99	1843606224
The Warlord's Gift	Veronica Chadwick	$13.99	1843609541
Tied With A Bow	Jennifer Dunne Dominique Adair Madeleine Oh	$13.99	1843607433
Ties That Bind	Jaid Black Lora Leigh	$10.99	1843606194
Touch of Gypsy Fire	Shiloh Walker	$11.49	141995007X
Trek Mi Q'an 4 & 5: Conquest	Jaid Black	$12.99	0972437789
Trek Mi Q'an 3: Enslaved	Jaid Black	$11.99	0972437770
Trek Mi Q'an 2: No Mercy	Jaid Black	$11.99	0972437746
Trek Mi Q'an 1.5: Seized	Jaid Black	$8.99	0972437738
Trek Mi Q'an 1: The Empress' New Clothes	Jaid Black	$15.99	0972437703
Uncharted Waters	Jodi Lynn Copeland	$10.99	1843607492
Violet Among The Roses	Crickett Starr	$10.99	1843608928
Waiting For It	Rhyannon Byrd	$11.49	1419950045
Warrior	Julia Templeton	$12.49	1843603942

Ellora's Cave Titles In Available in Print

Title	Author	Price	ISBN
Way of the Wolf: The Northlanders I	Shelby Morgen	$17.99	1843604485
Wicked Wishes	Stephanie Burke Marly Chance Joanna King	$14.49	184360406X
Wildfire	Cheyenne McCray	$11.50	1843607506
Winter Pleasures	Anya Bast	$8.49	1843605562
Wonderland: King of Hearts	Cheyenne McCray	$10.50	1843607514
Wonderland: King of Spades	Cheyenne McCray	$10.99	1843608995

Printed in the United States
23008LVS00003BA/67-153

9 781843 608967